It TAKES TWO *to* TANGLE

THERESA ROMAIN

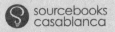

sourcebooks
casablanca

Published by Sourcebooks Casablanca, an imprint of Sourcebooks, Inc.
P. O. Box 4410, Naperville, Illinois 60567-4410
(630) 961-3900
Fax: (630) 961-2168
www.sourcebooks.com

Printed and bound in Canada.
WC 10 9 8 7 6 5 4 3 2 1

One

IT WAS NO GOOD. THE CANVAS STILL LOOKED AS though a chicken had been killed on it.

Henry Middlebrook grimaced and stepped back, casting his eye over his work. In the cooling light of early evening, his vermilion paint looked ghastly.

He dragged his brush over one corner of the canvas and regarded it again. A slight improvement. Now it looked as if someone had killed a chicken on it, then tried to clean up the evidence.

No matter. He could fix it later somehow. Or hide it in an attic.

As he stepped forward again, ready for another artistic attack, Henry's foot bumped the fussy baroque table on which he'd set his palette. The palette rattled perilously close to the edge of the table, and Henry swooped for it before it tipped. He lost his grip on his paintbrush and could only watch, dismayed, as the wide brush flipped end over end and landed with a faint thump on the carpet.

Well, damn.

"How lovely!" came a cry behind him, and Henry turned.

His sister-in-law Emily, the Countess of Tallant, was standing in the morning room doorway smiling at him. She wore a gown the watery, fragile pink of rose madder, with some part of it pinstriped and some other part of it beaded, and her auburn hair arranged with a quantity of pink-headed pins.

Henry did not understand all the details of women's fashion, having spent the past three years learning the significance of shoulder epaulets, forage caps, and stovepipe shakos. Still, the effect of Emily's ensemble was pleasing to anyone with the slightest eye for color—which Henry had, though no one looking at his canvas would possibly think so.

"Good evening, Emily," he said, shifting his foot to hide the fallen paintbrush. "I might say the same to you. You look very well."

"Nonsense, Hal," she said. "This gown is a full year out of fashion and is suitable for nothing but lolling around the house. I must go change for the ball, as must you. What I meant was that it's lovely to see you painting again."

She craned her neck to look behind him. "And it's even lovelier to see you resting your palette on that dreadful table. Jemmy's Aunt Matilda gave it to us as a wedding gift. I can only conclude she must have hated me."

Emily walked over to Henry and held out her hand for the paintbrush, which he sheepishly retrieved from the floor. She scrutinized it, then began to daub the gilded table at Henry's side with red curlicues.

"I'm not the expert you are, of course, but the texture of this red seems a bit off."

"Yes, it's too oily. I'm out of practice."

"Well, that's easily enough fixed by time. I'm glad we still had some of your supplies left from… well, before." Emily signed her name with fat, bold brushstrokes to the ruined tabletop. "There, that's the best this table has ever looked. If you can stand the sight of the beastly thing, then you must have it for your own use while you paint. Surely we can find a studio for you somewhere in the house. You could even keep painting here in the morning room if you don't mind rolling back the Axminster, of which I'm rather fond."

Henry looked at the heavy carpet guiltily. A splotch of warm red paint marred the fine sepia pattern of scrolls and bouquets. "I should have done that first thing. I'm sorry, Em."

She waved a hand. "I understand artists are remarkably forgetful creatures. Once the creative mood seizes you, you cannot be responsible for your actions."

"Are you giving me an excuse to be an aggravating guest? This could be entertaining."

Emily's mouth curled into the cunning smile that meant she was plotting something. "You're much more than a guest, as you know. But you're right. I should demand that you pay me a favor for spilling paint all over my possessions."

Henry took the brush from her and laid it carefully across the palette, atop the newly adorned table. "Let me guess. You already have a favor in mind, and you are delighted I have ruined your carpet, since now you can be sure I'll agree to whatever you ask."

Emily looked prouder than ever. "Excellent! We shall slip you back into polite society more easily than I could ever have hoped. Already you are speaking its secret language again, for you are correct in every particular of your guess."

"I'm overjoyed to be such a prodigy. What, precisely, have I guessed?"

"Tonight, I am going to introduce you to your future wife. What do you think?" She beamed at him, as though she expected him to jump up and start applauding. Which was, of course, impossible.

Henry gripped the edge of the fussy little table tightly. It was difficult to imagine feeling comfortable amidst the *ton* again—as difficult as it had seemed to leave it three years ago.

But he was just as determined on the former as he'd once been on the latter. Choosing the right wife could be exactly the key he needed to unlock London.

Emily passed a hand in front of his face. "You didn't answer me, Hal."

Henry blinked; stalled. "Don't call me Hal, please."

She raised her eyes to heaven. "You know perfectly well that I shall never be able to stop calling you Hal in my lifetime, just as you cannot stop calling your brother Jem. We are all far too set in our ways. But that's not the answer I wanted. What do you think of my idea about finding you a wife? Actually, it was Jemmy's suggestion, but if you like it, I shall claim it for my own."

Fortunately, Henry's elder brother Jeremy, the Earl of Tallant, poked his dark head into the doorway at that moment, saving Henry from a reply. "Em?

Aren't you ready yet? I've already had the carriage brought around."

In his sleek black tailcoat, mathematical-tied linens, and waistcoat of bronze silk, Jem looked every inch the earl. Every inch, that is, except the one between his forehead and nose. His eyes—a bright lapis-blue, the only feature the brothers had in common—held an ignoble amount of doubt just now. "Hal? Are you sure you're ready for this?"

Henry decided on deliberate obtuseness. "For Lady Applewood's ball? No, I still have to change my clothing."

"I'll send my man up to help you," Jem replied too quickly.

Emily crossed her arms and regarded her husband slowly, up and down. "You look very elegant, Jemmy. But why are you ready? We aren't leaving for an hour."

Jem's expression turned puzzled. "An hour? But I thought—"

"We must make a grand entrance," Emily said in a hurried hush. "I told you we shan't leave until nine."

Jem shrugged, squeezed by his wife, and came to stand next to Henry. "It's too dim in here," he decided as he regarded the painting. "I can't tell what you've painted."

Henry swept his arm to indicate the baroque table. "This table, for a start. And your carpet. And my breeches a bit." He regarded his garments ruefully.

Jem nodded. "Rather ambitious for your first effort."

"Yes. It's served me well to be ambitious, hasn't it?"

Jem managed a smile as his eyes found Henry's. "I suppose it has. Well, best get ready. Em's told you about our grand plan, hasn't she?"

"If you mean the plan to marry me off, then yes. I can't say I'm shocked. I'm only surprised it took her two weeks to broach the subject."

"She's been plotting it for weeks." Jem sighed. "Quite proud of the scheme."

"I'm still *right here*," Emily said from the doorway. "And I *am* proud of it. It's just…"

When she trailed off, both brothers turned to her. Emily's merry face looked sober all of a sudden. "We think you'd be happier, Hal. If you were married."

Henry pasted a smile across his face. "Don't worry about me. I'm quite as happy as can be expected."

Emily studied him for a long moment, then nodded. "One hour, Hal. Jemmy, do come with me. You may help me decide which dress to wear."

The earl followed his wife. "It doesn't matter, Em. You always look marvelous. Besides which, you never wear what I choose."

"That's because you'd send me out with no bodice. Honestly, Jem!"

Their voices quieted as they moved down the corridor, and Henry allowed the smile to drop from his face. He could guess what they'd begun talking about: just how happy *was* he?

He'd given them a truthful answer on the surface of it. He was as happy as could be expected. But a man in his situation had little enough reason for happiness.

Still, he had determination. Surely that was even more important. With enough determination, happiness might one day follow.

He dragged his easel to the edge of the morning room and gave his painting one last look.

Just as horrible as he'd thought. But in time, it would get better.

With a rueful shake of the head, he left behind his first foray back into painting and went upstairs to prepare for his first foray back into London society.

⌒

Frances Whittier was too much of a lady to curse in the crowded ballroom of Applewood House. Barely.

But as she limped back to her seat next to Caroline, the Countess of Stratton, she found the words a gently bred widow was permitted to use completely inadequate.

"Mercy," she muttered, sinking into the frail gilt-wood chair. "Fiddle. Goodness. *Damn.* Oh, Caro, my toes will never recover."

Caroline laughed. "Thank you for accepting that dance, Frannie. The last time I danced with Bart Crosby, he stepped on my toes twelve times. Oh, and look—I think I've cracked the sticks of my fan."

Frances wiggled her feet. "He's improving, then, for I'm sure he stepped on mine only ten." She exchanged her own unbroken fan for Caroline's. "And if you would quit batting everyone with your fan, it wouldn't break."

"I can't help it," Caroline said. "Lord Wadsworth puts his hands where they don't belong, and the only way to remove them is by physical force."

"In that case, we should have a new fan made for you of something much sturdier than ivory. A nice rosewood should help him remember his manners."

"Or wrought iron, maybe?" Caroline replied, and Frances grinned. Caroline was in quite a good humor tonight and more than willing to share it.

The role of companion to a noblewoman was often seen as thankless, but except when her toes were trod upon, Frances found her position quite the opposite. Maybe because her employer was also her cousin, or maybe just because Caroline was cheerful and generous. The young countess had been locked away in the country for the nine years of her marriage; now that her year of mourning for her elderly husband was complete, she collected admirers with the deliberate joy of a naturalist catching butterflies.

Frances enjoyed helping Caroline sort through the possibilities, though she knew her cousin was as determined to guard her independence as Frances had once been to fling hers away.

"What's next, Caroline? Are you of a mind to dance anymore?" Frances leaned against the stiff back of her chair. It was not at all comfortable, but it was better than having her feet stomped on.

"I think I will, but not just yet." The countess leaned in, conspiratorial under the din of hundreds of voices bouncing off a high ceiling. "Emily has told me she's bringing her brother-in-law tonight, and she intends to introduce us. He's a war hero, just back in London after three years on the Continent."

"A soldier?" Frances said faintly. The hair on her arms prickled from a sudden inner chill.

Caroline shot her a knowing look. "Yes, a soldier. That is, a former soldier. He should be intriguing, don't you think?"

"I have no doubt of it." Frances's throat felt dust-dry. "At any rate, he won't be one of your tame puppies."

"All the better." Caroline adjusted the heavy jonquil

silk of her skirts with a practiced hand. "They're so much more fun when they don't simply roll over, aren't they?"

Frances coughed. "I can't really say. I haven't *rolled over* since I was widowed, you know."

Caroline raised an eyebrow. "Maybe it's time you changed that."

"Believe me, I've thought of it."

Caroline chuckled, though Frances's smile hung a little crooked. Any reference to her brief, tempestuous marriage that ended six years before still trickled guilt down her spine. Which was probably why she hadn't *rolled over* in so long.

"How do I look?" Caroline murmured. "Satisfactory enough?"

Frances smoothed the dark blue crape of her own gown, then cast an eye over Caroline. With quick fingers, she tugged one of the countess's blond curls into a deliberate tousle, then nodded. "You'll do very well, though I think you've lost a few of your jeweled hairpins."

Caroline pulled a droll face. "Tonight's casualties: one fan, an undetermined number of hairpins. I don't suppose a soldier would regard those as worthwhile, but I rather liked them all."

"They were lovely," Frances agreed. "I saw Lady Halliwell hunting the same hairpins on Bond Street after you last wore them five weeks ago."

"Oh, horrors." Caroline frowned. "She'll remember that I've worn these before."

"If she does, it won't matter, because she admires you greatly. Besides, she wasn't able to get any for herself. I'd already put the remaining stock on your account."

Caroline looked impressed. "You do think of everything, don't you?"

"I do. I really do." Frances permitted herself a moment of pride before adding, "But if Lord Wadsworth calls on you again, he'd better bring you a new fan."

"And himself some new manners," murmured Caroline. "Oh, look, I see Emily now."

Frances squinted, picking out Caroline's good friend Lady Tallant pushing through the crowd. The countess wore a grin on her face and her husband on one arm. A tall, fair-haired man followed a step behind. The war-hero brother, no doubt; his taut posture was military-perfect, his handsome face a calm cipher.

Caroline lifted her—well, Frances's—fan as soon as the trio were within a polite distance. "Emily! You look beautiful, as usual. How do you keep your silks from getting creased in the crowd?"

Lady Tallant did a quick pirouette to show off her indigo ball gown. "Jemmy uses his elbows to keep the crowd away. Isn't he a wonder?"

"Elbows, Caroline," muttered Frances, "would work much better than your fan the next time Wadsworth becomes too free with his hands."

Her cousin gave a short cough of laughter. "Ah—yes, he is indeed a wonder. Jem, never let it be said there's no place for chivalry these days."

"I won't," said the earl gravely. "After all, I sacrifice the tailoring of my coat each time I drive out an elbow."

His wife rolled her eyes, then inclined her head to the man at her side. "Caro, Mrs. Whittier. We're here to make an introduction."

Frances could have sworn Caroline wiggled a little, though she managed to keep her face calm. "Oh? To a friend of yours?"

"Much better than that." The earl bowed. "To my brother, Henry Middlebrook. He's quite a war hero. Perhaps you've heard of his adventures on the Continent?"

The fair-haired man shot his brother a look so filthy that Frances made a little *ha* of surprise. He cut his eyes toward Frances and quickly composed his expression.

Lady Tallant must have noticed her brother-in-law's glare, because she swatted her husband with her fan. "Jemmy," she hissed.

Lord Tallant blinked. "Er, ah, forgive me. Er, Hal has been recently traveling on the Continent. For, ah, personal enrichment."

Another filthy look from the brother, another swat from the wife's fan. Lord Tallant looked positively discombobulated now. Next to Frances, Caroline was beginning to shake with suppressed giggles.

Frances grinned. The cipher of a soldier was actually rather entertaining. Interest crackled through her body, the fatigue of the long evening seeping away.

"What, Emily?" said the earl in a beleaguered voice. "God's teeth, stop hitting me. You'll mar my coat if you keep that up."

"Well, you'll mar my fan," retorted his wife. "Never mind, Jemmy. You are hopeless. Caro, here is Henry. He is positively salivating to meet you. You too, Mrs. Whittier."

The man stepped forward with a wry smile. This close, he proved to be just as tall and well made as he had appeared from a distance. His eyes crinkled with good humor; his hair glinted as gold as Caroline's under the hot light of the chandeliers.

"Do forgive my salivation," he said. "Having been away from London, I suppose I've forgotten the proper manners."

Caroline shrugged. "Have you? Well, if you're living with Emily, you won't need manners."

Lady Tallant smirked. "And if he spends more than a minute with you, Caro, he'll need smelling salts."

"I doubt that," Mr. Middlebrook said smoothly into the middle of this friendly volley. "I rarely get the vapors."

"Nor do I." Caroline gifted him with a sunlit smile and extended her hand. "I'm delighted to meet you, Mr. Middlebrook. Perhaps we shall be good friends."

He returned the smile and bowed over her hand with impeccable military bearing.

And his right arm swung down, down, loose as the limb of a puppet.

When he straightened, his face pale, Frances noticed what she had failed to see before: his right arm hung stiff and wasted within its sleeve, facing painfully backward.

Two

Damn it.

Henry straightened as quickly as he could. He had forgotten again. This gentleman's uniform he wore tonight, the finely tailored black coat and breeches, made him look and feel like his old self again. When really, he was the only broken-winged blackbird in the flock.

Lady Stratton—a guinea-gold vision, as painfully beautiful as Emily had told him—simply stared, dumbstruck.

The woman at her side recovered first. Dark-haired and olive-skinned, she had a roguish look as she extended her left hand to shake his. "I'm pleased to meet you, sir. I am Lady Stratton's cousin and companion, Mrs. Whittier, and I am generally thought to be terrifying."

For an instant, warm fingers clasped his. Henry looked at his left hand as it released hers, feeling as though it belonged to someone else. "Thank you, Mrs. Whittier." His shoulders unknotted a bit. "I am accustomed to obeying my superiors. I shall do my utmost to be terrified."

"You shall be, Hal," interjected Jem in a relieved babble. "God help me, the woman never forgets a thing. She can tell me what I wore to a ball, say, last summer. Me or anyone else."

"That is no trick, my lord, as you always wear black," Mrs. Whittier said. "As for any other feats of memory, I can assure you, they are grossly exaggerated. I am well aware that a too-good memory is unforgivable in a friend."

Lady Stratton had recovered her aplomb, and she dimpled. "It is far worse in an enemy, Frannie, which is why we keep you as a friend. Mr. Middlebrook, would you care to sit with us, or do you intend to dance?"

Now it was Henry's turn to stare. "I'm not precisely suited to dancing, but I'd be glad to sit with you."

"I'll fetch lemonades all around, shall I?" Jem was already poised to battle through the crowd again.

"Two for yourself," Henry said, knowing his brother's love of sweets.

"Wine for me, Jemmy, if you can find it," Emily said, shoving a nearby chair into position next to her friend, then another. "Lemonade will give *me* the vapors."

Jem dropped a quick kiss on her forehead and set off.

"Use those elbows!" Emily waved at Jem, beaming when he shook his head at her before disappearing into the crowd.

She plumped down into one of the light giltwood chairs with a sigh. "It is rather fun discombobulating Jemmy, isn't it?"

"I've always thought so," Henry agreed, taking the other empty seat.

A silence fell as they all smiled at each other. Henry's thoughts unrolled swiftly:

I cannot stand it if they speak of it. But I cannot bear it if they don't.

Surely Lady Stratton must want a man who is whole.

But after living through the hell of Quatre Bras, surely I've earned the right to pursue whatever—whomever—I desire.

Surely no four people have ever sat in silence this long within a full-crammed ballroom.

After an endless few seconds, Lady Stratton spoke. "As you are a soldier, I must thank you for your service, Mr. Middlebrook. All London has been celebrating because of men like you. To have Napoleon vanquished at last—can it really be true?"

She waved her fan as she spoke, a fluttering gesture that drew his eye to the clean lines of her gloved fingers, her arm. The effect was rather marvelous. She could sit for a painting, just as she was.

Henry gathered his stiff right arm into his left hand, wishing it could paint that picture. "It can indeed be true. But please don't credit me with any significant contribution."

Too bleak. He summoned The Grin, a blithe expression that had eased his way through society in former years. "Though I thank you for your kind sentiments. It's very good to be back in London, and this is where I intend to make my mark. Emily and Jem are allowing me to stay with them as long as I care to, even though I have already ruined Emily's favorite carpet."

His soldiering had done him some good; he was adept at parrying and shielding, even in conversation.

Lady Stratton nodded her fair head and accepted this new topic. "You've made a mark on London already, then. That is admirably quick work. I've been trying for years to ruin Emily's carpets, as I am terribly jealous of their fineness. Were you roughhousing with the boys?"

Jem and Emily had two young sons, good-natured boys who were abominably full of energy.

"If only it had been that," Emily sighed. "No, he spilled paint on it. But he did also help me ruin a table I hate, *and* he came with Jemmy and me tonight. So I suppose I'll forgive him eventually."

"Spilled paint? You are an artist, then?" Mrs. Whittier's tilted hazel eyes grew bright, lending her features a glow.

Henry nodded. "I was, once. I hope to be again. Though today's effort was, shall we say, not sufficient to get me into the National Gallery."

Lady Stratton shrugged. "I've never had a painting accepted there, either, so that is nothing to be ashamed of."

"Do you paint?" He felt a quick flash of yearning.

She shook her head, smiling. "No, I don't. But that is nothing to be ashamed of either."

It took him a moment to sift her words; then he laughed. *Flirtation.* Just as in the old days, before he had left.

He settled into his too-small chair and regarded this widowed countess, this friend of Emily's who seemed to have wrapped all London society into a ball and put it in her pocket. "I wonder, Lady Stratton, if you consider anything worth being ashamed of."

She tilted her chin down and fixed Henry with the full force of her blue-green eyes. "Oh yes. But nothing that I'd admit to such a recent acquaintance." Her mouth curved in a secret half smile. "If you wish, you may call me Caro, and perhaps I'll tell you more."

"Outrageous, isn't she?" Emily murmured in Henry's ear. Mrs. Whittier covered a grin with one hand.

Henry rather suspected Lady Stratton was less so than she seemed, that she had carefully honed her act on all the suitors who had come before. When one had wit and wealth enough, the edge of propriety could prove astonishingly flexible.

He was more than willing to tread that flexible line with her. With such a woman at his side, he could walk anywhere—and eventually, the *ton* would follow along.

It was time to employ a little strategy; he would set the pace. "You do me a great honor, my lady," he said, "but as I cannot yet be *Caro* to you, I shall not ask that you be so to me." Not yet *Caro*; not yet dear. Someday, though. Maybe.

She was surprised by this small rebellion, because her eyes widened before she smiled again, slow and appreciative. "You keep me at a distance, Mr. Middlebrook. How am I ever to learn anything of you?"

"Simply ask me, Caro, and I'll tell you all his secrets," Emily said. "For one thing, he's a rotten caretaker of a carpet."

"That's one fact," Mrs. Whittier agreed. "And we know he has two occupations: soldier and painter."

Lady Stratton coaxed her fan closed with careful fingers. Her golden hair glinted, pale fire under the crystal-spun light of the chandelier. "I'll grant that," she said slowly. With a quick snap, she flicked the fan open again. "Very well, you've revealed three inconsequential facts about yourself. Perhaps you'll call on me tomorrow and share a fourth?"

"Inconseq—" Henry's brows shot up. "My lady, you are hard to please indeed if you think I've revealed nothing of consequence."

"I'm not always hard to please," the widow said with another of those veiled smiles. "It simply depends on what's being revealed."

"Honestly," said Emily *sotto voce*. "It almost makes me wish to be widowed so I could be such a scandalous flirt."

"She's got a rare gift," Mrs. Whittier replied. "I *am* widowed, and I couldn't possibly manage it."

The mischievous Mrs. Whittier seemed entirely capable of managing a scandal if she wished, but Henry dutifully pretended not to hear her aside. He considered her words, though. Yes, Lady Stratton did have a rare gift. She had already conquered society; if he could conquer her, then her triumphs would be his as well.

Emily thought they would suit one another; after all, she had said he would meet his future wife tonight. And Emily was usually fairly astute about such matters.

Very well. "Lady Stratton, I'd be honored to call on you and reveal as many inconsequential facts as your heart desires."

She pursed her lips in a cherry-ripe bow. "Excellent. Perhaps I'll reveal a bit more about my heart's desires when you do. After all, a woman can't live by facts alone."

The hairs on Henry's left arm prickled. Possibly on

the right too, though he couldn't tell. It only hung numb and useless at his side, as it had since Quatre Bras six weeks before.

Jem shoved his way back through the pressing crowd just then, trailed by a red-faced footman in a crooked wig. The footman hefted a tray of beverages, which Jem handed around their small party.

Emily held up a glass of cloudy, pale liquid. "If this is wine, there was a serious problem with the grapes."

"It's orgeat," Jem stated proudly. "Delicious."

Henry took his own cup and gave it a sniff. It smelled syrupy, like almonds boiled with sugar. Emily looked faintly nauseated as she handed the glass back to her husband, who drained it in one swallow.

Just then, a young man with a determined expression and a still more determined cravat, striped and starched up to his cheekbones, poked his face into their little gathering. "Lady Stratton? Our dance is about to begin."

Lady Stratton—*Caro*, as she would have it—turned to him. "Oh, Hambleton, thank you for fetching me." She stood and shook out the heavy silk of her gown, sunny and bright as gamboge pigment. "I must leave you all now. I've enjoyed our little tête-à-tête very much."

Henry received a proper nod as the countess accepted the arm of her new suitor. "It was a pleasure to meet you, Mr. Middlebrook."

And with a parting smile, she allowed her escort to pull her into the crowd.

So. She was a strategist too, as determined as he to set the pace for their flirtation or... whatever it might become. She would have him know she was quite willing to exchange his company for that of another. Even with Emily's encouragement.

It was time he formed another alliance, then. The companion, Mrs. Whittier—she would be best, if only he could remove the audience to their conversation.

Emily sighed and stretched out her arms. "Jemmy, care to have a seat? If you aren't going to bring me wine, you must amuse me in some other way."

"Why not have a dance?" Henry encouraged. "I know you'd like to, Emily." Indeed, the toe of her slipper was peeping from under the hem of her gown, wiggling in time to a sprightly scrape of strings.

Jem and Emily both regarded him with that bizarre expression he'd seen so often on their faces lately: half hope and half apprehension, with a seasoning of worry. "Are you certain? You won't mind if—"

"Go on, enjoy yourselves. I'm sure Mrs. Whittier won't eat me," he replied.

"Don't assume too much," that lady said with a shrug. "All the world has told you how terrifying I am." Her cheeks darkened from rosy madder to velvety alizarin, Henry's favorite reddish pigment. A lovely effect with the fair olive of her skin and the stark, earthy brown of her hair, the ink-dark blue of her gown.

He regarded her closely as the chairs around them emptied, as the cream of London society crammed onto the dance floor.

"Mrs. Whittier, you might be surprised by what terrifies me."

෴

Frances studied the face of this man who regarded her with unnerving seriousness. His brows were determined slashes over eyes of a startling blue, his hair as fair as Caroline's. Faint lines had been burned into the corners of his eyes, no doubt by months under the sultry sun of Spain or southern France. So faraway and lovely that a shiver ran through her body.

He had been a soldier, just like Charles.

"I reckon I have a fair idea of what terrifies you," she said smoothly, slinging a friendly smile onto her face. "As you're a soldier, it must be eminently practical—a boggy field or an empty powder horn."

His mouth curved. "You give me credit for more sense than I actually possess. I'm no longer a soldier, for I've already begun the process of selling my commission, so I can no longer have a soldier's fears."

"Ah, but you must have good sense all the same, or perhaps a remarkable persuasive ability. After all, I know you've staked your claim to a room of Tallant House, and somehow you managed to paint one of Lady Tallant's carpets without incurring her anger."

"That was no triumph of my own. My sister-in-law happened to be distracted by a scheme." He took a breath as though he was going to continue, but nothing else followed. The dark lashes of his eyes lowered, shadowing his face.

For a long moment, Frances studied him in silence, then began to tease apart the cracked sticks of Caroline's fan. This former soldier was pleasant to look on—more than pleasant, to be honest. But his pause wasn't for Frances's benefit. If her guess was correct—which, after years of observation, it usually was—the scheme in question involved matchmaking Mr. Middlebrook with Caroline.

Frances wasn't sure if Lady Tallant had done him a service. Caroline was eager to flirt but little interested in allowing anyone to achieve a conquest.

"Anything you care to discuss?" she finally asked.

"Actually, yes." Once again, he gathered his stiff right arm into his left hand, shielding himself behind a wall of limbs. "I want to court Lady Stratton."

Ah. So she'd been correct. It ought to feel gratifying; there was no sense in a little pang of disappointment.

After all, this was to be expected. Everyone wanted Caroline. Though there was something painfully deliberate about the way Middlebrook spoke that simple sentence, as though he'd clipped a long list down to its bare essential.

While Caroline was a virtuoso of flirtation, Frances was a conductor, orchestrating social interactions so that they ran smoothly and pleasantly. "If you only want the opportunity to court her, then you'll be very easily satisfied. As she's invited you to call tomorrow, all you need to do to achieve your heart's desire is accept the invitation."

He shot her a sharp look. "I didn't say it was my *heart's desire*. It's simply something that I would like. After all, she's not *Caro*—or rather *Cara*—to me yet."

Not yet his *dear one*. His tone was tinged with dry humor, and Frances smiled, though she knew he would care little for the smile of a passably attractive widow of twenty-nine. When a man had Caroline's fair flawlessness on his mind, *passably attractive* was nothing of the sort.

"She'll probably become so," Frances said. "She does to everyone." Her voice sounded weary rather than confident, and she batted her own hand with the cracked fan. Though Mr. Middlebrook wanted what everyone else did, that didn't mean his desire was any less sincere.

And it was not Frances's place to question it. It was her place to ensure that he called tomorrow.

"Excuse me," she murmured. "What I mean is, I'm sure you'll enjoy her company if you call."

Middlebrook leaned back as much as his frail chair would permit, narrowing his vivid blue eyes. "If you'll permit me to be frank, Mrs. Whittier, I would rather have *her* enjoy *my* company. And I ask for your help ensuring that she does so."

Frances twitched. "You—what?"

He shrugged, a lopsided gesture as he still held his right arm tight. "You are her cousin and friend as well as her companion, are you not? You live in her house, sit at her side. You must know her better than anyone else. I would like your help as I..." His straight brows yanked into a vee as he searched for a word. "Pursue her."

Frances could only stare. "No one's ever asked for my help before."

Now he looked surprised. "Really? But it seems so obvious."

A brittle laugh popped out. "To you, perhaps, but not to the *ton*. I assure you, Mr. Middlebrook, there's nothing obvious about looking to the right hand of the most sought after woman in London."

She realized her blunder at once, and her cheeks

went awkwardly hot. "I'm sorry, I shouldn't have
referred to… oh, that wasn't well done of me."

The earl's brother tilted his head, then shook it.
"Please don't feel you must avoid common figures
of speech. I'm well aware that our language includes
many references to right hands and arms."

Frances drew in a long breath. "Thank you for that.
I must say, your manners are quite as pretty as anyone
could hope."

His mouth curved on one side, denting his cheek.
"It's not good manners, but frankness. I'd much prefer
not to have people ignore my injury. I won't be able
to rejoin society if others pity me."

Pity. The word was so small yet so terrible. Frances
had met pity before, and the two had parted as
enemies. "I understand. And I assure you I meant only
to apologize for something that might have seemed
unfeeling. I've known other soldiers before you. None
of them wanted pity as much as they wanted a good
meal and a quick tumble."

He choked. "You really *are* a little terrifying."

"Am I wrong?"

She had thought his face stern, his smiles carefully
measured. But now it broke into a grin, quick and
sunny and full of mischief, and she caught her breath
at the sweet suddenness of it. "No, you're quite right,"
he said. "Add a soft bed, and I do believe you would
capture every soldier of my acquaintance."

"A good thing you're not a soldier anymore, then,
as London offers beds and meals and tumbles aplenty."

His shoulders shook. "I hadn't expected such plain
speech in a ballroom, I admit."

Her stomach gave a sweet little flip. He hadn't exactly given her a compliment, but it was a tiny triumph to surprise this man. She was beginning to find him intriguing, with his wounds and his frankness, his humor and determination.

And *intriguing* was not something she came across very often when talking with Caroline's suitors. Frances was famished for *intriguing*. Especially when *intriguing* had intent blue eyes and captured her in conversation.

She dragged her thoughts back into crisp order. "Caroline tolerates it, fortunately. As a companion to a countess, frankness serves me well. I am her second set of eyes and ears, and if I do not report accurately, I cannot help her."

He raised an eyebrow. "Will you be reporting on me, then? Perhaps I ought to fetch you some wine instead of the orgeat my brother inflicted upon you."

"You needn't get me inebriated in order to get a favorable report."

"Oh? What must I do?"

Nothing more than you already have. She flexed the sticks of her fan again, far too hard, and the cracked ivory snapped. "You've told me the truth about what you want, and you've asked for my help. That's singular enough."

"You've broken your fan," he said with a nod at the wounded accessory.

"It's not mine," Frances blurted. Her fingers felt clumsy on the fragile, ruined ivory. "Please, never mind it."

He studied her for a long moment, and she drew herself up as tall as she could. She was a baronet's daughter by birth, after all. There was no need to become agitated under the scrutiny of this golden man, who asked and noticed things that no one else did.

So she told herself—yet as he studied her, her blood seemed to rush a little more quickly through her veins. Though she sat carefully straight, she thought of… *rolling over*.

Ridiculous. It had been far too long, that was all; her imagination was as overheated as this ballroom. "About Caroline," she said in a voice that was all business. "You want my help in courting her."

He drummed the fingers of his left hand on the arm of his chair. "Help with courtship sounds a bit excessive. What if we limit it to advice?"

"Oh, certainly. I'm excellent at giving advice."

He smirked. "I've heard that often this evening."

Frances drew her chin back. "What? That I inflict advice on people?"

Again, that quick mischievous grin. "No, no. I can't speak to that, having only just met you. But the whole of the *ton* has been remarkably free with advice tonight, much to my good fortune."

Ha. She could well imagine. Everyone would want to be the first, the closest to a man retrieved from the violent mysteries of war—whether he returned as a prodigal son or a hero.

"That is indeed fortunate," Frances replied. "That the advice has been free, I mean. Few could bear the cost if the *ton* began to charge for its helpful instructions."

Henry's expression grew self-conscious. "Indeed, yes. Within one minute of entering the ballroom, our hostess recommended several remedies that she swore could not fail to restore my youthful glow."

Frances would have laughed if she had not thought he might take it amiss. If there was anything he lacked, it was not a youthful glow. His skin shone the healthy brown of long days spent outdoors, while under the stark cut of his austere black and white clothing, his muscles showed long and lean. No one who really looked at him could think Henry Middlebrook was anything in the common way.

Her stomach did another little flip, but she managed a calm tone. "Do you plan to take all the advice that has been shoveled upon you?"

He shifted in his chair, hitching one foot across the other knee. "I could not if I wanted to. I have been advised both to take rest and take exercise, to eat heartily and to starve myself. I am not to closet myself away, nor should I monopolize the attention of the young ladies."

A shadow flitted over his light eyes for a second, then the satirical glint returned to them.

Frances nodded as though this recitation made perfect sense. "You must be the most fortunate man in this ballroom. Not only to be so taxed by the good wishes of caring friends, but then to be able to discard all of their contrary advice without a bit of guilt. I hope you've found the evening enjoyable despite the burdens placed upon you."

He settled himself more firmly against the back of his chair, considering. "Do you know, I think I have. Will I see you tomorrow at Lady Stratton's house?"

"Of course. I'll be the one flinging advice at people and breaking all the fans. Someone must play that essential role."

He studied her through narrowed eyes. She narrowed hers right back, and he grinned, then turned his head toward the couples winding their way through the final patterns of the dance.

"You would have made a good soldier, Mrs. Whittier," he said. "I shall be fortunate if you agree to fight on my side."

Frances did not pretend to misunderstand. "A word in Caroline's ear at the right moment? Tell her how fond you are of starving and gorging yourself?"

He rolled his eyes. "Not that, please. But any and every other inconsequentiality that might be of help. If you don't mind, of course."

"I don't mind. I'll be happy to help if I can."

"I'm sure Lady Stratton values your opinion."

"She might if I dispensed it less freely. But I shall give it to her, for what it's worth." She offered him a smile, wishing for a little more of Caroline's verve.

"I won't press you for more than that," he said. "You're very generous. Only keep her from forgetting my name, and let me know if she has any particular likes or dislikes. I shall endeavor to do the rest."

Forget his name? Surely not. Would he remember hers, though?

The music came to an end, and the ballroom began to shift in new patterns as a hubbub of voices replaced the tune of the orchestra. Frances caught a glimpse of Lord and Lady Tallant through the swirl of the crowd. They'd be back in less than a minute, all curiosity. *What could Hal and Mrs. Whittier have to talk about for so long?*

"Not roses," Frances said in a rush. "Caroline doesn't

care for roses because they're so often given. Bring something more unusual when you call."

Middlebrook studied her again. "Thank you. I'll make sure that I do."

With Lord and Lady Tallant now almost at his side, he stood and inclined his head, a gesture of farewell that she realized would not draw attention to his injured arm.

Frances wanted more than a distant nod; she wanted to reach him. Before she thought, her hands stretched out to clasp his—first the left, then the twisted right.

She had never done such a thing before. Her own body startled her.

It startled her too that she felt the pressure of his fingers so deeply; they warmed her with a heat nothing like the crush of the summer crowds. His gloved hands were strong within hers.

He stared at her, his lips parted as if he were about to speak, but the words had melted before they reached the air. She realized her face wore the same expression, and she pressed her mouth into a proper smile and released his fingers.

"Until tomorrow," Frances said in a louder tone to cover her bewilderment. Thoughts in a tumult, she looked down at the sensible dark blue crape of her gown as though it required all of her attention.

She still had no idea what terrified him. And that terrified *her* a little. In a good way.

Oh, she was intrigued.

Three

ALBEMARLE STREET, HOME TO LADY STRATTON, WAS A jostling, vivid lane at the edge of London's most fashionable residential area. Carts and carriages trundled past, pulled by high-stepping horses that graced the crushed-stone macadam with their droppings. Coal soot powdered the sky, and vivid blooms tumbled from window boxes.

Henry loved it. He absolutely loved London. Its familiar scents and sights were more precious to him than a masterpiece in tempera paint.

Though with only one hand, the simple social act of calling on a woman was not so simple as it ought to be. To carry flowers, Henry had to clutch them to his chest as if they were themselves a desirable female. To sound the knocker, he had to set his precious flowers on the ground. Then stand, knock, crouch again, and retrieve the flowers—all, he hoped, before a servant opened the door and caught him scrabbling on the steps. The waiting was the only part of this simple ritual that he could perform as well as anyone else.

It was rather annoying. Especially since Henry had never enjoyed waiting.

He had composed himself with his flowers—not roses, as his new ally had forewarned him—by the time the door opened. A butler bowed him in and showed him up to the drawing room, where Henry entered the presence of the dazzling Lady Stratton.

And ten other people.

Henry had not expected such a clutter of suitors and opulence. From the outside, Lady Stratton's narrow Albemarle Street house resembled its neighbors, all sedate stone trim and stucco. Inside, the drawing room was as full of lush blooms as a hothouse, and alive with booted feet and blinking eyes.

Against the far wall of the Prussian blue–papered room, Lady Stratton held court amidst a bower of roses as big as baby cabbages. A wide bay of windows draped and valanced in fringed brocade framed her, the sooty afternoon light giving her the dreamy look of a *sfumato* painting. Graceful and otherworldly, a fairy tale princess with hair as fine as spun flax and eyes the color of new grass in spring.

"Mr. Middlebrook!" Lady Stratton cried, extending her left hand to him. "How wonderful that you have come. I was hoping to see you."

"You honor me." He inclined his head—thank God, he remembered not to bow his greeting—and handed her the flowers. The heavy scent of the roses around her punched him in the nose.

"Violets! Oh, delightful. I haven't been given violets in ever so long." She held them to her nose, her eyes closing as she breathed their faint scent. "How lovely. Thank you very much."

Henry noticed Mrs. Whittier sitting in a

straight-backed chair tucked into a discreet corner. At Caro's speech, the companion winked at him, her hazel eyes merry and rebellious in her demure face.

Henry suppressed a grin. "I'm glad you like them." He shook Caro's hand, admiring the ease with which she had accomplished the small social trespass of left hand rather than right.

With that, his moment at court was over, and he turned to find a seat. Caro was boxed in between the determined forms of Misters Crisp and Hambleton, cousins who often dressed identically for effect. They stared back at Henry with identically set jaws over their leaf-green cravats: *Don't even think about it.* Very well—next time he would call earlier, so he might claim a closer seat.

He found his way to a chair by Bart Crosby, a mild-mannered baronet who had been one of his closest friends before Henry went to war.

"Hal," Bart murmured as Henry settled down next to him. "About the ball yesterday. I didn't know about your…" His dark eyes didn't meet Henry's as one of his hands flailed.

"Don't give it another thought, Bart." He clapped his friend on the shoulder in their old reassuring habit. "I'm the same man I always was."

The lie was kindly meant, so perhaps Henry could be forgiven it. He wasn't the same man he had been before Quatre Bras. *Four arms*, the name meant. The place was a crossroads. Ha. He was only twenty-six; he might live another five or six decades with the damage Quatre Bras had wrought.

Not that Bart wanted to hear about that. Nor did

beautiful Lady Stratton. Nor did Jem, who had never wanted Henry to purchase an army commission in the first place, who had offered him a lordly allowance to remain in England.

Henry couldn't bear to be the type of man who stayed home and stayed safe, taking money from his brother. But if he had, at least he'd have been able to take it with both hands. Fist over fist, taking and taking.

"Would that were so," Bart said at last in reply to Henry's assurance. "If you're the same as ever, we could go out on one of our adventures, just as we did when we were boys. Unless... unless you have had enough adventuring lately?"

Henry shook his head. "I would not say I have had any adventures at all."

He tried to smile, to reassure Bart, who had looked up to the Middlebrook brothers. Bart was the youngest in his family, and his mother and three older sisters had always been brimful of schemes for his betterment. Bart had been more interested in hunting and fishing, muddy boots and windy gallops.

"But we can certainly remedy that," Henry added. "I must get to know the city again. You'll have to be my guide."

Bart's expression turned relieved. "Certainly. I've got a new curricle and pair. We'll take it out sometime, shall we?"

"If your horses are up to the task," broke in a new voice. Lord Wadsworth, a viscount with whom Henry'd once had an uneasy nodding acquaintance. Wadsworth had sauntered over unnoticed and perched on the arm of a tapestry-covered chair. "Oh, wait. I forgot. Your mother helped you select them, didn't she, Crosby? In that case, they must be marvelous."

He grinned at Bart, who returned the smile hesitantly. Henry only watched Wadsworth, wondering whether the man meant to be rude or polite. It was always hard to tell with Wadsworth.

"Lady Crosby has an admirable knowledge of horseflesh," he finally ventured. "One that her son shares."

From the corner of his eye, he could see Bart's shoulders shift. "Of course," Wadsworth said blandly, and Bart's shoulders relaxed.

The viscount squinted at Henry, his gray eyes bright. "Haven't seen you for a long time, Middlebrook. You look well. Except for your arm, of course." He made a tutting sound. "Did a Frenchie do that to you? It must be the very devil to have a coat tailored with your arm like that."

His voice was sympathetic, and Henry saw Bart nodding along. But Henry had grown accustomed to looking for weapons, and he considered his reply for a careful second. "I find the tailoring of coats to be a matter of insignificance. You are fortunate indeed if this is all that occupies you, Wadsworth."

The viscount slid his feet in an impatient gesture. "Nonsense, Middlebrook. That's not the only thing on my mind. I merely—well, I know you want to fit in again, and I fear it won't be easy for you."

"How thoughtful you are to fear on my behalf," Henry said just as sympathetically as Wadsworth had.

Wadsworth waved a hand. "Simply condoling with you, Middlebrook. I thought you'd have enough fear for two, coming home from war all mangled."

His eyes were narrowed, scrutinizing Henry. With his dark hair brushed forward over his forehead, Wadsworth looked vulpine, and Henry remembered why he had always felt uneasy around the viscount. Wadsworth always studied people a little too long, a little too closely. His words were barbed, but not so pointed that any injury could be deemed deliberate.

And maybe it *wasn't* deliberate.

Maybe.

"As I've come home alive and well, I can't imagine what you mean by *mangled*," Henry replied carelessly, leaning back in his chair. It was another spindly gilt contraption, far too frail and feminine to allow him to lean his full weight against it. So he held his abdomen tensed, supporting his weight with his own muscles as he strove to keep his expression bland and calm.

"If you don't, I can't imagine who does. Such a serious injury must positively unman you." Wadsworth smiled again. "Come now, Middlebrook, we're all friends here. I'm only offering my... sympathy."

If there had been anything warm and friendly in his eyes, as there was in Bart's, Henry would have believed him. Actually, Bart was looking stricken. Pitying, almost.

Enough of this. Bart already felt wounded enough on Henry's behalf. It was time to go on the defensive.

"And what's been occupying you during the three years I've been away, Wadsworth? Have you made any worthwhile conquests?"

Wadsworth shrugged and pulled his pocket watch from his waistcoat. "Worthwhile? No. Not yet. But I aim to catch Lady Stratton if I have my way about it." He spun the timepiece, twirling it one way, then the other on its short gold chain. "Want to see something really amusing? Watch this."

He winked at his audience, then turned toward the corner of the room. "Mrs. Whittier, could I have a word with you?"

Henry scanned the room, noting how Caroline still spoke with her bookend dandies; how a plate of sandwiches was handed from man to man, laughter spilling forth at each gesture; how Mrs. Whittier rose from her chair and walked toward them with a companion's dutifulness and a great lady's hauteur.

"Lord Wadsworth." She inclined her head. "Sir Bartlett. Mr. Middlebrook."

"I was just telling my friends," Wadsworth said, "that I'm pursuing Lady Stratton. Have you any opinion to express?"

She opened her mouth, then slammed it shut again and shook her head. "Any opinions on the subject of her courtship are best expressed by the countess herself."

"You're right, of course," said the viscount. "I really needn't consult you at all. I know it seems unlikely to ask one such as yourself, but Lady Stratton relies on you so. And so I'm willing to overlook the disparity in our station and allow you to express your opinion."

"You honor me," she said drily. "But I doubt I have anything to say that you'd want to hear. Excuse me."

She threaded her way across the room to Caroline and bent her dark head down to her cousin's fair one. With a nod, she seemed to accept some order. She moved across the room again and consulted with a servant in the doorway.

All without another look at Henry or Bart or

Wadsworth. It was well done—but Henry had hoped for some small sign of friendship. Another wink, another smile. They were allies, after all.

Wadsworth snorted. "I do enjoy that woman. She is the prickliest female. Quite a guard dog for her employer."

"If Lady Stratton has any undesirable suitors, then a guard dog is precisely what is needed." Henry shoved himself forward in his chair, then stood. "If you'll excuse me. Bart, I'll see you soon?"

He wasn't sure exactly what he ought to say to Mrs. Whittier, but he had to say *something* to let her know he welcomed the help Lord Wadsworth scorned.

Or seemed to. Damn, maybe Henry was tilting at windmills, ready to imagine enemies everywhere. This was London, not the Bossu Wood. No one was hiding, ready to fire at him.

"Mrs. Whittier," he said softly as he came up behind her near the doorway of the drawing room.

She started, then turned. "Oh. Mr. Middlebrook." Her eyes seemed unwilling to meet his, and she had plastered her tall form against the wall, as though she could shove herself through and into the corridor if only she tried hard enough.

"Call me Henry if you wish," Henry offered. "My friends do. Well, some of them call me Hal, but I hate that."

The bright eyes lifted to his, and her expression turned shrewd. "This is what your friends call you? And yet I heard Lord Wadsworth call you Middlebrook."

"Exactly." Henry wanted to sigh. "Lord Wadsworth is not the kind of man to set people at their ease. In fact, I think he prefers to do the opposite."

She drew in a long breath. "Yes, I know that about him. I suppose I'm rather too proud for my own good. You probably don't understand that from someone in my position."

Henry let out a quick bark of laughter. "Too proud? Mrs. Whittier, I had my turn under his quizzing glass before you did. I'll wager I can muster as much pride as you can."

At last, he won a smile from her. "Frances."

"Pardon?"

"If you like, you may call me Frances. Caroline calls me Frannie, but I cannot abide it."

"Frances, then," he said, shaking her hand in his left. "Since we are soldiers together."

She caught her breath, and her cheeks darkened, the blush of a plum on the skin of a peach. She was all brights and darks, this woman. Such coloring would require much layering to capture it well in oils, but she would look well painted, with her determined features and elegant carriage. He wondered if a portrait painter could capture the snap of defiance in her eyes, though, or the wry curve of her mouth.

Her fingers moved within his, twisting, and he realized he still had hold of her hand. "Pardon me," he muttered.

"It's quite all right," she said quickly. "So, we both have dreadful nicknames. Is it not odd how the people who are closest to us persist in addressing us as if we are six years old?"

"That may be the last time they saw us clearly."

Frances looked thoughtful. "You may be right. And

that might not be a bad thing. I was a much better person at the age of six than I am now."

"I find that hard to believe."

Her brows lifted. "You need not say things to me just because you think politeness requires it, Henry. I am sure you too are not the innocent you once were, for good or ill."

Probably she meant the statement to be taken lightly, but Henry turned it over in his mind.

For good or ill, she said. The edges of the words tumbled roughly, snagging his thoughts. "Do you truly see good in it? The way one changes over time?"

To Frances's credit, she did not look surprised by his odd question. She caught her lower lip in her teeth and shook back a lock of coffee-colored hair that had fallen free from its pins.

"Yes, I do. At least, I think there is always the hope and possibility for good." She smiled, looking rueful. "I know as well as any that such hopes and possibilities are not always fulfilled. But that is what tomorrow is for, is it not? To try again? Or so I tell myself in my most ambitious moods."

"Awfully cozy, aren't you?" Wadsworth's voice drawled into Henry's ear. Henry jerked, caught unaware.

Wadsworth nodded silkily to Frances, then turned to Henry. "So, Middlebrook. Have you decided to leave Lady Stratton to better men?"

Before he could reply, Frances lifted her chin. "Lord Wadsworth, I doubt there are any better men here than Mr. Middlebrook. And as you are aware, Lady Stratton trusts my opinion implicitly."

"I am aware," Wadsworth said. "It is her ladyship's

only fault." He kissed his fingertips in the direction of Lady Stratton, who was still holding forth to a rapt Hambleton and Crisp.

Frances bristled, and Henry felt the urge to jump to her defense, just as she had his. "Wadsworth, you cannot insult this lady in that way."

Wadsworth smiled. "But I just did, did I not? It seems I can do as I like. Pity you can't do the same."

And with a final flick of his eyes over Henry's arm, he strolled back to the center of the room. Back to Lady Stratton, who had heard nothing of what had just passed.

He was efficient, that Wadsworth. It took him a scant minute to abandon even the pretense of politeness; even less time to eviscerate Henry's tentative peace.

Frances's cheeks were vivid with color, and her chest caught with shallow breaths. She looked like she wanted to claw out Wadsworth's throat.

Henry found her fingers again, pressed them for an instant. "You must tell Lady Stratton he speaks to you this way."

"He's never done so before." She ground out each word through clenched teeth. "He's always been civil. He's…" She drew in a deep breath and slapped a smile on her face. It didn't reach her eyes, and it began to fade at once. "Well. Never mind. I can handle him myself."

"Why should you have to?"

She folded her arms, then pressed herself against the wall again. "I'm only a countess's companion, Henry. He's a viscount. He's just having a bit of fun at my expense. As long as he treats Caroline well, that's all that matters."

Henry wanted to shake her. "That is *not* all that matters. If one doesn't stop a bully, he will continue."

She frowned. "He's not Bonaparte, Henry. He's only a bored aristocrat. If Caroline enjoys his attentions, it's not my place to send him away."

"Surely she owes you the respect of her friends."

Frances turned her head away, as though the gilded plasterwork that framed the doorway deserved every bit of her attention. "No, it is I who owe her everything. And she gives me her own respect. She cannot be responsible for the behavior of others."

She drew herself up straight. "Besides, it is no worry of yours. Wadsworth is not the first such man I've encountered, and he probably won't be the last."

Her smile trembled, and Henry actually reached out his hand to touch her cheek, to offer some comfort.

But his hand didn't reach out. His right shoulder flexed, his arm dangled and seesawed numbly. From the corner of his eye, he saw Wadsworth lift his eyebrows, then turn toward Caro. He murmured something low, and a burst of laughter succeeded from the men around him.

In the clear afternoon light, the countess's fair hair shone richly, the bright ruddy gold of Indian yellow pigment. Precious and rare. For her, only the best.

In this room—in London—there might always be people like Wadsworth, who doubted Henry could resume his place in society. Who doubted *him*. The war was over, and its tactics were of no use anymore. He couldn't win the esteem of the men in this drawing room by offering them meager privileges like dried-out snuff or extra biscuit; they could do better for themselves simply by stepping out the door with a shilling in hand. And he could hardly soothe and train Lady Stratton to follow his will, as once upon a time he had been able to command a horse.

He had lost his easy place in this world, and he did not yet see his way to a new one.

He could not stand still any longer; his muscles jumped to act. "I must leave," he blurted to Frances.

She sank a little against the wall. "Yes. Yes, I understand."

If so, that was more than Henry understood.

He bade Lady Stratton a proper farewell; he managed that much. Lord Wadsworth muttered in his ear as he left, "Deserting the scene of your defeat? I would have expected better from a soldier."

His words crawled over Henry like stinging insects, and he shuddered them off, annoyed, as he left the house and began to stride the few streets back to Tallant House. His feet fell naturally into the swift pattern of wheeling step: one hundred twenty paces in a minute, each a perfect thirty inches long.

He halted, forced himself to walk more slowly—the pace of a gentleman, not a soldier. He must remember the kind of man he was now.

Or was it only the man he had once been? He was beginning to suspect that his old self had been trod into the mud of Belgium, burned away under the unforgiving sun of a Spanish siege. He might feel the ghost of the old Henry here, but Wadsworth had just proven: it would be difficult to resurrect his place in society.

He was determined, though. He was haunted by many ghosts these days; the old Henry would merely be one more.

❧

Naturally, Jem and Emily wanted a full report over dinner on his call at Caro's house.

"I brought her violets," Henry said, looking over the dishes scattered across the table. He had yet to re-accustom himself to the amount of food served for a simple family dinner. Two courses, multiple meats and vegetables, all prepared and seasoned well.

An everyday luxury. Heaven on a plate. He selected beef, creamed peas, and a fricassee of chicken as tonight's particular heaven.

"Violets were a good choice," Emily said, cutting slivers of sole. "Really, anything except roses is a good choice. You wouldn't believe the number of roses Caro gets. She has a horror of them."

Jem paused with his fork halfway to his mouth. "Em, I thought you liked roses."

"I do, Jemmy. But I don't get hundreds of them every week."

He stared. "Hundreds? Where does she put them all?"

Emily shrugged. "In the privy, for all I know. Never mind, Hal; you've made a good start. Did you speak to her much?"

"Not much." Henry didn't want to discuss the afternoon again. The unexpected alliance, the unforeseen attack. He forked through his chicken and found pieces small enough to spear without cutting, then turned his attention to the beef.

"Why not?" Emily pressed.

Jem shot her a look.

"What?" Emily countered. "He went there to talk to her. So why didn't he?"

"She was… *busy*," Henry grunted as he struggled to cut the beef without the aid of a fork. "She had at least ten other callers. *Gah*." The sauced beef had shot from his plate into his lap, spattering wine-broth down his shirtfront and on his breeches.

Good God. He looked like a baby playing with its food. He glared at his right arm, but it was insensible. As always.

He would have glared at his brother, at Emily, but they both studied their plates tactfully as a footman helped Henry clean up the worst of the spill.

"The fish is quite good," Emily said when Henry reseated himself. "I asked Cook to make it salty, just as you always preferred it, Hal."

She passed him the platter with a smile, though her eyes didn't meet his.

If she or Jem had offered to help Henry cut his meat, as though he were one of their young sons, he might have left the table. But this—well, she meant to be kind. And she managed it beautifully, as she managed everything she put her mind to.

Such kindness could strangle him, though. Jem and Emily had wondered whether Henry was ready to be back in London, to mix with society. Now they couldn't even look at him.

A pity, Wadsworth had said. It was pity that terrified Henry. And it was lurking everywhere today.

Except in the dark eyes of Frances Whittier.

Jem cleared his throat, studied the crest on the handle of his fork. "You know, Hal, I was wondering how Winter Cottage was looking these days. No one's been there since you… ah…"

"Left for war." Henry's voice was flat.

Winter Cottage was a small property in Sidcup, a short ride outside London. Jem had deeded it to Henry when he reached his majority.

Jem was the opposite of subtle; his every emotion flickered across his mild countenance. And just now, he had that worried look again. Henry knew what he was up to.

"The season can be awfully exhausting," Jem continued. "Right, Em?"

"Oh—yes, indeed," his wife agreed. "Very much so. Yes, I only wish *I* could go to Sidcup for a few weeks."

Henry folded his arms—well, one arm—and grimaced, waiting for them to make their point.

Jem widened his eyes, trying to look as though he'd just had an idea. "I say, Hal, you could wait out the season at Winter Cottage. Come back in a few weeks when the City's thinned out. Er, more relaxing that way, you know."

"I'm not here to relax," Henry said. What he *was* here for, he wasn't sure. He'd wanted to conquer, to win London. He deserved a victory; he craved one. But not even his family had faith in him anymore.

Why should they, though? If he couldn't get through a family dinner without dumping food on himself, how could he mix with the *ton*? How could he dance at a ball or take a lady in to supper? How could he ever again clasp a woman in his arms when he had only one?

"Just think about it," Emily pleaded. "It would be such a pity to have that lovely cottage unused."

Pity.

"I'll think about it," Henry sighed, and she looked relieved.

And maybe he really would. Leaving for Winter Cottage wasn't ideal, but then, neither was having a paralyzed arm.

Henry could think of nothing better to do. And surely it was better to do *something*.

But that night, the first letter arrived, and that changed everything.

Four

THE FIRST SURPRISE WAS THE FACT THAT A LETTER HAD arrived for Henry at all. Since his recent return to London, he had often been included in Jem's and Emily's invitations, but he had no correspondents of his own.

The second surprise was the way it was delivered. Jem's butler brought the letter to Henry's bedchamber with a disapproving glare, the first facial expression Sowerberry had ever permitted himself in Henry's presence. The letter had been, the servant declared, left by a saucy-looking boy for "the soldier what had the gamy arm."

Henry halted his inventory of his possessions—not that he was *definitely* leaving for Winter Cottage, just *considering* it. "My arm is not gamy," he protested as he accepted the letter from the butler, who drew himself up tall with offended dignity. "Nothing of the sort, or I would have lost it."

"I am aware, sir. Nevertheless, I judged you a more probable recipient for this missive than Lord or Lady Tallant, who have suffered no such unfortunate injuries," Sowerberry sniffed, bowing himself out.

Henry hardly noticed his departure, because the letter itself was the third surprise. The manner of its delivery had led him to expect a note from someone who had known him in the army. Maybe one of the men who had fought under him, God help the poor fellows. But this letter was on heavy linen paper, faintly cross-hatched from the netting on which it had been dried. A quality such that a soldier would never have dared scrawl on a single sheet.

The folds of the paper were sealed with a generous blob of red wax dropped in a deliberate circle and pressed with the image of a hill topped with a cross.

The seal of the Graves family. Of Caroline Graves, Lady Stratton.

Another surprise; by now Henry had lost count of them. He could not imagine why she would write to him. Apart from giving her violets, he had surely done nothing to make an impression on her this afternoon.

Henry pressed the letter against his body and worked open the seal with one awkward thumb.

The handwriting was feminine but bold and clear, the lower loops angular, as if dashed off in haste.

Dear Mr. Middlebrook,

I hope you'll forgive the impropriety of a private correspondence. I wanted to say more to you earlier today, and I must now resort to paper rather than speech. It is a poor substitute, but I shall imagine your face as I write. Did you know you are positively transformed when you smile? You seem to carry a heavy weight inside, yet I know you are a young man. Several years younger than I, since I can be strictly honest on paper.

A note might be better than a conversation, after all. You are a soldier—or were until very recently—so I know you require proof, facts, evidence. Here, then, is the evidence of my friendship. I believe that your own is well worth having, and I hope you will grant it to me.

I thank you for your call earlier today. The beau monde can, I know, be unmannerly, and that is their misfortune. But do not let it be yours. We all hide our wounds here, but that does not mean they do not exist. Some are very deep indeed. Your wound is simply visible to everyone. For that, you must be even braver than the rest of us. I know you have lived in this world before, and you shall again with great success.

Your company has given me great pleasure, and I would like to see you again, often. I would appreciate your assistance in keeping this correspondence a secret, but if you wish, I will write to you again. Often.

Sincerely,
Your friend

Good lord.

Lady Stratton had noticed him. Even more unexpectedly, she sought his company. Without pitying. With "great pleasure."

His left hand felt as nerveless as the right, and he sank into a convenient chair. The letter dangled from his hand as if trying to escape, and he made himself hold it in front of his eyes again to prove that it was real.

It *was* real. The ink had bitten into the heavy, soft paper, and the words were dark and clear. They were proof, facts, evidence that he had made more of an impression than he thought. That he had succeeded in some small way.

She wanted to see him again.

She, the most desirable woman in London. Caro, the foundation for rebuilding his life.

Before Quatre Bras, the day that changed everything, Henry had made a habit of stretching out on the ground during his few leisure hours. He and his men were accustomed to long hours of work and long hours of monotony: ninety-nine days of drudgery for each day of terror. As soon as fires were lit and shelters built from whatever brush or wood was at hand, Captain Middlebrook always sprawled on the ground, looking as though there was nowhere in the world he would rather be.

His soldiers thought nothing of it, then, when they brought him terrible news—orders gone astray, enemies drawing near, no sleep again tonight—and Henry was leaning on one elbow or lying with his hands clasped behind his head. Leaning, sitting, or lying down, he took the unexpected from them as easily as the everyday.

Henry alone knew that when the unexpected hit, it shook him like an earthquake under water, deep within until he felt he'd crumble. So he used the ground as his support, ever ready. He had been only twenty-three when he went to war, and he had neither seen bloodshed nor learned courage.

Now he was twenty-six, and he had seen much bloodshed, and he still felt shaken to his marrow when he was struck by the unexpected. And he had not expected this letter.

He hoisted himself from the chair and sat on the floor, leaning against the bed with its ivory damask cover. A carpet was as apt a surface for sitting as was dirt chewed by hooves and marching boots. It reminded him that his world was different now—this familiar society, which had so suddenly tilted askew.

Caro's letter itself was not much more than a friendly note, but it set the world straight again.

He ran his fingers through the loops of the Brussels carpet. Jem's carpet, in Jem's house. He was even wearing Jem's clothing today. Everything he had was Jem's, really, except for Winter Cottage. Henry could slide out of London without leaving a trace of himself behind.

But no. It was no more right for Mister Middlebrook to turn tail and run now than it would have been for Captain Middlebrook to do so in Bayonne or Brussels. Or Quatre Bras.

Very well, he would answer the letter. He would take her confidence for his own. And with enough letters like this, she might make herself dear to him yet, and he might become so to her. *Caro*.

He would compose his reply right away. He stood and reached for pen and ink from the compact desk in his bedchamber.

Except he didn't. His right shoulder flexed inward from his collarbone, the ghost of the movement he'd commanded, and his numb arm jerked and swayed like a pendulum.

Damn it. He had forgotten again, in his anticipation. He stared at his disobedient limb, hand, fingers. They would not act; they could not flex to hold a pen.

His insides tipped, sudden and watery as a ship sliding down a wave.

He clasped the back of his chair and breathed in and out slowly. This was nothing nearly as serious as Quatre Bras. This was simply putting ink to paper in a comfortable house in London. He could do this.

He sat at the desk, and with his left hand, he wrenched open the inkwell. Ink spattered onto the painted wood of the desk and speckled his hand.

"Damn it," he muttered. This blunder slightly damped the pleasure of answering Caro's letter. Ink was the devil to clean up.

He dipped a quill that felt wrongly shaped against the curve of his hand. His unpracticed fingers shivered once the pen took on its load of ink, and black blobbed onto the page.

No matter. He was just writing a short note; he could cut off the damaged section of the paper.

But his fingers slipped, dropping more spatters of ink, and filling the D he'd tried to write—just Dear, that was all—in a misshapen circle. And he'd gotten ink on his shirtsleeve too.

He glared at the paper for a moment, as if the force of his gaze would move the particles of ink where they ought to belong. But the few letters he'd scrawled stayed stubbornly malformed, impossibly childish. Illegible, really. And his sleeve was still ruined.

He scratched away determinedly for half an hour, shaping letters until he had managed to write "Dear

Caro" in handwriting at least as good as that of a five-year-old child. It took seven full sheets of writing paper, and his cuffs were completely ruined.

Of course, they were really Jem's cuffs, as he had borrowed this shirt from his brother.

The thought cheered him at once.

Henry leaned back in his chair and regarded the fruits of his labor. Jem's shirt: ruined. His desk: in need of repainting. His hands: speckled as a quail egg.

All for two meager words. That wouldn't do.

He wiped the pen and put it away, the habit of order too strong for him to dismiss even as his mind stumbled around for a solution. He couldn't ask Jem or Emily to write out his reply. They'd be so delighted for him, they'd be buying a special license by morning. And Caro had asked him to keep her letter a secret.

Then he had an idea.

He *could* answer this letter with a little help from the right person. From someone who held Caro's full confidence and whom he thought he could trust with his.

He stood, smoothed his clothing, and rang for Sowerberry.

"Could you please," he asked the butler, "ask Lady Tallant to summon Mrs. Whittier for a call tomorrow?"

Five

FRANCES SUCKED IN HER BREATH, HARD, AGAINST THE tight lacing of her stays. "This is completely ridiculous," she gasped. "I can wear one of my own gowns."

"No, *that* is completely ridiculous, because this gown will be perfect," Caroline said as she and her lady's maid gave the laces another determined yank. "There, that should do it. Goodness, Frannie, you've got a sweet little waist. It's got to be some sort of crime against good society for you to wear plain clothing."

Frances passed her hand down the smooth sweep of the stays. "The only crime is the one you just committed, suffocating your own cousin."

"If you'd truly been suffocated, you wouldn't be able to talk such rubbish," Caroline said, picking up the bronze-green silk from Frances's bed. "Besides, it's not like this is a court dress. It's simply more elegant than your usual." She held it up to Frances's chin. "Millie, I told you the color would be ravishing on her."

"Yes, mum," the maid agreed, and began helping Frances into the garment.

"I've no idea why Emily summoned you, but it

must be important," Caroline mused, sinking into a chair next to Frances's bed. "Perhaps she needs your help recalling something."

"Lord Tallant always wears black," Frances replied in a singsong voice.

Caroline grinned, but Frances couldn't manage another joke. She could barely draw breath, struck as she was by a sudden fear that squeezed her inside her stays.

It was the letter. Lady Tallant knew about the letter Frances had written to Henry, and she disapproved. She intended to warn Frances away, wanting something better than a widow of no family and means—well, not anymore—for her one and only brother-in-law.

In her distraction, she hadn't noticed that Caroline and Millie had finished their assembly. "I knew it," Caroline said. "Ravishing."

"Then it's a shame I won't be doing any ravishing today." Closer to the truth than it ought to have been, since a call at Tallant House was almost a call on Henry.

Maybe she would catch sight of him while she was there. Maybe he would like the way she looked in this borrowed silk.

Maybe she was letting her imagination gallivant around when it ought to tread sedately.

Caroline smirked. "You never know what the day will bring, Frannie. There might be ravishing in it yet. Look how the gown brings out the color in your cheeks. Do you see?"

As Frances knew exactly why the color in her cheeks had suddenly blazed high, she spared herself no more than a glance in the mirror. "All I see is a sow's ear tucked into a silk purse."

"You just feel that way because you ate an embarrassing amount of ham for breakfast," Caroline said. "Now go find out what Emily wants, and tell me everything as soon as you come home."

After five minutes in Tallant House, Frances was fairly sure Lady Tallant didn't want anything at all. She had barely greeted Frances, only welcoming her into the morning room and then excusing herself in a hurry.

So, the call wasn't about the letter to Henry. Probably.

Whatever the mysterious reason, Frances knew how to deal with the whims of the aristocracy. One waited them out. Calmly and as comfortably as possible.

She found a gold velvet chair that looked promising. The bronze-green gown's heavy skirt rustled as she sat.

Hmm. That was rather a pleasing sound. She stood again, then sat with more force. *Shussshh* went the dress against the nubby golden upholstery of her chair.

Good advice; she probably ought to *shush* and behave with dignity. At least she had a pleasant space to mull over her social mystery. Frances loved the morning room in Caroline's house, and this space was just as sunny. Three of the walls were stenciled, white filigree over buttery yellow, and the wall opposite the door was covered with a lush mural of the goddess Athena soothing the Ithacans and their long-lost warrior king Odysseus to peace with one another.

The old soldier returning home to such unrest and ingratitude. Poor man. Still, he had been able to return home to his family. It was more than many were able to do.

"Thank you for your call," said a low voice behind Frances.

She had not heard the door open behind her. She would have startled at the sound of the voice had she not been so pleased to hear it.

"Henry-not-Hal." She turned, a smile tugging at her lips. "How are you?"

He need not even answer; she could see he looked well. More than well. His eyes were crinkled from a grin; his hair was the rich shade of old gold in the coal-smudged daylight filtering through the tall windows. Surprisingly, he wore no coat, and the fine linen of his shirt and silk of his waistcoat lay lightly over the lean planes of his shoulders and chest.

She felt a little warmer within the swaddle of her borrowed gown. She'd been summoned here the day after sending a letter... he wore no coat... they were alone...

She knew the parts of a logical argument: premises, inference, conclusion. Given those premises, there was only one inference she could make... and one way to carry this encounter to its conclusion. He had read the letter; he had liked the letter; he wanted more. More what?

She felt *very* warm.

"I'm quite well, Frances," he said, "though I'm also greedy and presumptuous."

Humor rather than heat? This did not follow the same fluid line as the other premises. She tilted her head. "How delightful?"

"Well, maybe. You see, I have to ask a favor of you." His grin slipped sideways, rueful and crooked. "I need to write a letter."

"To me?"

When he stared at her in surprise, she knew she'd blundered somehow. A new heat of embarrassment colored her cheeks. "Of course not to me. Here I sit, so there's no need for a letter. To whom, then?"

A secret smile brightened his face. "Caro. She sent me a letter last night, and I wish to answer it. The sooner the better, before she forgets about me."

Frances was suddenly very glad for the punishingly tight lacing of her stays. Their stiffness was the only thing that held her upright. "You got a letter… from Caro?"

He dropped into a chair across from her, then leaned forward conspiratorially. "It came under her seal. Quite a lovely note. I hadn't realized she cared so much for my friendship."

"Oh." Frances's head seemed stuffed with cotton. "Yes, she's very kind." She drew in a breath as deep as her lacing would permit. "But the letter—"

"In truth," Henry broke in, left hand gripping the arm of the chair, "I'd rather lost confidence after the call at her house. The letter was just what I needed, at just the right time."

"A letter from Caroline was just what you needed?" She was ransacking the conversation now, looking for some small shard of hope that she'd misunderstood.

He nodded, and his expression softened. "She has a gift for kindness without pity."

Frances sank against the back of her gold-velvet chair. *Shushhhhh* went the dress.

Yes, what else could she do but *shush*? If she told him the truth—that *she* was the one who had reached out to him—she didn't know whose embarrassment would be greater: hers or his.

Probably hers. And she had too much pride to watch his delight turn disappointed. If he needed a letter from Caroline so badly, it was better to let him think he'd gotten one.

She swallowed that pride, the thwarted hope, the flush of humiliation. It was a lot to choke down all at once, and it caught in her throat. She coughed, cleared her throat, and took several seconds to reply again. "I'm glad you liked the letter."

That, at least, was true. There was no need to lie to him at all. His own enthusiasm set the tone of the conversation, and all she need do was play along.

She slipped on her companion's mask, capable and cheerful. "So, you want to write her a letter. Or rather—oh, blast, your right arm. Do you want me to write the letter for you?"

He looked a little taken aback. "No, indeed. I must maintain *some* pride. I might ask for secret insights and hints about gifts, and I *might* inflict my first name on you, but I would *never* ask you to write a letter of courtship for me." That rueful grin again. He was more at ease with it than other men were in all their puffery.

"Of course not." Frances returned his wry tone. "I beg your pardon. I'd quite forgot the rules of assisted courtship." Her nervous hands smoothed her bronze-green skirt again. *Shhhhhhh.*

Henry's eyes flicked over the garment. "That's an

excellent color on you, if you don't mind my saying
so. It's the precise shade of your eyes."

There was no need for Frances to feel a squirm of
warmth again. Certainly no need for it to shoot through
her body from scalp to toes. It was, after all, merely an
observation from an artist, who could be expected to
notice color. "Thank you. It's Caroline's. She insisted
it would be acceptable with my complexion."

There was no way she was going to repeat the
word *ravishing* to Henry. Not when his face had
just softened a little, as though he had only required
this evidence of Caroline's thoughtfulness to fall
completely in her thrall.

"So." Frances spoke up before he could begin
rhapsodizing about Caroline. "If you don't want me
to write your letter, why *have* you summoned me?"

He drew himself up straighter, and his withered
arm sank into the cradle of his left. "My handwriting
is atrocious. Infernal, really. I hoped you could help
me assemble an acceptable reply with a minimum of
misshapen words."

He cleared his throat, shrugged, and looked faintly
mortified. "You were right about not bringing roses,
after all. So I thought you'd know what to—ah, now
that I've said this aloud, it sounds rather... well. You
know, maybe we'd better forget the whole thing."

"No, indeed." Perhaps it was unworthy of her
to want him to fidget a little. "I understand you
perfectly. You want me to write you a love letter to
Caroline, and then you'll transcribe it. And it must be
very short."

She put a hand on her chest and intoned dramatically,

"'*Bed me, my sweet.*' There, we're done. Shall I ring for tea?"

Henry's lips bent in an expression of wicked humor. "If that's your idea of a love letter, perhaps you *had* better ring for tea, and I'll write it myself." He shook his head. "What am I saying? I'm not even writing a love letter. It's a reply, that's all. It's a possibility letter."

Frances permitted herself another jibe. "Still, Henry. This is one of the oddest things I've ever been asked to do, and I once helped Hambleton and Crisp tie their cravats together."

He rolled his eyes. "I don't want you to compose it, only to advise. And you needn't do anything with my cravat."

So of course, she had to look at his cravat when he said that. The starch-white points against his tanned skin, his blue eyes, the sun-golden of his hair. He was a bright palette, all stark colors and clean lines, and his faint scent of soap and evergreen woke something eager within her. She wanted to draw closer to him, breathe deeply, and remember how it felt to be near a man.

He began tapping his knuckles against the arm of his chair, a pillowed pat that pulled her attention back to his words. "I've never written with my left hand before, and I hoped you could help me learn how. My first foray was not a success. I didn't manage a single legible letter, though I did spoil a very nice desk and cuff with ink."

Frances chuckled, and he added, "Ah... that's why I've taken the liberty of removing my coat. I hope you are not offended."

"No, certainly not." *Not at all.* Her eyes wanted to rove over his form again, but she fastened them to his face with admirable tact. "It wouldn't do for formal company, of course, but we're in your home and we're quite alone."

He seemed to become aware of that fact as well. "I apologize if this is not an appropriate request. I thought since you help Caro in so many ways, that this would not be wrong. To help her receive her reply."

She relented at last. It wasn't his fault he had misinterpreted the letter. It wasn't his fault that he wanted Caroline. As Frances truly did like him, she ought to give him the friendship he seemed to want so keenly.

Even if she would rather be selfish.

"No, no. I was only teasing. I always deal with Caroline's correspondence, so there's nothing wrong with this, Henry." Frances savored the taste of his name, of the intimacy he had granted her.

But that wasn't why she'd been summoned here. Apparently.

She drew two chairs over to a graceful tambour writing desk positioned near a window to catch daylight. It held pens, ink, paper, and sand for blotting. Everything they needed.

"Do sit," she said, sinking into a chair. "Take this pen in your hand and see how it feels."

He hefted it sharply in a clenched fist. "It feels wrong."

Frances pressed her lips together to hide a smile. "It's not a riding crop, you know. Just wrap your fingers around it the same way you always did with your right."

She slid the quill between his second and third

fingers. He looked surprised at the contact, and Frances drew her fingers back. "It would be easier if we had a quill from the right wing of the goose, for those fit the left hand better. But these will work well enough until you can lay in a supply. Try forming some letters—very large, at first, just to get accustomed to the movement."

He didn't move; he only stared at his left arm.

"What is it?" Frances asked.

A sideways flick of his eyes. "I'm sorry to ask this, but would you roll back the left sleeve? This is my brother's shirt, and..." He trailed off, ruddy from chagrin under his tan.

"Oh, of course," Frances blurted. "Writing with the left hand does tend to make a muck of one's hand and wrist. How thoughtful of you to consider the fate of your brother's garment."

"It's a kindness to his valet, actually. The man almost wept when he saw what had happened to the shirt I wore last time I wrote. To say I ruined it is an understatement; I don't think it'll even be suitable for dustcloths."

As nimbly and dispassionately as a maid or valet, Frances slipped his cufflink from its moorings and turned back the light fabric of the sleeve, once, twice, to the middle of his forearm. Tendons played under his skin as he flexed his hand at the wrist. The back of his hand grazed hers, and she pulled away a little too quickly, self-conscious.

A second of awkward silence followed. Henry broke it by saying, "Thank you."

Frances only nodded, her throat closed on a

reply. Where his bare hand had grazed hers, the skin tingled, eager.

Gingerly, Henry dipped the pen and began to scrawl the alphabet in large, untidy capitals. The edge of his hand slid through the ink of the first letter he drew, smudging paper and skin.

"Try angling the paper to the right," Frances suggested. "Your hand will travel down in a line, rather than across what you've just written. Yes, exactly. That will save your cuffs from now on."

His hand flexed on the pen as he drew another letter, almost sideways. The hairs of his arm were fine, bleached gold against his sun-darkened complexion.

"How is it you know so much about writing with the left hand, Frances?"

"In the likeliest way you can imagine. I was inclined to use my left hand as a girl."

"You don't anymore?"

"No, my governess was adamant that I use my right. I resisted making the change, but she triumphed in the end. She had the ruler, and I the lashings, you see."

Henry's hand stilled, and he stared at her. Frances smiled. "Don't feel bad for me. I assure you, I made her job as difficult as I possibly could. I can be quite stubborn."

"I believe your determination, but you don't strike me as the disobedient type," he said, studying her face. "Or as someone who once favored her left hand. So you were sinister as a girl, were you?"

"I am still sinister," she said. "I frighten everyone I meet. You must be extraordinarily brave to sit so close to me."

Teasing to cover the import of the moment.

Not since Charles was alive had a man chosen her company. Yet here she sat in a chair pulled as close to Henry's as space would permit, their hands bare, not even inches apart. It might have been miles, though, for all that she could not bring herself closer. He had only chosen her company for the sake of another.

Her hands became busy trimming a pen, shaving away bits of the quill with a penknife until the nib point was whittled so fine as to be useless.

"You know," Henry said, sitting back and holding up his work to the window light, "I think that's a bit better. The angle of the paper helped. Here, see what you think."

His fingers brushed hers as he stuffed the paper into Frances's hand. She bobbled it, grazing her skirt. "Damn it."

Henry lifted his eyebrows. "Good thing you're my fellow soldier, or I'd be shocked by your language."

"Oh, stop," Frances muttered. "I told you, it's a borrowed gown, and I mustn't get ink on it." She laid the paper down on the desk and smoothed the fabric tightly over her thighs. "No, I don't think I did."

She looked up to see him studying her oddly. "What? Did I?"

"No," he said, still looking at her in that strange way. "You look very well." He shook his head, then gave her the paper again, holding it tight at the edge until she grasped it.

She could see on the paper the effect of her hard-won, palms-being-smacked experience. Though Henry's letters were still large and unformed, they grew tidier and less blotchy as they marched down the page.

"I think you've got the idea," she said. "Only lay in the right kind of quill, and you'll find it much easier."

He nodded and took back the paper, laying it on the desk again. "I'm glad to know it. You're a good teacher."

"Oh." She waved a hand. "Well, thank you. I actually *was* a teacher once, during my scandalous youth."

"A palm-smacking governess?" His head tilted, as though he were trying to imagine it.

"Nothing so formal as that. My good memory meant I was just the girl to help the squire's young son brush up on his Latin or teach the village children the names of every flower in the field."

Henry looked surprised, and Frances added, "Don't credit me with any great charity. I thought it my duty to help, yes, but I also dearly loved to be right."

His mouth made a wry curve. "Loved, past tense? I think not."

He bent his fair head over the paper and *skkkriiik-kked* another line. A fine spray of ink dotted his face, and he squinted, dropping his pen to grope in his waistcoat pocket for a handkerchief. "Right now, for example, you are perishing to tell me why I can't draw a neat line for anything." He rubbed at his face. "Go ahead. I'm ready to hear it."

Frances pursed her lips. "You're quite wrong."

"Oh?"

"Yes. I first wanted to tell you that cotton rag would clean your skin much more effectively than that slippery silk."

He emerged from the handkerchief, face still smudged. "My apologies, then."

"Not necessary." A grin broke across Frances's face. "The writing was a close second."

Henry snorted, crushing the ruined silk square in his hand, and she took out her own handkerchief of cotton lawn. "May I try this?"

He shrugged. "All right. I'd rather not look like I've been splashing in ink, even if that's the case."

Frances smiled, but his words were dim in her ears. *She might touch him again.* She held her breath, wondering why it should seem so important. Maybe because it was so rare, actually being invited to touch another person. She watched her hand, feeling as though it belonged to someone else, someone with the right to learn the shape of this intriguing man.

The hand reached up, stroked the frail fabric across Henry's forehead, down the strong bone of his cheek. Over the bridge of his nose, then down, to rub over the stern curve of his mouth, work it into softness. Then his chin, with its stubborn point. His neck, and just a slight rub under the edge of his cravat. She could feel the faint catch of stubble against the light fabric, the leap of muscle and tendon as he shifted under her touch. Beautiful as a statue, yet beautifully warm and human.

By the time she was done, her breath came a little faster. At the nape of her neck, between her breasts, a faint sheen of perspiration had formed. Underneath her stays, her skin felt sensitive and abraded, her nipples hard.

Henry's throat worked, and he turned his head away. "Thank you," he said in a choked voice. His skin looked flushed.

Frances folded the ruined handkerchief. "You're quite clean now." A brisk voice to banish the trespass of the honey-slow moment.

"Thank you," he said again, more quietly. He turned back to look at her, those vivid blue eyes searching her expression. "It seems you were right again, just as you love to be."

She stilled under his scrutiny, and after a few endless seconds, he pulled in a deep breath and picked up his quill again. "You'll probably be right about my abysmal handwriting too, then."

Back to normal, then. She shrugged, trying to dispel shivers of want. "I'm sure I will be," she said crisply.

He stopped in the middle of drawing a ramshackle letter *K*. "Is your own writing clear, Frances? Is it possible to learn to write well with the hand that feels wrong?"

"Yes, with enough practice. Probably you won't even have to be slapped across the hand, since you have a more pleasant incentive." That was *one* way of describing Caroline.

"Will you show me?" His blue eyes looked deep into hers. "I want to know this will work."

A simple enough request, but Frances understood what it meant. Every day, she realized, he must encounter something that had changed because of his injury. Losing an arm meant losing so much more: independence, comfort, even the easy courtesy of one's acquaintances, as they had seen yesterday.

Frances knew this well, for she had once lost too. Not a limb, but a whole person. A whole family. The finest part of herself.

Oh, she knew the sick dullness of loss. And anything she could help Henry gain, she would, even if it earned her nothing but his gratitude.

"All right," Frances agreed. "I'll write something."

She selected a quill, dipped it in the ink, then wiped the nib. She drew each letter deliberately, rounding it into a perfect feminine copperplate, loops and vowels as open as the model script in a writing primer. Bearing no resemblance to the writing in the letter she'd sent.

HENRY IS TOO DEMANDING.

He laughed. "I see there's nothing wrong with your handwriting at all."

Frances sanded the letters as carefully as she would an invitation for the queen, then set the paper aside. "As I said. You couldn't believe me without seeing it for yourself, could you? Is that because you're a solider or an artist?"

He narrowed his eyes, the look she now knew meant he was collecting details. "I've always been that way, so maybe it is an artist's curse. But I am curious, why do you speak so readily about soldiering? You seem to understand the life as many women do not."

His words startled Frances, silencing her for a too-long moment. No one had asked her about her past since she'd come to London with Caroline. It was scarred over, but not truly healed. Most wounds she had unwittingly inflicted herself.

She mustered a reply. "Yes. My late husband, Charles, was a soldier. He died during the siege of Walcheren." A quagmire. Pointless.

"I am sorry for your loss," Henry said.

"You need not be. It was almost six years ago; I've had plenty of time to come to terms with it."

This was quite true. Nearly six years was enough time to stop missing the man himself, whom she had long since grown past in years. Charles had died at twenty-two, and Frances would be thirty in a few more months.

"He must have been a marvelous man to deserve you," Henry said. He really did have fine manners.

"He was far too handsome for me," Frances murmured, "but I was more than willing to allow the imbalance."

Her eyes flicked over Henry's face—hair like morning sun, eyes like afternoon sky. He resembled night-tinted Charles not at all, except that both were far too handsome for her.

Charles's face had not been the only imbalance in their marriage. For Charles, Frances had tipped so far from her center, she hadn't righted herself for years. In some ways, she still hadn't. But she'd found a new equilibrium instead.

Or had, until Henry started studying her with those clear eyes of his, making her think of *rolling over* again. She knew from long months of watching the *ton* just how many secrets people betrayed without realizing.

She wondered what Henry saw in her now.

"After Charles died," Frances said, tugging her eyes down to the safety of the paper on which Henry had been writing. *ABCDEFGHIJK. Blot.* "I used to look over everything I had of his every day: a sketch of him, some letters. But I have not needed to for a very long time."

It didn't bring him closer to look through his things,

and it didn't send him farther when she kept them hidden away. Sometimes she didn't want him close at all; she only wanted to forget what she'd done to him.

But she couldn't forget anything, ever.

Henry's left hand tightened around his pen, then he laid it aside. "I am honored by your confidence."

She gave him a tight smile and smoothed a lock of her hair trying to uncoil from its pins. If only it was so simple to tidy up unruly emotion. "I probably spoke out of place, Henry. Your wound is much fresher than mine." Charles, after all these long years, awoke more guilt than grief.

Henry's clenched left hand unfolded, so close she could almost touch it. And so she did, just a brush over the back of his hand.

Their hands were freed from formal gloves, and Henry was warm skin under her skin—solid bone, sinew, all working perfectly together. To touch him was a wonder. A hand was a living miracle. She supposed Henry knew that better than anyone.

Again, she met his gaze. He was watching her closely as she traced lightly over his hand, his eyes deep and blue enough to drown in.

She sputtered for words, resisting the undertow. "Do you want to talk about it? Your injured arm?"

"No," he said, but his eyes did not cool with this refusal. "Though I thank you for asking about it. It's a part of me now."

He twisted his living left hand beneath her right—she thought at first to free it from her grasp. But he simply rotated it, placing his hand palm to palm with hers. Fingers wrapped around fingers, their sensitive pads awakening each other with pressure as light as the feather on a quill. The contact was simple, everyday, yet almost unbearably intimate.

And it was too uncertain; it could mean everything or nothing. A naked hand to a naked hand was a pact between business partners, a promise between friends, a beginning for lovers.

It was with Caroline he wished a beginning. And Frances had promised to help.

That was better than a pact, at least.

"Well." She freed her hand, found a quill they hadn't ruined yet. "Let's write that letter. You can start again with *C*."

My *caro*, she thought, though she could never say it now.

Six

"TOO BAD YOU REMEMBERED TO COVER THE CARPET this time." Emily sighed from the doorway of the morning room. "I could use some guilt ammunition."

Henry turned to look at his sister-in-law, more relieved than annoyed by the interruption. His latest effort at painting—this time with watercolors—was not going nearly as well as had this afternoon's writing lesson. "Emily. You're plotting something again?"

"I'm always plotting something." She trailed into the room and stood beside him, lowering her pointed chin to fix him with the full force of her bright eyes. A vivid green touched with blue; nearly the same shade as Caro's.

There was a pigment for creating just such a color. Paris Green, Henry had heard it called. It was a new formula, no more than a year old. Derived from copper and arsenic, and remarkably dangerous to work with, as so many of the richest colors were.

"Aren't you going to ask what I'm plotting?" Her eyes narrowed.

He set down his brush and turned to sit on the edge

of the baroque table they'd painted a few days before. "Aren't you going to tell me what you're plotting?" he mimicked. "I can tell you want to. You're all swelled up like a pufferfish."

"I'm—" She looked down the smooth line of her alizarin-red gown. "I am *not*. Hal, you're as bad as my boys."

He grinned. "No one could ever be as bad as your boys." He loved his nephews deeply, but they were an exhausting pair.

"True, true," Emily granted. "This is the plan: since you've decided to stay in London, Jemmy and I are planning a ball for you."

Henry lurched, then scrabbled at the edge of the small table to steady himself. "A ball. You're planning a ball for me."

"Yes." Emily looked pleased. "The *ton* is marriage-mad during the final gasps of the season. It's gasping longer than usual this year, for everyone's staying through Prinny's birthday. I am sure that, with a ball in your honor, we can draw all the attention to you that you deserve."

Henry looked down at his right arm, waiting for a movement that never came. A constant reminder of Quatre Bras, of his failure. "I already have what I deserve."

Emily began to pace; he could hear the rustle and shush of her skirts as she paced around the dimming confines of the morning room. "You won't have what you deserve until you're as happy as you were before you left. If your brother and I can do anything to help, we will. And that includes finding you a wife. And *that* includes hosting a ball for you."

Henry continued to stare at his arm. Bundled in a coat sleeve, it looked almost normal, except for its eerie stillness. "It's not up to you to remake my life, Emily."

The sound of her pacing stopped, and Henry looked up. She was facing the mural of Odysseus, blinking hard. "I really ought to have this painted over with something more pleasant. Perhaps a pastoral scene."

"It'll still be there, even if you paint it over," Henry murmured.

Emily pressed her lips together. "It doesn't matter what's below, as long as one can recreate the surface anew."

Her voice fell, and she added low, "Please, Hal. Let us do this. We must do something."

He knew that desperate feeling well enough. The need to escape the present, to change it in some way. That slippery discontent had almost pushed him all the way to Winter Cottage.

But there was one unavoidable flaw in Emily's plan. A flaw that unpinned his knees, made him want to sit down on the cloth-covered floor.

"I can't..." He swallowed, hating to have to say the words. He jerked his head toward his right shoulder, and Emily's face softened with understanding.

"Dear Hal," she said, walking back to his side. "We shall open the ball with a traditional minuet. You need hardly use your arms at all. And after that first dance, you may use your arms however you wish."

She winked at him roguishly, then patted his cheek, her smile lopsided. "I hope you know that we only want your happiness."

"I know," Henry replied. His insides had not yet

returned to order. His stomach was twisting, his heart thumping. He was to open a ball—he, with one arm, dancing before the whole *ton*.

Jem and Emily had never thrown him a ball in all the years before the war. They had always wanted his happiness, but they'd never felt the need to intercede with such a heavy hand. Another reminder that the world didn't see him as it once had.

For good or ill, just as Frances had said.

Somehow, he would have to make sure it was the former.

"Now that you're acquainted with my scheme," Emily wheedled, "do tell me about your painting. Is it some sort of jungle creature?"

Actually, it was a first attempt at a human. But considering the elegant brutality of the *ton*… "Yes, it is," Henry answered with a sigh.

"Delightful! And might I paint Aunt Matilda's table some more?"

෴

When Bart Crosby called an hour later, Henry was more than ready to leave behind his snarled-up painting and Emily's persistent discussion of the ball's details. He followed Bart down the front steps of Tallant House, where waited the new curricle of which he'd heard so much.

The small open carriage was a graceful, glossy rocker perched atop high spoked wheels. Its reins were held by a tiger in a snug coat and immaculate buckskin breeches; a boy so small that he looked unable to hold the horses if they should bolt. But the two fine grays, matched to the very blaze and stockings, stood with a calm that spoke to Lady Crosby's—and her son's—light and skillful hand with horseflesh.

The whole affair seemed precarious and fragile; Henry thought he could have pulled it himself without much effort. It looked far more hazardous than the sturdy gun carriages and supply wagons that had rolled next to Henry for hundreds of miles and hundreds of days.

Bart tapped a crop in the palm of one gloved hand, waiting for the verdict.

"It's just as fine as you described it," Henry said, knowing he'd given the right answer when Bart grinned.

"I wanted a phaeton," Bart excused in a quiet voice, so the wide-eyed tiger would not overhear, "but, well, you know how mothers are. Always sure a fellow's going to overturn and break his neck. Ah—beg pardon, Hal. You know. About your mother." He swatted his crop against his thigh, marking the pale dun nap of his buckskin breeches.

"There's no need to apologize," Henry said. "The loss of my mother is hardly a fresh one. Besides, your mother has an excellent eye. I am sure this is very modish."

"Modish isn't the word, old fellow," Bart said with a waggle of his dark brows. "It's *all the crack*. Don't you know?"

No, he didn't. He felt a heavy, sliding awareness that he had missed out on a great deal.

He shook it off and summoned a smile. "So even modish words are modish now. Well, well. Such is life in the *beau monde*."

"Where do you want to go?" Bart asked. "We can go anywhere you like." He rubbed the neck of the near horse, which whickered and bobbed its finely molded head.

"What sort of places do you go? I don't know what's all the crack this season." This cant sounded odd on Henry's lips, as wrong as if he'd lisped in a Catalan accent or tried a Scottish burr. But Bart grinned again.

"That's the spirit, Hal. Let me think. There's Jackson's, for one, but I don't know if you could spar with your... er..."

Henry rescued him before he could apologize again. "No, not Jackson's. What else?"

"Shooting or fencing. But... er..."

"Maybe another day," Henry said in a voice as mild and smooth as butter. "If my brother were with us, we could go to Gunter's for an ice. Jem is fiendishly fond of sweets."

"And what about you? What are you fond of nowadays?"

Blinking, Henry took a moment to reply. "I...oh. Many things?" It ought not to have sounded like a question.

Bart whisked his crop one more time, then swung himself up into his polished carriage with the ease of a man born to driving. The well-oiled springs made not a sound as Bart shifted into position and took up the reins. "Hop in, Hal," he said. "We'll find somewhere that suits you."

He sounded so sure of himself that Henry almost believed him. With a heave and a tug and a quick catch from Bart, Henry settled his unbalanced body into the high, rickety perch of the curricle.

And off they headed to someplace that would suit him. Though where such a place might be in a London of fencing and boxing and *all the crack*, he couldn't imagine right now.

～

Bart Crosby was a quiet fellow, and therefore the world did not regard him much. With a voluble mother and three still more voluble sisters, it was a wonder he had ever learned to talk at all.

It was not a wonder that Bart was not sure what to say right now. He would usually have offered to turn the reins over to Hal. But his oldest friend had only one arm now, and there were two spirited horses. The math did not add up.

Bart took great comfort in the steadiness of routine. Every spring, he came to London. Every autumn, he brought a passel of friends to Lincolnshire to shoot at his country estate.

Over the years, change had inevitably come. Bart's sisters had each married and left the ancestral home, which Bart found very bearable. Then his father had died, which was a shattering loss. His parents had ruled the world as Bart knew it, and now Bart was expected to step into his father's place and serve as a baronet.

Sir Bartlett, everyone should be calling him now. The idea was laughable, even to himself. He was still just plain "Bart" or "Crosby" to both friends and strangers. Maybe because his mother had continued to run things as she saw fit, just as she had when Bart's father was alive.

Since the years of their boyhood, Hal was the only one who had ever trusted Bart to make up his own mind. *Where do you want to go?* Hal would ask. *We'll go anywhere you like.*

It became a game, to listen at doorways and gather clues from their elders. London seemed full of places with odd and wondrous names. Boodle's. Jermyn Street. Hatchards. The Star and Garter.

And so would begin one of their adventures. Hal always knew where to find their quarry. He and Bart would slip out of Tallant House and run through the streets of London, their feet crunching on stone macadam or raising puffs of dust. Sometimes they wore no shoes, and every scratch, every cuff, every time someone shook a fist at the two dirty ragamuffins felt like a victory. They were in disguise. They were not young scions of the gentry; they were simply free.

"Do you remember how we used to knock on the windows of Boodle's?" The question slipped out, unleashed by Bart's reminiscing.

Bart wrapped the reins once more about his hands, as if taking hold of himself. His grays tossed their heads in protest but slowed to a walk. Pall Mall was two walls of brick and stone rising on either side of a clutter of foot traffic and carriages. Hard to believe that he and Hal had once run through here. No taller than the curricle wheels, they could easily have been crushed by a careless driver. But Hal had always let him choose where to go. It was wonderful, such trust.

Bart darted a look at his friend. Hal was sitting very

straight on the padded curricle seat, squinting at some huge building. "Sorry, Bart. What was that you said?"

"Nothing." Bart chucked and turned the horses onto St. James's Street. This plan might not work. He hadn't known where to go, so he went where they always used to go. Where, as boys, they'd thought all men went. A square formed by four bustling streets of clubs, grand houses, cigar stores, bookshops. It seemed the beating heart of the city once.

Hal seemed to wake up in his seat. "Boodle's. Yes, you're right." He leaned forward, looking for the familiar brown-brick building, the dramatic white arch of its huge central window. Lit at night by a massive chandelier, its brightness was a beacon, drawing small boys to make mischief.

Hal laughed, a short, startled exhale that little resembled his old explosions of mirth. Before the war, no one could laugh like Hal. His laugh was hearty and deep; it made the world want to laugh with him.

It made Bart sad to hear Hal laugh now.

But Hal looked pleased. "How angry Jem used to get when we'd hang over the iron railing and rap on the window. Do you remember how I used to steal his malacca cane to do it?"

"Salt in the wound, Hal. Gad, he was proud of that thing. A swordstick, wasn't it?"

"Oh, yes." Hal settled back against the padded seat. "He had it made when our father died and he became Tallant. Something about the title meaning 'good with a sword.' I believe it was granted in the long-lost past for heroism in battle."

"I don't remember your brother ever being much

good with a sword. Probably because we were always stealing it from him."

"Poor Jem. He always was a good brother, you know. He deserved better than such teasing from me. A man should be able to sit down with friends without being tormented." Hal's posture grew taut; Bart could tell from the way the seat shifted.

"They were just boys' pranks, Hal. Nothing more." Bart glanced at his friend, trying to read Hal's expression. Either it was blank or Bart was out of practice.

"Oh, I know. Did you know that Wellington's a member of Boodle's?" Hal sounded strange, and the smile he gave Bart was strange too. Bart wanted to sigh as they drew past Boodle's and turned onto Piccadilly.

Here was Hatchards, tall and gray, where they'd once bought horrifying novels, telling the bemused clerk they were for Bart's sisters.

And next to it… "Fortnum's," Hal said. They had never run here, never had the slightest interest in a store where no pranks could be played, nothing bawdy bought. But the adult Hal had had much to do with Fortnum's, which had fed the army for years.

It seemed there was nowhere Bart could drive that would allow them both to think nothing had changed.

And why should there be? Everything had changed. Bart was the one asking, *Where do you want to go?* And Hal didn't trust Bart anymore. Bart could tell from the too-hearty cheer of his voice, nothing like real cheer at all.

When Bart was a boy, a youth, the Middlebrooks were everything he had wanted to be: friendly, confident, and clever. Bart never had succeeded in becoming what he wished. But this Hal in the curricle—he wasn't that sort of man either anymore. He seemed but a portrait of his old self, baked brittle in an oven and cracked all over.

Which reminded Bart of something that might jolt Hal out of his reverie. "Hal, I can make the circuit back to Pall Mall. We could stop in at the British Institution and look at the new paintings."

"The British Institution?" Hal was caught; he leaned forward eagerly. "Yes, excellent idea. Let's go there. Though I thought you hated it?" He cut his eyes at Bart, his mouth curving.

Clever Hal. Bart *had* always hated the British Institution. He had hated every endless afternoon he'd ever spent in its quiet pinkish-walled rooms, waiting as Hal studied painting after painting and the promised "just one hour" inevitably turned into three or four.

Pink, to Bart, would always be the color of tedium.

But Hal wanted to go. He'd given an answer at last. And that must mean he trusted Bart, at least a little.

Maybe not *everything* had changed.

"We'll go anywhere you like," Bart said dutifully, diplomatically, and chucked his horses into a trot back toward Pall Mall.

❧

Henry came back to Tallant House more tired than he had expected to be, and more hot and more… well, more glad.

The drive hadn't started well. As they'd driven down Pall Mall the first time, Henry had noticed only two things. Cumberland House, a stretching Palladian mansion that seemed to loom up into the sky and stare at Henry as he passed by its seven bays of windows. Here squatted the Board of Ordnance, the army's mapmakers, the ones who ensured that weapons and powder got to soldiers—or didn't.

And the Guards' Club, as inconspicuous as the other building was eye-catching. It was a narrow town house, quoined and pilastered in tasteful style, home to a new club that the other officers in the Foot Guards looked forward to joining someday. Henry had turned his back on it when he sold his commission, yet here it was, in his face.

But Bart, good man, had opened Henry's eyes to the other buildings. Years, he had lived in this square of Town, and he'd run down these streets, and he'd loved London. Everything he'd loved about the city—its noise, its life, its vitality—was still here.

Visiting the British Institution had been painful yet sweet, like looking on the picture of a beloved dead relative. Henry knew he could never set up an easel within its galleries again, copying paintings with eager energy. He would never win the coveted prize awarded to the artist who could create a fitting companion to the Old Masters.

But he still had eyes in his head. He could look and wonder and admire. He could study color and scrutinize brushstrokes.

And he could still prod Bart through room after room and watch his old friend try to stifle jaw-cracking yawns.

Yes, he was glad he had gone out. And when the fastidious Sowerberry gave Henry a letter after helping him off with his dusty, too-warm coat, Henry was glad he'd come back. A letter from Caro today was the essential extra that made everything just as it should be. A letter would help him capture this skittish optimism and cage it within himself.

Henry took the stairs to his bedchamber two at a time, leaping up them as if Caro herself would be waiting in his bed. Once he was alone, he cracked open the seal with a hand that felt cold. He was disappointed when he saw how short the note was.

> Dear Henry,
>
> Thank you for your reply to me. I know it must have cost you a great deal of effort, and I value it accordingly.
>
> I have been thinking over my last letter, wondering if I did right to persuade you to stay in Town when you might have desired to leave. But I cannot regret doing so, for I've gotten my way, and that means I shall see more of you.
>
> I have learned that your sister is hosting a ball for you in two weeks' time. I should be honored if we could dance together. Once again, you see, I am trying to persuade you, but I hope not against your wishes. We shall find out, once we are holding each other close.
>
> Your friend

Well. It was short, but it was everything it needed to be. He stretched out on the floor for a while after that letter arrived, grounding himself on the Brussels carpet of his bedchamber.

The last time he'd been in Brussels itself, he'd been anything but grounded. He had forgotten the troubles of war for an evening by flirting his way through a ball. The night before Quatre Bras, as it turned out. Hours of dancing turned into hours of marching turned into hours of pain.

But not every ball led to battle. Not every dance led to destruction. Sometimes they were simply meant for pleasure.

He leaned his head back against the side of his bed, remembering his younger self. The scandalous whirl of a Continental waltz, the winding pattern of a London country-dance. The tight thrum of *wanting* through his body and blood. He had lost the simple joy of it over time, but soon he could have it all again. He need only wait for the ball and for the chance to clasp a woman in his arms.

Arm. One arm.

But even remembering that the number of his working upper limbs had been decreased from plural to singular did not lessen his resolve. He would do everything to make this ball—and himself—a success. Even if he could hardly dance anymore, he would find the joys left to him. Caro would help him do it.

I would be honored, he wrote back, his printing still clumsy and slow. *You may have any dance you desire.*

Maybe he could have something he desired too. He had the hope of it, and he would promise anything just for the pleasure of having hope again.

Seven

"THIS IS SNUG. QUAINT. AND I DO NOT MEAN THAT as an insult, Hal, though those words usually mean social ruin."

Henry accepted this magnanimous praise from Emily, who perched at the edge of a delicate chair of gilded beech. Her hands were folded neatly in her lap as she surveyed her small domain.

Small their evening gathering was, at Henry's request. Only Bart, Caro, and Frances had joined the family party at Tallant House. Dinner now over, the six sat in the gilt-papered, lamp-lit drawing room. A low coal fire winked, banishing clamminess from the long reach of the room. A space for cards, a space for books, a space for music, a space for just sitting and wishing one had a cheroot to smoke.

Henry and Emily sat in the latter space, while the other four battled through a rubber of whist. "Would you care for a cheroot, Emily?"

Her eyebrows lifted. "You'd regret it if I said yes. Jem would have my head for it, and then he'd be hanged for beheading me. And then you would have to assume the care of John and Stephen. They can be absolute hellions, and I do mean *that* as an insult. Though also as a statement of fact."

"Just a suggestion," Henry said lightly.

Emily paused. "This plan of yours. Dinner at home. Hal… it was a good idea." Her brows puckered, an expression of doubt she wore with enviable rarity. "Perhaps I should have arranged more small events like this one, instead of the grand ball in the Argyll Rooms next week."

Such an admission was akin to Bonaparte saying that perhaps he should have stayed on Elba and not caused so much trouble on the Continent.

"It's all right, Emily," Henry said, hiding his astonishment. "Thank you for arranging the dinner tonight."

Her aplomb reappeared in an instant. "It's all part of the plot," she said with a dismissive flick of fingers.

"The throwing-me-a-ball plot?"

"*No.*" She peeked over the high back of her chair, then ducked down and whispered, "The finding-a-wife plot."

"Ah. Yes. That." Discomfiture knotted Henry's stomach. After his first introduction to Caro, he had wanted to take on the rest of his courtship without interference.

At least, without any interference besides what he sought out on his own.

It was damned difficult to keep up a wall of confidence when no one had faith he could rebuild his life. Maybe not even himself. Why else would he have asked Frances to help him win Caro, if not doubt that he could triumph alone?

He peered around the back of his own chair. Frances

was laughing and sliding coins across the card table to her partner, Bart. Caro gave an exaggerated sigh and tossed her cards down. "Jem," Henry heard her say, "we're going to be roasted and toasted, you and I."

Chagrin, confusion, unease—whatever one called it, it twisted through Henry's chest at the sight of Frances's smile. Already, he had wrapped her tightly into his fledgling courtship of Caro. He couldn't write a letter to Caro without recalling Frances helping him shape letters; he couldn't give her flowers without thinking of Frances's advice. He couldn't hear Caro's voice or see her face without his eyes seeking Frances, his ears sifting sounds for the careful speech and wicked laugh of his own ally.

And yet, with all the help Frances had given him, he had given her very little in return. It was hardly flattering to ask the help of an unmarried woman in winning the hand of another. It implied that she wasn't worthy of attention herself... didn't it?

He didn't mean to do *that*. It certainly wasn't true. She looked vivid in the low glow of fire and lamp, her strong features all shadow and light. Deep eyes and a mouth made for secrets. *Chiaroscuro*, that stark Italian technique, would be the perfect way to paint her.

If he could paint.

Which he couldn't.

Which was why he needed Caro.

There was no denying the countess was as lovely as Botticelli's Venus. If he could persuade her to look his way, it would be no hardship to look back at her.

That was the odd thing, though—she hadn't looked

his way much this evening. Certainly not as much as one would expect from the partner in a secret correspondence.

"Excuse me, Hal." Emily had perked up. "They finished their rubber of whist. I shall arrange things to further our plot." She called, "Jemmy, do deal me a hand. But I shall scream if I have to partner you."

She glided over to the card table, while Henry stared at the grate. The coals were glowing, not much more than ash now, occasionally split by faint fire. He could see the slanting flickers through the milky glass of the fireplace screen. It was walnut framed, painted with a snowy marble temple flanked by two sturdy oaks, their wavy branches intertwining.

It had been Henry's wedding present to Jem and Emily a decade before. He'd thought himself very clever, representing the story of Baucis and Philemon: the couple who grew old together, kindhearted, and were transformed into trees after their deaths so they could live on side by side.

The story was apt. But he hadn't been clever enough to fix his colors. The glass hadn't been fired well after he had painted it, and the paints had bubbled and dimmed, the colors smoky.

Oh, well. It still looked better than Aunt Matilda's greasy red-painted baroque table.

He heard Emily shriek, heard the others laugh, and realized his sister-in-law had been paired with Jem after all. So someone else would come to join Henry at the fireside now. Fair enough. He could handle these small bites of friendship, which he need not lift a finger to consume. Which was well, since he had only half the usual working complement of fingers.

He gritted his teeth. It was tedious how his mind worked sometimes. How dearly he would love to forget that anything had changed. Or barring that, have it not matter.

Enough.

He shoved himself out of the chair and joined the rest of the party.

"What's all the screaming about?" he said in a jovial voice as he skirted the card players.

"Oh, Hal," Emily collapsed into a chair at the velvet-draped card table. "I am ruined. Your brother can never remember the cards that have been played, and I shall lose all my pin money."

"And I shall win it," said Frances, snapping and bridging the cards before handing them to Jem to deal. "Or *we* shall, Mr. Crosby." She flashed a bright smile at her partner, Bart.

Henry suddenly wished very much that he were part of the game.

But if he was not, Caro was not either for this rubber. "So you have been dealt out, Lady Stratton?"

Caro smiled. "Indeed. I am not sure now whether I have been lucky or unlucky."

"You are lucky if you were partnering Jem. I only thank heaven Hal is not playing," Emily said with mock innocence. "He cheats."

"I do not," Henry protested.

"Good lord, Em," Jem interjected. "It's a good thing you're not a man. You'd be called out for saying such a thing."

Emily rearranged the cards in her hand. "My dear husband, it's a good thing I'm not a man for many reasons besides that one. Besides, I am only teasing Hal. I do it out of my bitterness, knowing that I am going to lose my pin money."

"I'll give you more," Jem said. "Only you must remind me what trump is. Hearts?"

Emily shot Henry a what-did-I-tell-you look. "Yes, my dear heart, it is hearts. Caro, would you be willing to sing something to keep us company?"

Frances didn't even look up from her cards. "I would consider Lady Stratton's singing to be a blatant attempt to undermine our concentration."

"Would it?" Bart sounded interested. "Are you very accomplished, my lady?"

Caro shook her head. "Not at all. I sound like a raven crowing. Or croaking, or whatever they do."

"Caw, maybe." Henry peered over Bart's shoulder. Not a trump in his hand, poor fellow. "Good lord, Bart. Seven trumps? Jem is clearly the one who cheats, since he's dealt you so many."

"You are a child, Hal," Emily said, her brow furrowing as she selected her next play. "You are almost as bad as my Stephen, who reads out everyone's cards, and he is only eight years old."

"I was the one who shuffled the deck," Frances said. "Does that mean I cheat at cards too?"

Henry smiled. "I would believe you capable of anything, Mrs. Whittier. You are sinister; you told me so yourself." He was inordinately pleased to see color rise to her cheeks.

Caro began to peep at the hands of each of the card players. "My, my, Emily. Your pin money is surely gone. Frannie is frighteningly capable. I believe she could have cheated at cards anytime, and none of you would have suspected a thing."

Frances slapped a low diamond onto the table with a frown. "If I truly cheated, I would have made certain that I got a better hand."

"Or that I did," Bart murmured. "I only wish I truly did have seven trumps."

Jem tossed his cards onto the table, facedown. "Jupiter's nightgown, how am I to think with you all talking? Is everybody cheating now?"

"Jemmy, how unkind of you. I shall call *you* out if you say such a thing again," Emily said. "Drat; no, I won't. With you dead, we would surely lose the rubber."

Jem blinked. "Was that a compliment, Em?"

She sighed. "I suppose, though I only implied that you played better than a corpse."

Before Jem could reply, there was a scratch at the door then the butler Sowerberry peeped his angular head into the drawing room. "I beg your pardon, Lord Tallant, but Master John and Master Stephen are asking you for a..." He paused and enunciated the next words as if they were in a language he did not understand. "A bedtime story, my lord. They insist that you promised them one if they spent the evening without breaking anything. They have requested that it be horrible."

Henry smirked. "Oh, it'll be horrible."

The cuff on his shoulder as Jem stood felt blessedly normal. But after Jem left, Henry felt slow and stupid as he tried to think of the perfect thing to say. Or anything to say at all.

Because if there was one thing he could *not* do, it was take his brother's place in the game and hold a sheaf of cards for whist. Not with one hand.

Maybe Emily noticed his sudden awkwardness, because she shrugged off the idea of further cards. "Well, that game was brief and combative. I am sorry for that. Though I am relieved not to lose any money to you flock of carrion crows. Mrs. Whittier, do come and play the piano, so Bart and I can have a dance." She laughed when Bart's face reddened at her teasing.

Briskly, Emily sorted them all out. Frances shuffled through music, and Caro joined her, exclaiming over a waltz. "Rather fast of you, isn't this, Em?"

She looked as light and lovely as one of Leonardo's angels as she shifted a lamp into place to study the music and began humming tunelessly. Next to her, Frances fell into shadow.

"Not a waltz, please," Bart said, growing still more red.

Caro laughed again and set the scandalous music aside. "Perhaps a reel, then, for two couples? Frannie could play for us." Her bright eyes twinkled as she held a hand out to Bart.

It felt like she'd slapped Henry with it.

So, she would write to him in private, but she wouldn't acknowledge their closeness even in such a small party? And yet *close* was exactly how she wanted to hold him. She had written him so.

He felt hot-headed and hot-blooded, wanting to cut in and take her hand, wanting her to extend it to him.

Instead, he beat a strategic retreat to the fireside, unwilling to watch himself be defeated.

"I think I'll sit out the dancing, ladies, if you don't mind," he said. "Though I'll be happy to observe and critique your form."

When all three women pulled faces at him, Henry knew his grin had stayed in place and no one suspected the truth.

Namely, that he had to fabricate a new kind of courage or he would never get even the ashes of what Baucis and Philemon had shared.

With a rustle of fabric, a woman dropped into the chair next to Henry. The faint, crisp scent of citrus told Henry it was Frances, even before he turned his head.

"Mrs. Whittier." He straightened in his chair, glad she sat to his left, his good side.

"Mr. Middlebrook," she mimicked. "I hope you don't mind if I sit with you. I have been evicted from the piano. As it turns out, your friend Mr. Crosby is by far the best musician of us all."

"So Emily is dancing with Caro?" He twisted, peering around the broad circular back of his chair. Hmm. So she was.

"Most women learn to dance with one another, you know," Frances said. "I do believe your sister-in-law is more comfortable at leading than at following."

"I completely and wholeheartedly believe that," Henry said drily. "What shall we do, then? Shall we play a game of our own?"

She raised an eyebrow. "Very well. I'm thinking of something with blond hair and a red gown. Do you care to guess what it is? It'll be easy because you're probably thinking of it too."

He narrowed his eyes. "Ha. You are riotously funny."

"A transparent attempt to dodge the question. You have no guess, then?"

He settled himself into his chair, wedging his numb right arm firmly in the angle where the seat back met the side. "Of course I have a guess, but you may not like it." He gave her The Grin, his most charming smile. The old, carefree expression hadn't sat so easily on his face for a long time.

"Try me." Her tip-tilted eyes looked roguish.

"The queen, of course. I'm a devoted servant of the Crown."

Frances snorted. "Nonsense; the queen hasn't been blond for at least thirty years. And why shouldn't I like that guess?"

"Because I spoiled your fun." He gave a little shrug. With his right arm wedged into the corner of the chair, he could almost believe its stillness was normal.

She held up a hand and ticked on her fingers as she replied, "At the present moment, I'm not losing money at cards, I'm not bumbling through a minuet on the piano, and I'm not racking my brain for the steps of a reel. So how could you think you've spoiled my fun?"

"If I'm the only remaining option, I should try to be more amusing."

"Please do." She folded her arms and looked down her nose at him in one of the haughtiest expressions he'd ever seen.

"Good lord, Frances, you're as stiff as a fireplace poker."

She relaxed, grinned. "At least I'm sitting in the right seat, then, in front of this lovely warm fire."

"It is lovely, isn't it? I painted the fireplace screen, you know."

"Well, it's only an early effort. You are still relearning how to paint with your left hand. I am sure you will get better with time."

His head reared back. "I painted the screen long ago."

"Oh. You did? It's… hmmm." She furrowed her brows, obviously trying to think of something kind to say.

"It's been damaged over time." Henry felt the need to defend himself, though a smile crept over his features. "It was never an astounding work, but I promise you when I finished it, it didn't look like an ash heap had been sick all over it."

"I'd never have described it that way." The dratted woman was trying not to laugh.

"No, but you obviously thought it. I've been insulted, and by my own fellow soldier."

"Oh, come now, you know it's not your best work. If you want a compliment, you can simply ask, and I'll think of a much better subject than an old, damaged painting on glass."

Citrus caught at him, a sweet scent that reminded him she sat only a touch away. The sound of Bart plunking out "Mr. Beveridge's Maggot" became dimmer in Henry's ears. "Would you, now? I wonder what you'd say. Are you trying to be terrifying again?"

"Why? Are you terrified?"

A little. "Of course not," he huffed. "It would be beneath my considerable dignity."

"It *is* considerable. Maybe that's what I'll compliment you on. Many men in the *ton* would be helped by a little more dignity and a little less vanity. Have you seen the dandies who can't even turn their head within their high collars?"

"Yes, but surely it's worth it. Isn't that fashion *all the crack*?"

When she laughed, he felt a hot clench of pleasure in the center of his chest.

"I don't know," she laughed. "I haven't been *all the crack* for over a decade, Henry."

"Now who's angling for a compliment? I know this is false modesty, because you notice and remember everything. You could easily be whatever you wanted to be."

Her smiled dropped. For a too-long moment after this speech, she watched him, her eyes slightly narrowed. If he'd had ten fingers at his disposal, he probably would have embarked upon a world-class fidget under her scrutiny, drumming his fingers and shifting in his chair.

Instead, he sat carefully still, and he spoke lightly in a moment that had mysteriously turned heavy. "What is it, Frances? You're acting like I just transformed into a wolf and howled at the moon."

"I'm just wondering," she answered quietly, "if you meant what you said."

"That you had false modesty? Of course."

Her mouth curved into a wry little smile. "Never mind. Forgive my distraction. I suppose I'm just distraught over being banished from the pianoforte."

That armor of humor she kept—he knew it, because he wore it too.

It looked well on her. Her rich dark hair was pulled

back by a celadon bandeau; her gown was cut low across her bosom, edged with lace of a darker green. Her skin glowed in the wavery light that penetrated the unfortunate fireplace screen. Subdued but so touchably lovely that he wanted to stroke her. Feel her warmth, take it in. He felt it, the want—a clenching hunger low in his stomach.

"You might be surprised," she said with a sigh, "at how aggravating it can be to remember everything. Sometimes I can't get to sleep for all the thoughts jostling at the inside of my head."

"I know that feeling."

She shot him a quick sideways look. "Yes, I suppose you might."

"If you recall—which I'm sure you do," he said more lightly, "I did give you a genuine, unsolicited compliment."

She shot him another look, this one wicked. "On my memory, which is nothing but a parlor trick? Come now, Henry. You must know that women want only to be praised for their bonnets and gowns. There are quite a few common synonyms for *you look very nice*, you know."

With a rueful smile, she turned back to the fire, watching a coal crumble into cinders. Henry saw it lick hotly at the thick glass of the fireplace screen; then its light vanished.

"You do look very nice," he said slowly, "but to give or receive a common compliment is no real honor. Anyone might look lovely, but I've never met anyone with your gifts of memory or your talent in teaching left-handed writing."

The words swelled within him, filling him with an

unexpected heat. She *did* look lovely. She *was* uncommonly gifted. He felt a pull to her, an ease in her presence, that he hadn't felt since returning to London. He wanted to capture this feeling, to hold it close, as in a lover's embrace. His shoulders flexed involuntarily, and he felt the inevitable tug at his right shoulder, the pendulous weight of his still right arm.

The heat turned into a chill reminder of all that had changed.

"As you've never needed to learn to write with the left hand before," Frances said, "I don't suppose you could know how skilled a teacher I am."

"But I do know," he said, not wanting to explain how much she had helped him answer Caro's letters. "And surely such compliments are within the bounds of friendship."

"If you say they are, then they are." Frances slapped her hands onto her knees, pushing herself upright. "If you say we're friends, then we're friends."

So abrupt suddenly. Had he offended her? "Ah… no, you have a say in the matter as well."

"Consider this my compliment for you," she replied with a smile. "You may take my friendship for granted."

"I will never take you for granted," Henry said. When her face softened, grew warm in the firelight, he wondered if he'd said far more than he knew. She looked at him with her deep eyes, all the tumbled browns and greens of the Bossu Wood, and he felt stripped bare, known and understood, as he had not in years.

He had never thought to be stripped bare again.

Her lips had parted in surprise, and he could almost

feel the warmth of her breath, the very essence of her life, pulling him closer.

"I would not take you for granted either," she murmured, and reached out a hand to brush, so lightly, over his fingers.

Another touch, just as she'd given him when they first met and when she showed him how to write. Each time, he showed her a weakness, and she still reached out to him. That was a miracle in itself, and the sensation of her touch, forbidden and strange and sweet, woke his skin. Heat arrowed through his body: wistful desire, blessed hope.

Yes, hope. He had hope that he could rebuild his life. Though he knew he could not do it on his own. He needed Caroline for that.

It was hard to remember his carefully calculated reasons, sitting here in front of the fire.

Perhaps Frances sensed his sudden confusion; maybe he'd tensed. She pulled her hand from his, looked back at the fire again, and said in her damnably calm voice, "Doggedness." Her tip-tilted eyes crinkled in a smile, and he knew she wasn't annoyed. "That's my answer to your dignity. Doggedness is probably the best quality I have, though also the worst."

The change of subject was a relief; they'd been growing a bit too fraught. They couldn't begin grabbing each other's hands at every opportunity or people would talk, and that wouldn't do either of them any good. A companion was in a precarious position in society; it wouldn't take much to send her tumbling.

A quick tumble, that made him remember. Frances's words about soldiers the first time they had met. It had been so long since Henry'd had a tumble, he could hardly remember the sensation. Understandable, then, how much it was on his mind; how tense his body felt, how aware of Frances's closeness, of her every touch.

But this wasn't the time or the place or the person for such thoughts.

"Come now, it can't be both best and worst." His voice came out clipped as he tried to quit thinking *tumble, tumbled, tumbling*. He waved a hand for a servant. "What do you care for, Frances? Tea or sherry?"

She thought for a moment. "Tea would be a wiser choice than sherry. You are always trying to get me intoxicated so you can learn secrets from me, aren't you? One would think you'd been a spy."

Henry snorted and asked for a tea service to be brought over, then turned back to Frances. "If I'd been a spy, I'd have much subtler methods. But I've never been very subtle. Not even before the war."

"Maybe that's *your* best and worst quality, then." She smiled a quick thanks at the footman who set a tea tray down on a low table between their chairs. "Sugar for you, Henry?"

Henry considered. He'd gotten out of the habit of drinking tea sweetened—or indeed, regularly at all— during his tent-centered life in the army. "Yes," he decided. "Two spoonfuls, please." He had a taste for something new.

He watched her pour out the tea, her movements efficient and graceful as though they had been practiced thousands of times. And probably they had.

She'd once said she was the daughter of a baronet, had she not? He wondered how she'd tumbled into the role of a companion.

Damn it. Tumbled *again.* His whole body felt tight and eager.

Frances held out a cup and saucer to him, and he tugged his mind back to the tea tray. The cup rattled faintly in its frail willow-patterned saucer, and he extended his hand, then paused. How to take it with one hand? If he held the saucer, he wouldn't be able to lift the cup.

After cutting his eyes sideways to ensure that the tune of "Mr. Beveridge's Maggot" was still issuing from the pianoforte, that Caroline and Emily were still practicing their steps with the glee of debutantes, he shook his head at Frances. "Just the cup, please."

"Oh, of course." She rolled her eyes at her own mistake. "Sorry about that." She twirled the teacup so he could grip its tiny handle, then laid the unneeded saucer on the tray again.

He took a too-sweet sip, then returned to the thread of their conversation. "So. You think subtlety isn't always necessary?"

Frances stirred milk into her own teacup as she considered. "Not for men, no. Subtlety's probably more important for women. We're permitted only the flimsy weapons of speech rather than anything really satisfying. Sometimes I think it would be much easier just to shoot out our troubles instead of keeping a smile pasted on all the time."

Henry let out a low bark and wiggled his fingers against the porcelain cup, trying to keep its hot contents from burning him. "Shooting isn't always the fun it may seem."

Another gulp drained his tiny teacup to the dregs. It was syrupy at the bottom, with sugar grains not yet dissolved.

Well, he could use some help to sweeten his speech, because he had something difficult to say to Frances. He was getting too distracted by his alliance with her when it was secondary to his true strategy.

"Frances." He leaned forward and set his teacup down on the tray. "Look, I've got to tell you something."

Her cup clattered in her saucer. "Then tell me."

They had just excused the male sex from the need to be subtle, yet Henry didn't want to be too blunt. "It's about Caroline. I—well, I'd prefer to court her on my own from this point."

He stared at his teacup, lonely and saucer-less on the silver-plated tea tray, as though its dregs held all the mysteries of the universe. He didn't want to watch her face change at his words; whether it was disappointed or relieved, it would be better not to know.

"You don't care to have my help anymore?" The question sounded light enough, simply seeking information. He looked up, and her face was a sweet mask.

He sidestepped the question. "I've been honored by your help. But I think it would be fairest to all of us if I proceeded alone."

"You want to be fair? How so?"

"None of the other suitors have ever received assistance from you," he said lamely.

"I see," she said with that careful smile on her face

again. "You don't want to give yourself an unfair advantage in winning Caroline."

"That's not what I meant. I'm well aware that Caro isn't in the slightest danger of being swept off her feet by me or any other suitor."

He turned in his chair to regard Caro. She and Emily now stood by the pianoforte, laughing as they shuffled through the sheet music, making a snowstorm of paper around Bart. In truth, Caro looked just as happy plunking sour notes on the pianoforte as she had playing cards, dancing at a ball, entertaining suitors. Her mood was constant sunshine—never a cloud, never a storm.

This was why the *ton* loved her and admired her and sought her company. But did Henry have any idea what lay below that sunny surface?

Yes, he did. He had the letters.

He looked back to Frances, whose odd smile had begun to unbend. "What *do* you mean, then?" she asked.

"Just that… well, it's my puffed-up dignity." It rather magnified the indignity by having to speak of it, so he leaned forward, spoke lower. "I'd rather see whether I can court her successfully on my own."

She picked up her teacup again, wrapping both hands around it as though pulling warmth from the tiny vessel. "So, just to be perfectly clear, you don't want me to intercede at all."

"Right," Henry said, relieved when she nodded. "And I'll tell the same to my sister-in-law."

Frances shrugged. "All right, I understand. I won't interfere anymore."

Again, there was something strange about the way

she spoke, as though she chose her words carefully to hide something.

He thought he could guess what she was covering up: pity. Why else would her eyes skate away from his? Why would she agree so quickly to his ungracious request to distance herself?

Maybe she too had felt they'd been bound a little too closely. Or maybe distance was what she preferred. He had too much dignity and not enough bluntness to pursue an explanation from her when it was sure to end in another embarrassment. The latest in a long series since he'd returned to London.

With a dissonant crash of keys and another peal of laughter, the trio at the piano called for Henry and Frances to join them. They both stood quickly, not quite looking at one another.

"Don't forget," Henry said in a whisper. "It's all up to me now."

She gave a little sigh. "I never forget, Henry."

❦

The rest of the evening went by pleasantly. When Jem returned to the drawing room, the six took turns giving dramatic readings out of a book of plays. An aggressively safe activity, as no one could be tugged into an intimate conversation, or even an intimate *glance*, with anyone else.

That was all right with Henry. He had the letters to rely on, to look forward to.

Or so he thought.

But write to Caro as he might, in the week leading up to his ball, not a single letter came in response to his.

Eight

"I LOOK LIKE AN IDIOT," FRANCES HISSED AS SHE followed Caroline through the crowds in the Argyll Room's lengthy ballroom.

Plentiful witnesses to Frances's overdressed presumption were on hand, for all of London seemed to be in attendance at Lord and Lady Tallant's ball for Henry. The ballroom was brightly lit, richly ornamented, crushingly full. Curious guests peered down from the tiers of boxes overlooking the grand room and chattered from rows of benches surrounding the dancing area. Frances felt pinned by their curious gazes, as though she were a butterfly in a glass case.

Yes, tonight she was a butterfly, or at least had the coloring of one. For this ball, Caroline had insisted in fitting Frances out in one of her own evening dresses, a deep red sarcenet with black trim to flatter Frances's dark complexion, and she had lightly rouged Frances's cheeks and lips.

"I told you that you looked wonderful," Caroline tossed back over her shoulder as she waved at a friend.

"My feelings will be very hurt if you continue to question my judgment."

"I'm sorry to hurt your feelings, but I have to," Frances muttered to her cousin's back. "If I can't say I look like an idiot, then what about a clown? I'll start juggling the biscuits if you let me into the refreshment saloon."

Caroline stopped short and turned to face her. "I'm going to pretend that I didn't hear any of that. And *you* are going to pretend that you think you look lovely. Because you do." She held up a hand against Frances's protest. "You do, Frannie. Why won't you believe it?"

Frances opened her mouth, waiting for an explanation to fall out. She wasn't exactly sure how to answer Caroline, who always meant well.

"I guess it's because I don't feel like myself." She made a helpless gesture at the dress. "The color, the cut. It's so conspicuous."

As though proving her point, a young man in starched shirt points jostled her heavily and righted himself with a grab at her waist.

Frances fixed him with a filthy glare, then turned back to Caroline. "See? Clown. That fellow certainly expected me to entertain him."

Caroline winked. "What better mood for a ball than a willingness to entertain? Tonight, you shouldn't hide on a chair against the wall. You ought to have a dance, and not only when my toes can't stand Bart Crosby's boots anymore."

Frances's fingers worked around the slim rectangle of her folded fan. "What if you crack your fan? Or what if you need my help with something?"

Caroline flicked open her own fan, an elaborate affair painted with an image of Venus reclining amidst a flock of Cupids. Gracefully, as though unconscious of the movement, she fluttered it in the area of her shoulder, forcing back a trout-faced man who was about to step too close for propriety. "I think," Caroline said with a tolerant smile, "I shall be able to bear the inconvenience. I'm not completely helpless, you know."

"I never thought that," Frances said.

"Off with you." Caroline wiggled the fan. "Shoo. Go. Enjoy yourself. That's an order, Frannie. I don't want to see you again unless it's in the middle of a country-dance."

She gave Frances a friendly wave before turning away, and Frances was left alone, with nothing to do but stand there in a too-red gown and pretend she belonged in the middle of a crushing ballroom.

Which she had, once. Almost a decade before.

Her stomach clenched under the fine fabric of her borrowed gown. Ah, how she would enjoy being a girl again, of whom nothing had been expected but dancing and flirtation. She hardly remembered that blithe girl anymore. Single-minded and selfish, and delighted to be so.

That was before she had learned the consequences of being single-minded and selfish.

"I've been looking for you." A male voice sounded in her ear, making her jump.

"Henry." She turned. "Why, where is your adoring throng? I saw you next to Lady Tallant not five minutes ago, smiling down a pack of rabid debutantes. Surely you can't have escaped them so quickly in this crowd."

He raised his left arm to the level of his eyes. "Elbow. A little trick I learned from my brother."

"Ah. I should have known." Frances smiled.

So he had elbowed his way out of the receiving line to join her? She looked him over from short-cropped golden hair to bright eyes, to black-clad shoulders and stark white linens and… oh, good Lord, he was a delicious sight, all elegance and nobility.

Her mind vanished in a puff of lust, and she stood there gaping at him, a crimson-gowned statue.

"I need to speak with you," he said, and she noticed at last that he wasn't smiling back.

Lust squirmed again before reluctantly bedding down. "As you wish. Not here, though? It's rather loud."

"No, not here." He frowned. "I—"

"Oh, Hal, thank heavens." Lady Tallant, elegant in butter-yellow silks, had come up behind her brother-in-law. "I've been hunting for you. It's time to start the dancing. Did you ask Mrs. Whittier to stand up with you for the minuet? Excellent, come with me."

She charged through the crowd, using her elbows with as much determination as her husband, and Frances and Henry could only stare at each other and shrug.

"You're going to dance?" Frances followed Lady Tallant, walking on her toes so that her words might travel directly into Henry's ear. "I didn't realize you planned to…" She trailed off. No, he hadn't come over to ask her to dance, or he would simply have done so. He had something else on his mind. Probably something to do with the letters—or lack thereof.

"You don't have to dance with me," she said

hurriedly. "I know I was at hand, but I won't be offended if you ask someone else."

His eyes cut sideways for an instant. "Don't worry yourself about that. This way I can make sure you don't escape me, and after our dance is over, we'll have a chance to speak."

Her mouth fell open. "I... well, all right. I assure you, I won't try to escape."

That was an understatement if there ever was one. She could only hope she remembered the steps of the dance while her mind was so preoccupied with furtive longing. Her fingers tingled within their gloves, wanting to touch and hold. For a few minutes, he would be all hers.

The violins scratched the warning that the minuet was about to begin, and Henry threaded through the crowd a step ahead of Frances. The crush was, if anything, intensifying as the polite world pressed against the edges of the immense room to clear a large oblong for dancing. Couple after couple fought free from the crowd and took the floor, waiting for the guest of honor so they might begin the music.

At the edge of the crowd, Henry and Frances passed a tall figure that shot out an arm to arrest Henry's progress. "Middlebrook," said a silky voice.

Henry halted and turned his head slowly. "Lord Wadsworth. Ah, Caro. You intend to dance together?"

Caroline stood at Wadsworth's side, wearing her favorite ballroom smile. Frances recognized the expression, useful for crowded rooms in which Caroline wished to appear friendly but not inviting.

"As you see," Frances said to her cousin, "we *are*

meeting on the dance floor, just as you ordered in that dictatorial way."

"I'm delighted by your obedience," Caroline answered. "Good girl, Frannie."

"I hope *you* don't intend to be a good girl, Caro," Wadsworth said in the oily voice that Frances had come to mistrust. "What pleasure would there be in that?"

"I'm always a pleasure to be around, Wadsworth. Whether I behave myself or not. But in a ballroom, I rather think I shall behave myself. Don't you?" Her fan hung from its loop at her wrist, and she shook it, setting it to swinging.

The viscount's gray eyes widened just a bit, and Frances guessed that he was remembering a sharp rap on the hand.

"If you must, Caro," he replied with a tight smile. "Middlebrook, congratulations on your ball. I hadn't realized you'd be able to dance at all, considering the extent of your injury. I'm happy to be wrong. I know you'd be devastated not to be able to take part in society events anymore."

"I'm happy when you're wrong too," Henry said in a disinterested voice. Through the sleeve of his coat, Frances could feel the tension in his left arm. The tendons in his forearm were corded, the muscles clenched.

Wadsworth squeezed his eyes in a feline blink. "Caro, shall we take the floor over here? We must give Middlebrook and his partner room to show us what they are capable of."

He turned on his heel then, and Caroline shrugged

and waggled her fan at Frances as they stood in formation for the minuet.

Henry stood still for an instant, then drew in a deep breath. His eyes found Frances's. "Well. Shall we?"

He took her hand in his, warm through their gloves, and drew her into the center of the ballroom. More than ever, Frances felt conspicuous and odd, wondering whether Henry had wanted to be here with her or whether she was just a happenstance.

She pressed her mouth into the shape of a smile as he inclined his head, released her hand, and a bright string arpeggio signaled the beginning of the minuet.

And Henry showed her and Wadsworth, and everyone else, exactly what he was capable of. Though his right arm hung still at his side, not rising gracefully with the dance, his steps were as light and sure as if his feet had never left a ballroom to march heavily through a foreign country. She followed his lead, their feet crossing, their legs bending, turning in a large slow circle against the genteel pulse of the instruments.

Frances noticed every detail, as though the scene was drawn in her mind in indelible inks and colored with vivid paints. They wound through the other dancers, turning counterclockwise and catching their left hands together at the level of their eyes. Connecting with other couples, then breaking free to twirl and cross again. A tangle being combed into order. A regimented display. After Wadsworth's veiled taunts, this seemed a new type of march to war, only instead of the punishing swiftness of the infantry's wheeling step, they were wheeling slow about a giant circle. Sinking down in the bouree step, rising again in a half coupee, allowing everyone sitting on benches to have a look at them. That was what this ball was about—and this dance. Henry had something to prove to London society, and he was proving it.

At least, he would have with a proper partner.

A quick stab of panic tangled Frances's feet as they slid past one another. She wasn't suited to this extravagant dress, to a dance in the center of this ballroom. She had relinquished that right long ago. And she was definitely not suited for a dance with Henry, who wanted to court Caroline, who sought Frances only because she stood at Caroline's side.

All of this in an unbearable instant. But the minuet was forgiving; it was old-fashioned, winding and slow and precise, and Henry had pivoted with her, hiding her stumble with smooth grace.

He would be much-desired after this night. If he stayed in Town, he could have almost anyone he wanted.

"Thank you for dancing with me," Frances said dutifully to Henry when next she drew near him.

His eyes flicked over her face. "I am delighted to be dancing with you."

"And I am delighted by your manners," Frances said. "It's kind of you to pretend you wanted this, considering Lady Tallant invited us to dance together before you got the chance."

He tilted his head a little. "I might have asked you eventually."

She almost missed another step. "Might have? *Eventually?* Any more of this praise and I shall swoon."

His mouth pinched at the corners. "All right, I

would have. I told you I needed to speak with you." He stepped, stepped through the minuet, ever tracing a slow path with his feet. Pulling away, then turning back.

"Please do, then. The suspense is unbearable." She spoke the truth so lightly that he was sure to assume she was teasing.

"It has to do with the letters."

She had been correct, then. His expression looked as pained as she felt. "Frances, I haven't received any more letters. I can only assume Caro has decided she doesn't want…"

His head tilted to the right, just the smallest gesture toward his stiffened arm. His step flattened into a heavy tread. Anyone else watching might have thought the subtle shift only a part of the dance, but Frances hoarded his every movement with eyes long trained to be watchful.

Step carefully, Frances. Step, step, step. She caught his hand again and they twirled in a deliberate circle. She did not have much time to reply; surely the dance was almost done.

"No one would care for your injury," she said. "That is, they would not hold it against you. It does not change who you truly are."

His jaw clenched, and a dented smile—scarcely a decent attempt at the expression—flashed across his face. "Sometimes I think no woman will ever hold anything against me again."

No, no, he could not think so.

But it was too late for protests; the dance was over. They stilled, facing each other, as the final notes wavered into silence. Applause was distant in Frances's ears; the shapes of other dancers were dim shadows at the edges of her vision. The only clear thing was Henry, standing before her, looking at her with those desolate eyes. A battlefield with all the soldiers gone. No more fighting.

But he would fight again; she knew that. He could not be held back for long. He would leave her in another instant and find Caroline, or someone else, and Frances would be nothing but a fool in a borrowed gown.

She took a deep breath and took a chance.

"Come with me," Frances said, full of a heat that had nothing to do with the press of the crowd. "There is something I must tell you."

Nine

THE BRONZE EAGLE THAT SPREAD ITS WINGS ACROSS THE sky-dark ceiling of the Blue Room, clutching a chandelier in its claws, had overseen many an assignation. The wink of its eye and the sardonic curve of its beak seemed to approve of such clandestine activities.

Only a dozen yards outside of the door to this side parlor, hundreds of the rich and powerful now whirled and stamped their way through a country-dance. In the Blue Room, though, there was only Frances, and Henry, and the eagle that had seen so many of the bold seduce so many of the willing.

Frances knew she could be bold if only Henry was willing. She had only to reach him with word or touch to prove his fears misplaced.

But she wasn't the one whose touch he wanted; her words were not the ones he craved.

"Sit, please," she said in her most crisp, not-at-all-lust-struck voice. "In here we'll have a bit of privacy to talk over your concerns."

Henry's straight brows yanked into a vee. "You sound as starchy as my brother's butler."

"And why not? I too am employed by the nobility."

He gave her a searching look but said nothing. He only walked to one of the blue-velvet sofas that bordered the room, then trailed a finger over the plush upholstery. Within this room, the glitter and confusion of the ballroom were nothing but a patter of sound, as though Henry and Frances were swaddled within a cloud.

She made another venture, her voice still brisk. "So, you're concerned about the effect of your arm on Caroline."

Again, that searching look. "We don't really have to talk about it."

Left hand extended, he guided her to a seat on one of the sofas. He sat to her right, then leaned his head against the wall and closed his eyes. There were fine lines at their corners, burned into his skin by long days under the sun. His scent was clean, of evergreen and soap. With the deep-blue ceiling above, she could almost fancy them outside—perhaps alone in a garden at night, with a pine tree whispering in a gentle breeze.

A swell of peace made her greedy for more, to learn what he wanted, even as her body provided its own answer. As though she were a leaf, she absorbed every bit of warmth radiating from his body. She was ready to unfurl if the time was right.

"You did say you needed to speak to me," she reminded him. It was easier to badger him when he had his eyes closed and couldn't look back at her as if he suspected something amiss. He cracked her careful reserve, her cool governess's voice, when he looked at her with those ocean-deep eyes.

"You're right," he said, eyes still closed. "I did say that. It seemed more important before the minuet."

"You don't need to talk to me anymore, then? Should I—" She didn't really want to offer to leave. She made herself stop talking.

His eyes snapped open, and he stared at the cruel-beaked eagle chandelier. "How honest do you want me to be, Frances?"

"Perfectly honest, of course." Maybe.

"To be *perfectly honest*," he said slowly, "I thought you might have been piqued after our conversation last week, in which I said I didn't need your help. I thought perhaps you discouraged Caro from returning my letters."

She began to protest, but he raised his hand. "Hear me out, Frances. Because then I thought, well, if Caro was so easily discouraged, perhaps she never enjoyed corresponding with me. Maybe it was the intimacy of the small dinner party that convinced her she wanted nothing more to do with me, since I can't dance or play cards."

He rolled his head to the side, looking at her from a scant foot away. "But when we danced the minuet together, and you were so easy-mannered and lovely, I knew you couldn't have done anything to deceive me."

"Oh," Frances said, not sure whether she was struck dumb by his misapprehension or by the fact that he'd called her *lovely*.

"No, I realized if Caro has lost interest in me, it's because of me. It's some shortcoming in me that she didn't see before. And I can't fault her for that. The fault lies within me, and it is only by some happy accident she did not see it at first." His mouth pulled tight and grim.

"Henry, no. That's not—*no*."

Damnation, what a tangle. She *had* felt piqued after their conversation, and she *had* put a halt to the letters. But Caroline had nothing to do with that and never had. Frances had only taken Henry at his word: as he had requested, she did nothing to advance his suit with Caroline. As Frances's every letter seemed to coax Henry deeper into Caroline's thrall—not that Caroline noticed or cared—Frances could almost convince herself that she was doing him a kindness by ending the deception.

But there was no way to be kind about it. Not if the letters had truly ensnared him, not if stopping the letters convinced him that the world saw him as less than whole.

No, there was no way to be kind about the truth. So Frances took a deep breath and lied her head off.

"As a matter of fact, I am in Caroline's full confidence in the matter of the letters. I usually handle her correspondence, you know, and I asked questions when I saw her write and seal letters of her own. And I asked more questions when she stopped."

"Of course you did," he said drily. His mouth looked slightly less grim.

"Of course I did," Frances agreed cheerfully. "I knew about your correspondence from the time of our writing lesson, but I didn't know the degree to which it had flourished."

"Ah." Henry looked self-conscious.

"She admitted to me that she wished she hadn't

begun a secret correspondence. That she... well, she admires you greatly, but she can't give you more than she already has."

"Because of my arm."

"*No.* Because she can't give more to any man. She enjoys having suitors, but she doesn't plan to remarry. It was only a mark of her great regard for your family, and for you, that led her to write to you in the first place."

There. That was a decent enough explanation. Frances vowed she would keep silent until Henry was ready to reply, even if it took minutes on end.

He turned his fine head back up to the gloating eagle. His shoulders shrugged and he tucked his left arm across his body, annoyance creasing his eyebrows. Frances realized he was trying to cross his arms across his chest, the memory of an old protective gesture he could no longer make.

"I would welcome her letters if she would consider sending them again," he said at last. "They kept me in London when I had almost decided to leave, and they've been a tremendous comfort since."

He had told her he'd lost confidence after his first call on Caroline, but she had no idea he'd been wounded so deeply as to beat a retreat. "Caroline's letters have helped you that much, then?"

"Yes."

"And you want them still, even if she can never give you more than friendship?"

"She might *say* that," he said, "but she might not *mean* it. Perhaps she hasn't met the right man yet."

"And you believe you are that man."

"That's for her to decide." He stretched out long legs and crossed his ankles. "Without the letters, though, she'll never decide in my favor. There are too many other men cluttering up her life. The letters are the only way I may capture her alone."

"So you do want an unfair advantage, after all." She must have sounded bitter, for this seemed to needle him.

"It's only unfair if no one else has the ability to write her a damn letter. Which they all do." He sounded cross now, gathering his right arm into a white-knuckled grip. "Pardon my language, but her choice in correspondents really is up to her, Frances. Not you."

If you only knew.

No, it would be cruelty to tell him the truth now— cruelty to both of them. She couldn't watch him grow angry and disappointed at losing not only his would-be lover but a supposed friend.

She couldn't disappoint him. And she didn't want to admit her wrongdoing.

Just as she'd done with Charles so long ago, wasn't it? She hadn't learned her lesson; she didn't want to. Maybe there was still a little of the younger, selfish Frances in her after all.

"You're right," she said smoothly. "We don't have to discuss it anymore."

No. She hadn't learned her lesson.

"I'm sorry; I was too harsh." He rubbed the bridge of his nose. "I must be on edge from the ball."

A good choice of topic. Frances could prolong a conversation about social matters infinitely. And as long as he permitted it, she would be here. With him. Alone.

She settled back against the wall, wondering if the Prussian-blue plaster would leave a dusty mark on her gown. For tonight, Caroline had entrusted the costly garment to her.

She was entrusted with many responsibilities she'd just as soon abdicate. But she shouldn't. Wouldn't.

"A ball is often enough to set one on edge," she answered. "The heat and the noise, maybe."

"Being made to dance with one arm." He gave a choked laugh.

"Well, yes. That too."

They sat in silence for a few seconds, close enough on the velvety blue sofa that Frances could sense the coiled tension of his muscles. He was all stark angles and lines, yet his mood was so many subtle shades. Unwilling humor, unbearable pride.

She *knew* him, because she was the same way. And oh, how she wanted to close the distance between them, to tug off his austere black and white clothing, and reveal the man beneath. Her skin prickled under kidskin gloves, linen and sarcenet fabrics. She longed for the touch of this man, not just the luxurious barriers of her clothes.

Henry pinched the bridge of his nose again, then let his arm fall to his side. "Had Jem and Emily truly consulted my wishes, they would not have arranged a ball in this way. But I don't blame them. They didn't get back the same brother they sent away, and so there is not as much to celebrate as they had hoped. Thankfully, they are too generous to acknowledge their disappointment."

"No one could be disappointed by you," Frances

said, hoping the words did not sound rote and trite. "Your brother and sister-in-law love you deeply."

"I must sound ungrateful to you."

"Well… yes, a bit." Frances smiled to lessen the sting of her words. "But it is entirely understandable. Just because a person goes to great lengths to help, it does not follow that such efforts were welcomed."

"Exactly. I appreciate their intent, but not the way they've carried it out. Don't let that be known, though. They mean so well. I can't bring myself to tell them their efforts are wasted."

"Are you sure it's a waste? I thought you had an excellent time at the Applewood House ball. Maybe it's only the conspicuousness of your role in this ball that's left you unsettled."

His forehead creased in thought. "I had more hope at the Applewood House ball. I hadn't yet seen much of the *ton*, and I could hold to the illusion that they would welcome me back as if I'd never left."

"They *did* welcome you back, though."

"But not as if I'd never left."

"No, of course they didn't. They couldn't." At his sharp look, Frances explained, "The *ton's* changed in the last three years, just as you have. Even if you had lived in an icehouse for three years and didn't alter a bit, you wouldn't have come back to the same world you left. Different paintings hang in the National Gallery; different maidens make their come-out each year. There are new scandals. People lose face or gain fortunes. They topple in and out of love. Some of them leave; some die. That's just… normal."

Her throat closed on the word, and she fell silent.

He didn't need to hear everything she thought and felt. He only wanted a bit of perspective, not *History of Frances's Wrongdoing and Fall*.

Which was hardly a story she wanted to retell.

After an endless few seconds, his mouth twisted unwillingly up. "You really are terrifying, Frances. You put me very decisively in my place."

"I only seek to help you find it again."

"Yes, I realize that." He studied the deep blue ceiling as if it were the night sky, full of constellations to guide him. "I am coming to realize how much has changed every time I try to repeat an old pleasure. They cannot be recaptured, whether they are as simple as a dance or as elaborate as greeting a ballroom full of people I once thought of as friends."

The war, of course. It had changed Frances just as much, stripping pleasures from her like a forester slicing unwanted branches from a trunk. For her, the war had been a capstone to an old life. For Henry, it must serve as the foundation for a new one.

"Not all pleasures are lost, surely." The words stumbled from Frances's mouth. "You may not regain the old ones, but new ones will present themselves instead."

Look at me, she wanted to say. *I'll help you find them; we'll find them together.*

"I suppose you're right," he said, his brows knit as he held out his left hand, studied its form. He flipped it over and flexed his fingers, then let it sink to his side again. "I've found new joys different from the old."

Joys such as writing letters. Better yet, receiving them. "I think I understand," Frances said.

"Yes, I suppose you do." He cut his eyes toward

her. "What about you? What joys does your life hold? It must be an endless round of pleasures for you."

"My life is never dull, I can promise you that. Every day is different, as is every one of our daily challenges."

"And what are those?"

"Oh." Frances waved a hand. "You'd think them silly, probably. All the tiny, everyday mysteries that make up life in high society for women. But they do require a certain ingenuity."

"Having lived with Emily, I completely believe you about the cunning needed to succeed in society. Do you like life in London, then?"

"You can think of a better question than that, Henry. Good God, you don't have to act as if we've only just met."

He grinned. "Maybe it's a dull question, but I do wonder about the answer. Caro—and you—came from the country in a burst of fashion and charm a year ago, but what was your life like before then?"

Frances coughed. "Any bursts of fashion and charm are and always have been Caroline's doing."

"I wouldn't be so sure about that. Didn't you just hint at your own cunning?"

"You make it sound sordid."

"Oh, probably." He made an impatient gesture with his arm. "I didn't say it correctly because it was meant to be a compliment, and instead it turned you into a hedgehog. All prickles."

She snorted. "All right, I take your meaning. Yes, I like London, though I preferred the country. And now we may find a new topic of conversation or even return to the ballroom. Only please do not speak of my prickles."

Just… smooth them.

She must keep her thoughts more tightly leashed; Henry was more perceptive than most. His eyes were sky and sea and every unfathomable thing watching her, and she feared he could sense the heat in her, the wistful want.

"I don't want to return to the ballroom yet," he said. "Do you?"

She swallowed. "No, I suppose not. But I probably should."

"They're getting along quite well without us. Emily and Jem didn't really expect me to dance beyond the opening minuet, and I'd rather be in here than out in the grand saloon entertaining a pack of impertinent questions about my arm."

"I could manage a few impertinent questions if you think that would give you the full experience of the Argyll Rooms."

"There is no doubt in my mind that you could." His smile was faint, nothing but the specter of his bright grin. "If you put your mind to it, you could probably convince me to reveal my every secret."

"I'd never ask for a confidence you didn't want to give."

"I know you wouldn't," he said. "And I wouldn't tell you unless I wanted to."

"I know you wouldn't," she repeated. "You're an artist and a soldier. You see the underpinnings of every scene and strategy."

Except for the letters, of course. Hope could blind anyone.

She fairly ached, feeling such a distance between

them. She had brought him to the Blue Room to comfort them both, to hammer out a few truths. But she'd only given him more lies.

"I like the way you see me," Henry said at last. "You may be the only one who sees me thus." She was pinned by his eyes, as stark as memory itself.

"What did you want to tell me, by the way?" he asked. "When we came in here. Was it something about—"

"I wanted to give you the truth." In deed, if not in words, she could do this much.

The air seemed close and portentous, and Henry too far. She must pull him back to her, to the cool nightfall of this dim room. She shifted closer until she could feel the bone of his hip pressing into hers.

His eyes widened, and she caught his face in her hands and moored him with her body.

Ten

GOOD GOD, SHE IS LOVELY.

Frances's face was but a few inches from his, her fingers cradling the bones of his jaw. The room was all her bright hazel eyes, the gentle arch of her brow, her warm dark hair, her creamy skin.

He'd seen Frances, talked to her many times in the past few weeks. He'd even been alone with her, touched her, a not-quite-proper clasp of fingers. But now... he'd *really* talked to her. They were *truly* alone. And he was *finally* seeing her, clever and desirable—and oh God, did he want to touch her some more.

She held his face in light fingertips, waiting for him to say or do something. Her breathing was shallow and quick.

Henry was not sure he was breathing at all.

Before his brain could voice a contrary opinion, he leaned forward and brushed her lips with his. *Ah.*

Soft as the feather of a quill, faint as the line drawing that guided the form of a painting. It was an art, the touch of mouth on mouth, and he was out of practice, but it did not matter. Her lips parted for his, and her hands pulled his face closer with the desperate truth of her own desire.

He slid his hand up her side, finding her shoulder, tickling her neck with the lightest brush of his thumb. Up it whisked, then down, and she shivered and made a little sound in the back of her throat. *Mmmm.* Her fingers slid over his face, sweet and tender, then ruffled through his hair, her nails lightly raking his scalp.

All sense vanished beneath the primal triumph of pleasing a woman. Somehow he would persuade her to want him, this clever and mysterious woman who sat aside, who noticed everything, who let him kiss her when he'd feared no one would want him again.

He should not use her—not to fill his roiling emptiness. But it was *Frances*, and she always knew what to do. Her mouth felt so good against his; the taste of her lips almost unbearably sweet and intoxicating. Not since he was a youth had he grown so drunk on kisses. He could have kissed her for hours, exploring her mouth, winning precious little moans from her.

The hands fisted in his hair let go suddenly, and she pulled away, breathing quickly, and stood. In the shaded light of the eagle chandelier, he could see the darkening of her cheeks, the flush on the exposed portion of her bosom. He wanted to follow that color beneath her clothing, see where it ended, trace her nipples with his tongue.

But no—she'd ended the kiss.

Thump. He let his head fall back against the wall. "I'm sorry. Just… give me a moment to compose myself."

"Why would I want to do that?" Still standing, she began to wrestle with the heavy mass of her skirts.

She gathered and bunched them until her legs were bare to the knee, then plumped down again on the sofa next to Henry. "When I'm working so hard to *discompose* myself?"

With her legs freed from the long, elegant prison of her skirt, she turned her body to face his, hooking her knee up onto the sofa and bumping his hip again. And as she watched him with those bright eyes, shadowed under the candlelight from that mocking bronze eagle, she slid her hands onto his legs.

Henry held himself perfectly still, certain he was forgetting something important.

Oh, right. Breathing. Blinking. And probably eventually he should say something.

His throat felt rusty and dry. He could feel every one of her fingertips on his skin, as though they had burned through his trousers. Combustible as he felt, he might have burned through them himself.

"I can see the edge of your garter," he rasped. He couldn't look away from the loop of ivory ribbon peeking beneath her ruched skirts.

"An incidental bonus," Frances said. "The cursed skirts were in my way." Her fingers began to wander, stroke, dance up his thighs. If Henry had not been sitting down, his knees would surely have unhinged.

"Well. Shall we continue?" he finally managed to say.

Frances clapped her hands over her mouth, but not soon enough to stifle a snort of laughter. "Indeed, yes, Mr. Middlebrook. That would please me above all things."

Now it was his turn to groan. "Me as well."

Grinning, she found his thigh again, slid her hands up a bit more.

He flinched. He couldn't help it. He felt stung with disbelief, but this time… this time it was good. Amazing.

She froze when he flinched, and she started to lift her hands.

"Don't," he said. His voice sounded harsh. "Please," he said more softly. "Please." He sounded as if he was begging. He had no pride now, none at all.

She listened to him. She always listened. She leaned closer, just as he hoped, and she kissed him again as her fingertips clenched halfway up his thighs, clawing ten holes in his reserve.

She nipped at his lip, and he moaned. Her skin was as warm and soft as a peach under the summer sun, and he tasted her, sipping at her mouth, nibbling at her jawline until she sighed and pressed closer, her chest brushing his.

He wrapped an arm around her—his only arm, all he had—and tugged her closer, until she was almost sitting on his lap. He could not draw her any closer lest she notice his arousal. Kisses at a ball were nothing more than many people shared. They were a simple pleasure, as ephemeral as a breeze, soon forgotten.

But not to Henry. Not after three years gone and long years alone. If she knew how hungry he was, and how parched, she would be terrified by the force of his need. He was starving; he was dying of thirst, and she was a feast, and as crisp as cool water.

She had let him draw her close. She thought him strong. Oh, but she did not know how very weak he was now. He was so weak he could hardly keep his hand from stroking the length of her back, freeing her breasts from her stays. He wanted to taste them and touch them. He wanted to touch all of her.

He tightened his grip around her, crushing the fabric of her gown in his fist—wishing it gone and himself just a bit more controlled, or just a bit less.

Right now, less would be better.

"Henry," she whispered, and her breath heated his mouth. Her tongue tapped his, a teasing dance.

They were entwined, her legs over his, his arm around her. Such closeness was a strange sensation, as fizzing and frantic as the first time he'd kissed a woman. Every movement was a question, every feeling a revelation: the delicate spring of her ribs, the slickness of silk over the yielding curve of her breasts. She gasped and worked herself closer to him when his hand grazed her tight nipple through her clothing. When his fingers brushed it again, she caught his eye and gave her own naughty smile.

"Don't start what you don't want to finish," she murmured, and her hands found the fall of his snug trousers.

"Believe me, I want—" He choked as she slid her hand across his erection. Some sensible part of his mind said, *Stop, anyone could come in.*

Don't stop, said his body. *Never stop.*

"—this," he finished, hooking his forefinger under the edge of her bodice. Knuckle by knuckle, he worked it under the snug fabric, relishing the way her shoulders shuddered and the movements of her hands grew spasmodic. His questing fingertip stroked the velvety top of her breast and grazed the edge of her nipple.

She sucked in her breath, hard. "My damned stays are in the way."

Henry laughed. "You like this?" He knew the answer, but he wanted her to say it.

"Of course I do, you tease. Shall I tease you in return?" She wriggled against his fingers. Her own hands spanned the bones of his narrow hips, again a flicker away from the fall of his trousers.

"If you wish." His smile felt crooked, self-conscious; oh, how he hoped she would.

Her wicked hands danced upward, teasing him just as she'd promised. She stroked his chest, grazed his neck with her nails. Only his arms remained tactfully untouched.

Part of his mind was still drumbeating, *This can't be real, not now, not after Quatre Bras*, as a more hopeful part gulped in the evidence of his eyes, the sweet citrusy scent of her, the electrical vibrancy of his skin, every fiber awake and alive. Popping like fireworks of Paris Green in this blue room.

Paris Green. Treacherous and bright, the shade of Caro's eyes.

Thoughts flickered: the influential countess, the secret letters. The deliberate courtship that, right now, seemed to be nothing but a chore.

Quickly as that, the spell was broken. Henry's fingers pulled free from Frances's bodice with a faint *shup* against the rich fabric—a sound almost like the defeated pop of a cork being forced back into a wine bottle.

Swiftly, her hands lifted and wove together demurely in her lap. "What happened? Did you hear something?" she whispered.

"No." Henry raked his hand through his hair,

taming and flattening the wild peaks she'd made with her eager fingers. "No. I shouldn't have done this."

Frances's proud posture sagged. "You shouldn't have... what? Met me alone?"

"Yes, and—and touched you." He stammered, hating his own uncertainty. None of the social rules he remembered had prepared him for this: seeking advice about courtship, then mauling the advisor.

Carefully, she pushed away to a respectable distance. Her face fell into shadow against the deep blue of the wall. "I touched you too," she said in a bland voice. "Do you want me to apologize? Should I be ashamed of having kissed you?"

"I hope not," Henry blurted. He pressed his hand to his temple. It was far too hot in here suddenly; he wished he could lie down on the plush-carpeted floor and wait for his shuddering limbs to return to normal.

"You hope I won't apologize."

"*No*," he barked. "I hope you won't feel ashamed. That's not why I stopped." He drew in a hesitant breath, focusing on the minute physical sensations of his body: the soft abrasion of starched linen around his neck, the tight embrace of snug-buttoned waistcoat around his torso. His clothing kept him from pulling in a deep, down-to-the-toes breath. It also reminded him where he was.

"I... liked... kissing you." The words fell from his lips haltingly, as though it was the first time he'd translated such sensations into speech. "Very much."

"Oh." She bent forward, her long body folded up. Those tip-tilted hazel eyes wouldn't meet his, but at least he could see her face again. "I suppose that's something to be glad for."

"Is it?" He let out a harsh laugh. "Where can it lead us? Nowhere. You deserve better than…" He gestured wildly with his left arm, not knowing if he meant himself or something clandestine or something that wasn't completely wholehearted. Though it had felt awfully wholehearted for a few free, unfettered minutes, until he remembered the world outside.

"You have no idea what I deserve," Frances said with a wry smile. "None at all."

"We should go back," he said in a voice thick with thwarted arousal, sorrow, pain. He swallowed it all, and it stayed within him, deep and hidden. Deep enough that he could muster a smile, a courteous bow, and a graceful offer of a hand.

She took his fingers in hers, and he ignored the quick squeeze of longing. The light of the chandelier glossed her eyes with gold, and he could not see their true color.

So. That was that. He tugged her to her feet and escorted her to the door.

When they opened it, they were hit by a tidal wave of sound and heat. Stomping feet and shrill laughter and sawing strings and the light of a thousand candles.

This was reality. The blue room was nothing but an illusion of peace.

He could hide from the world for a few minutes, but eventually he had to live in it, to conquer it. And so he would have to keep his guard always up, more than ever before—because now he knew he could not ask Frances to help him. He could not be trusted to take from her only what he ought to take.

And he still didn't know what to do about Caro's letters, which might never come again.

Damn and double damn. He was more alone now than ever.

So it had come to this: he would have to ask Jem for advice.

Eleven

"Jem? Why did you choose to marry Emily?"

Henry supposed he should have knocked at the door of his brother's private study before he blurted out the words. Jem was startled; his hands jerked, and he nearly dropped the quizzing glass he was using to study caricatures in a society paper. "Gadzooks, Hal. Didn't see you there."

His surprise was understandable. Henry rarely entered Jem's study for any reason at all, much less to ask him questions about his choice of a wife.

Henry knew Jem did not mind the intrusion, though. He was always willing to talk, especially if he thought Henry was making a rare request for guidance. He set down the paper he'd been scrutinizing and drummed a hand on his wide mahogany desk, flexing his fingers in the circle of light cast by a bronze and glass Argand lamp.

"Come in. Sit, sit, sit. Does this have anything to do with the ball yesterday? Are you thinking to marry, Hal?"

Henry suppressed a sigh at the old nickname and

dropped into a chair opposite his brother. "No, not exactly. I am simply wondering how one knows how to choose a lady. Or how one ought to choose."

This afternoon, a messenger had at last brought another letter from Caro, a quick note of apology for her silence. But with the Blue Room holding Henry's thoughts like a firefly in a jar, he had not known how to answer it. It lay hidden under a book on the ink-spattered desk in his bedchamber, still awaiting a reply.

He was torn, more torn than he could ever remember feeling before. He had wrung intimacies from Caro on paper; he had stolen them from Frances in a hushed room the color of rain. He'd remembered the desire of the flesh, not just ambition—and ambition seemed a cold, lonely promise compared to the warmth of a woman.

With Frances, he could be himself and forget the world, but the world would always loom, waiting. Caro was a weapon against those who would deny Henry his homecoming. She was bright as a shield, sharp as a saber. More golden than any medal.

Yet he doubted her regard for him, mercurial as she was.

Yet… the more he succumbed to doubt, the more he needed the social certainty she held.

None of it made sense; none of it added up. Henry hoped for a bolt of clarity from Jem, who loved to offer advice almost as much as Emily did—and who would pry into Henry's reasons far less.

Jem had picked up his quizzing glass again and was twirling it in the fingers of his right hand, his arms slung lazily over those of his chair. His mild countenance was furrowed into an uncharacteristic expression of concentration as he considered his answer. *How do you choose?*

Jem knew everything—or thought he knew it, which, when one was a wealthy earl, came to nearly the same thing. "D'you know," he finally said, "I think what I first noticed about Em was her happiness. That's why I chose her."

"You're joking," Henry said flatly. "You didn't happen to take note of the fact that she was the most beautiful woman in London?"

Jem shook his head and gave the quizzing glass one final twirl before setting it aside, as if he'd seen all he needed to. "Of course I noticed she was beautiful. But there are scads of beautiful women, Hal. Every year more of them pike into Town. If you pay close attention, though—and I'm not saying you should, because they usually come with overeager mothers—most of them are tiring."

"You mean tiresome."

"Not exactly. *Tiring.* They *want* things, you see. They want to make the best marriage, or they want to have the most stylish gowns or the wealthiest admirers. All the fuss is exciting for a while, but it tires a man out, always having to compete."

"Yes, that makes sense," Henry said slowly. He felt that fatigue himself, every time he was caught in a crowd now. Especially within Caro's inevitable throng of admirers. As if he had to scrabble for her regard by shouldering others aside.

What was the alternative, though? "Jem, surely you're not suggesting it's better to pursue a woman no one else wants, just for the ease of it. That cannot have been true of Emily."

"Certainly not." Jem looked offended. "That's not what I meant at all. I'm saying that it's better to pursue a woman you *enjoy* pursuing. I'd never have chased after her for her looks alone, or her influence. There was something else about her that I admired." He raked a hand through his dark hair. "She was easy to be with."

Henry coughed, and Jem shot him a quelling look. In the shadow cast away from his lamp's flame, he was the image of their long-departed father. "Emily was beautiful, as you said. Still is, as much as ever. But she's happy too. She's not the tiring sort."

"I beg to differ. You must not have heard her badgering me about the guest list for last night's ball."

"*Hal.* What I mean is, she doesn't need to collect things for the sake of collecting them. She never has. She only wears gowns that make her feel beautiful, and she only spends time with people whose company she likes. She wants to please herself, not others. It doesn't matter to her if the things she likes are the ones other people think are the best."

"But other people do think so."

"Well, that's the effect of happiness for you. She's satisfied with her choices, so other people think they must be good choices. Then they imitate her." He lowered his voice, confidential. "She likes that too. I don't know if you've noticed, but she's fond of her own way. Rather enjoys being a leader in the *ton*."

"That has dawned on me once or twice," Henry replied drily.

Jem nodded. "That's the best I can figure. There's no other reason for so many females to start wearing yellow gowns, for one thing. Em loves the color, but it turns most other women into sick canaries."

Henry smiled at the description, but Jem needed no reply. He was warming to his subject now. "Just think of who makes you happy, Hal. That's probably the woman you ought to spend your life with. If you don't know that much, then you aren't ready to marry."

He leaned forward across the desk, his voice confidential. "Em would clout me for saying that. I know she wants to see you settled. If she ever gives you any trouble, though, you may just remind her that she waited almost an entire season before deciding on me."

Henry's thoughts were stumbling, falling behind Jem's words. "She did not always care for you, then."

He had been away at school when his brother married. He had always assumed Jem's courtship had gone smoothly because everything *always* went smoothly for Jem. His suit could never have involved the pain of veiled taunts or letters painfully printed out with an awkward hand. It would not have driven him to the guilty comfort of another woman's embrace.

"Not at first, she didn't want me," Jem said with a grin. He tipped his chair back on two legs, balancing himself by resting his hands on his desk. "I trod on her toes the first time we danced. I couldn't think of the steps while I was looking at her; she was that amazing. But that wasn't much fun for her, getting trampled, and she didn't want to dance with me again. I wore her down over time, though. I knew she was the one for me."

"You knew Emily was the right choice because she was happy."

"Yes." Jem let the front legs of his chair thump onto the floor again. "And I think that's why I felt happy around her too. I think everyone does. Don't you?"

Oh, certainly. That is, when she's not scheming to marry me off or turn me into a spectacle in front of the entire ton.

But Henry understood what his brother meant. Emily *was* happy. And because she loved Henry, she wanted him to find happiness too. She and Jem both wanted that, even if they did not know how to help him attain it.

How simple Jem made the whole situation sound when he reduced it to his essentials. *Think of who makes you happy.* But the *who* might not be the same as *what.* No woman on earth could bring back the use of Henry's arm or erase the pain of Quatre Bras.

What was left of happiness, then? He didn't know, but whether as an artist or a soldier, a lover or husband, he'd always planned to grasp for happiness with two hands.

He couldn't do that now. So he had to come up with a new plan.

"Did any of that help you?" Jem asked. His expression was eager.

"I'm not certain," Henry said.

But the seed of an idea was taking root. A strategy at last.

He just had one more letter to write.

Twelve

"I THOUGHT YOU'D STOPPED GETTING THOSE RIDICULOUS letters." Caroline handed a fat sealed note to Frances before draping herself onto her morning room's scroll-armed sofa.

Frances shoved the note halfway under her dark blue skirts, then took up her embroidery again. "I'd stopped sending them for a few weeks, so I thought I *would* stop getting them. Or *you* would, actually."

Her needle whipped quickly through Caroline's delicate lawn handkerchief, creating a monogram. *CS.* Caroline, Countess of Stratton. The lady to whom the note was addressed.

She shouldn't have sent that quick little note of apology following the ball. It was an atonement for mauling Henry in the Blue Room, even after she knew how much he wanted letters from Caroline.

But if he was sending letters again, then she hadn't really atoned for anything. She'd just compounded her sin.

The needle flashed faster. Its tip caught the edge of Frances's thimble, flicking it with a delicate *ping* across the morning room.

"I should never have allowed you to take my name in vain, but I thought the blasphemy would be short-lived. I never imagined your scheme would go on this long." Caroline stretched back on the green upholstery, chosen to match the shade of her eyes, and picked up the newest issue of *Lady's Magazine*. "Do you think a Pomona green gown would look well on me?"

Frances tossed aside the handkerchief again and dropped to the floor, squinting across the vine-patterned carpet for her lost thimble. "Yes, it would look lovely on you. And you know I meant to put a stop to the letters once it was clear to me that Henry was getting fascinated with you."

"Now there we differ, because that's not clear to me at all." Caroline snapped her periodical closed and dropped it on the floor, then hoisted herself up on one elbow. "Why are you scrabbling about on the floor? Are we playing charades?"

"Yes," Frances said. "I am playing a deranged fool. Could you not guess?" With a wrench of her arm, she laid hold of the thimble under a small writing desk. She then crawled over to retrieve Caroline's magazine, shook out the pages, closed it, and sat up.

Caroline peered down at her from the sofa. "It was a more than fair imitation, but I do not understand why the urge seized you."

"I lost my thimble," Frances said. "It was a perfectly normal reaction."

"And you got a letter from Henry," Caroline reminded her in a singsong voice.

"No, *you* got a letter."

"No." Caroline shook her head. "It's *your* letter, Frannie. They've all been for you, no matter the name on them. Whatever you've written is what he's become fascinated with. You ought simply to tell him the truth, then do the kind of thing to him that makes a man forget all about being angry."

The kind of thing they'd done last night... hard-muscled thighs, a firm mouth moving hot over her skin, hands stroking and groping in a twilight-dark room. Frances could have moaned at the memory.

"Your cheeks are turning pink."

Frances frowned and covered them with her hands. "So? It's hot today."

"Fine, lie to me." Caroline reached down an arm and patted around on the floor until she found her *Lady's Magazine*. "I'll just read about Pomona green and wait for the callers to start coming. We'll just have an ordinary day. We'll get far too many roses and we'll feed the blooms to the carriage horses. I wish for nothing else in the world."

"Nor do I."

Caroline rolled her magazine into a tube and batted Frances on the head. "Lies, lies, and more lies. I count on your advice, you know. If you're only going to tell me what you think I want to hear, I won't want to hear it anymore."

Frances rubbed at the top of her head and scooted on the floor out of Caroline's reach. "Right now I'm thinking of something you won't want to hear."

"Likewise." Her cousin waggled the rolled-up magazine. "Tell. Henry. You. Wrote. The. Letters."

Frances stood and brushed off her skirts. "So we're

back to that? Listen to me, Caroline. I'm not going to tell him."

She sighed and sank back into her chair, not caring that she rumpled her embroidery. "I *can't* tell him. Not after seeing how delighted he was to receive a letter he thought was from you. He said…" She made herself smile. "He said he'd been thinking about leaving London, but your letter convinced him to stay."

Caroline's mouth went slack. "What in God's name did you put in that letter? It must have been some sort of magical incantation."

"I don't recall, exactly. Just something that let him know I enjoyed his company." She gave a mirthless laugh. "But he didn't enjoy mine, did he? I signed it as 'a friend,' and he decided that meant you because your friendship was the one he wanted. He might have welcomed my words, but they held no power until he linked them with your name."

Caroline had shoved herself upright on the sofa. Under her crown of golden hair, her ocean-green eyes were huge and bright, and her mouth sagged.

"Don't make your lost-kitten face at me." Frances covered her eyes. "That's not fair. I'm not even going to look at you until you stop."

"Oh, *fine*." Caroline's voice sounded normal, but when Frances lifted her face, the countess still looked a little distressed. "I know you don't like that expression, but the feeling's real enough. I absolutely *hate* that you think you aren't everything he wants. And I hate him a little bit for making you feel that way."

"Don't hate him," Frances said. "It's not his fault.

This muddle is my doing. I wrote more letters knowing he thought they were from you."

"How silly of him. I suppose that's proof of male arrogance, because I've tried to give him no encouragement. Not since the first time I met him, and certainly not since you sent him a letter. If he had eyes in his head, he'd see that readily enough."

It *was* silly of Henry, maybe. But it didn't take much for a man to become fascinated with Caroline. Her ever-full drawing room was testament to that.

"Maybe he just thinks you're being devious," Frances suggested.

"I usually am," Caroline said, the lost-kitten expression now entirely vanished. "But in this case, you're being far more so."

"I'm not going to tell him the truth. I just told you why."

"Then I pity you both, because one day he'll find out the truth and he'll hate you for lying to him." Her hand fluttered to her mouth. "Oh, damn, and he'll probably hate me too, for going along with it."

"He won't find out. And please don't say that you pity either of us, Caroline." *Soldiers never want pity as much as they want a good meal and a quick tumble.*

Or a not-so-quick one.

"All right." Caroline slid to the floor. "The words will not come out of my mouth again. They might run through my thoughts, though."

With a quick swoop, she grabbed the still-sealed letter from the chair where Frances had left it. She cracked the seal and flapped the paper open in front of Frances's face. "Read it, you stubborn wench."

Despite herself, Frances laughed, and she took the paper from Caroline's outstretched hand.

> *Dear Caro,*
>
> *Thank you for your letter. I was pleased to see you at the ball as well. It's kind of you to write that you wished I had danced more. I found one minuet quite enough, though I hope in time to find other amusements that suit me just as well as dancing.*
>
> *I shall call on you this afternoon—with violets, of course—and must speak to you privately. Would you grant me a few minutes of your time for a discussion of a highly secret but not at all improper scheme?*
>
> *Yours,*
> *Henry*

Her fingers felt chilly, and they trembled. "Here." She thrust the letter back toward Caroline. "I told you it was intended for you."

As Caroline skimmed the lines, Frances made herself stand and roam around the room, tidying periodicals, folding up her sewing. If Henry intended to call today, he might be here in little more than two hours.

So. She had two hours to wrap her mind around the knowledge that Henry wanted a private interview with Caroline. The secrecy alone made it improper— just as was his supposed correspondence with Caroline.

Yet Frances was the one he had kissed and touched.

Frances was the one who had made his breathing rush, who had roused his body.

Or had he only kissed her back? He was the one who had pulled away first, though he pretended it was for her own good.

She creased Caroline's delicate handkerchief into a tiny square and crammed it into her sewing basket.

"A secret scheme," Caroline murmured. She cast the letter onto the floor with her usual carelessness, and Frances snapped it up and tossed it onto the morning room's small writing desk. "I can't imagine what it could be."

"Are you going to oblige him?" The tone of Frances's voice rang falsely bright even to her own ears.

"I'll see what he has in mind." Caroline frowned. "You don't think this is one of Emily's matchmaking schemes, do you?"

"I really can't say."

Caroline chuckled. "No, I really can't say what goes through Emily's head either. But still, this doesn't sound like one of her plots. If she had dictated the letter, I'm sure she would have been much more effusive about her ball."

"No doubt." Frances returned to her chair and folded her hands neatly, facing her cousin. "So. Violets. A secret scheme. Are you still willing to say he's not besotted with you?"

Caroline clambered back onto her scroll-armed sofa, *Lady's Magazine* again in hand. "I'm willing to hear him out. It might be something quite innocent. It could even be a surprise for Emily and Jem."

She leaned back and flipped open the magazine, then

laid it over her face. "Now do let me rest for an hour," came her muffled voice. "If we're to have a roomful of callers this afternoon, I need to prepare myself."

She tugged the paper down for a second. "Have Millie lace you into that ravishable bronze-green gown again, won't you? Just in case."

And with a roguish wink, she vanished again under the pages of fashion, leaving Frances with Henry's letter and far too many questions.

❧

Frances fully expected to see some change in Henry's face when he entered Caroline's drawing room that afternoon.

From her customary seat in the corner, she could read each arriving man like a book. Bart Crosby was a sweeping romance, all courtly admiration and puppy love. Lord Wadsworth was rather gothic in the way he squinted at everyone else, as though they were family skeletons he'd intended to shove back in the closet. Hambleton and Crisp were a farce, as always, dressed in identical high-starched cravats and waggling ivory-headed swordsticks.

But when Henry was shown into the drawing room at last, he looked annoyingly normal considering he was plotting a secret. Which made him a mystery.

There were no such shadows under his eyes as there were under Frances's: horrible gray-yellow circles that not even the bewitching bronze-green dress could banish. Henry's smile was bright and confident too, nothing of self-consciousness in it. He strode into the room with his left arm crooked around a bouquet of violets and swept into a bow before Caroline,

straightening before his stiffened right arm could swing
out of place.

"For me?" the countess asked—rather obtusely, in
Frances's opinion.

"Somewhat." Henry tumbled the violets into her
lap, then retrieved what Frances now realized was
one of two bouquets he'd been holding. "If you'll
excuse me?"

Caroline's smile widened to a positive sunbeam.
"Be off with you."

As seemingly everyone in the room stopped talking,
Henry strode over to Frances.

To her, he handed the violets with an entirely
different gesture. There was nothing theatrical about
the half smile, the simply outstretched hand. Frances
sat dumbly, watching, as he waited for her to take
the flowers.

"You deserve blooms of your own," he finally said.
"I would like you to accept these, if you're willing."

"If I'm willing?" She gave a little bark of laughter.
"I'm shamefully willing. No one's ever brought me
flowers before. Thank you." She took the bunch from
him with a clumsy, overeager gesture.

He gave her a searching look, suddenly a strategist. "Consider this an appeasement, to keep you
from ripping my head off in the middle of the
drawing room."

Her fingers tightened on the ribbon-bound stems.
"Why? Have you done something unforgivable?"

His mouth kicked up on one side. "I hope you
don't think so," he said in a quiet voice.

Under the armor of the bronze-green silk, Frances

felt suddenly conscious of every inch of her skin. "No, I suppose I don't."

The grin he shot her was pure mischief. "I am relieved to hear it."

"I'm not relieved in the slightest," she muttered, too low for him to hear. The tight, sweet tension of unfulfilled desire rippled through her belly at the sight of him, making her nipples harden.

Settle down, she told herself. These violets were meant to atone, their frail little blooms covering over a furtive interlude that should never have happened. He was too stubborn in pursuit of his countess, and she was too proud to throw herself at someone who didn't truly want her.

Probably. She was *probably* too proud for that.

"Is that all, then?" Her voice sounded brisk, as if she were truly the teacher she'd once pretended to be. And why not? If he thought to buy her off with violets, he must not know how glad she was for even this sign of his regard. Which was really a dismissal.

"For now." And with that brilliant grin that wiped her mind blank and muddled her thoughts into a froth of longing, he inclined his head to Frances and strode back to Caroline.

Only a few feet away, yet far enough that she had no idea where she stood with him.

Caroline had piled up cushions next to her to save a spot on the sofa for Henry. *All the better to scheme with you, my dear.* Wadsworth tried in vain to shoulder his way into their conversation, but every time he interjected something, Caroline found another small task for him to perform—a vase to relocate, a tray of dainties to pass among the guests.

Caroline was using him as a footman. It made a welcome distraction from Frances's own uncertainty.

The viscount grew distinctly sour as Caroline's indifference persisted through minute after minute. His courtly veneer thinned, then dissolved entirely as the other men ignored him, chatting about horses and boots and the cut of their coats, plucking sandwiches from the tray he held, granting him as little attention as they'd give a servant.

Finally, Wadsworth stalked over to Frances's chair, tray still in hand, and leaned against the blue-plastered wall.

"So you've learned one of the cardinal rules of good society," she said. "With the simple addition of a tray or a duster to one's hand, anyone can become invisible."

"You underestimate me, Mrs. Whittier," he said with a lazy smile, leaning so close that she could smell the floral-citrus of the bergamot with which he evidently anointed his hair.

"I'm sure I don't," Frances muttered, clutching her violets more tightly.

Wadsworth pretended he hadn't heard. "You know I am scrupulously conscious of manners. For example, I'm aware that I ought more properly to allow you to hold this tray. Since you are a servant."

He held out the platter of tiny sandwiches at arm's length. Before Frances could decide whether or not to take it from him, he released it.

Thump. The silver tray fell to the floor, sandwiches rolling every which way.

His expression was all solicitous concern; all except for the eyes. Those were cool and gray and sharp, like dirty icicles. "Dear me, Mrs. Whittier. What a state you're in. Well, we all have our little accidents sometimes; no need to berate yourself. Do you require help clearing those? I'm sure another servant could come to your aid."

Frances spared a quick second to glare at him before glancing around the room. Caroline and Henry were oblivious, talking head to head on the sofa. Caroline was grinning and nodding.

Bah. They didn't even need the letters anymore.

She swallowed a sick little heave of her stomach, then caught the eye of Bart Crosby. The good-hearted young baronet was hovering behind Caroline and Henry, but he noticed the food scattered over the carpet and made a convulsive movement, as though ready to come to Frances's aid.

With a quick shake of the head, she warned him back. Whatever Wadsworth meant by this game, there was room for only two to play.

"Since I'm Lady Stratton's companion," she said in her sweetest voice, "it is my responsibility to help her callers, even if their behavior is asinine and rude."

She gave Wadsworth a bright, innocent smile, an expression she'd learned from Caroline. "Not that I refer to *you*, of course. I am sure in your mind, it's perfectly normal to throw sandwiches onto the floor. Shall we leave them right there, or would you prefer to arrange them into a pattern? Do you mean to eat all of them? Shall I get you a cup of tea for you to wash down your floor sandwiches?"

Wadsworth's eyes narrowed until they were little more than slits. "I pity Caro the companionship of such a jade."

Frances narrowed her eyes right back. "If you mean to compare me to a precious stone, I thank you. And if there is anything else I can do to ensure your comfort, do let me know. I'll be standing across the room, next to Caroline, in whose house you have made such chaos."

She stood, savoring the luxuriant *shushhhhh* of the stiff silk skirts. She trod on the platter Wadsworth had dropped, then swanned across the room to stand by Bart Crosby.

It was a rather decisive exit, if she did say so herself. And just in time, because she could feel her face growing hot as if it had been slapped. Soon her throat would have closed, choking her, and she would have been unable to defend herself.

"Sir Bartlett," she murmured by way of greeting.

"You did excellently," he replied. His brown eyes squinted with suppressed laughter. "I'd never have thought of all that sympathetic tosh."

"You'd never have needed to." She could have sighed.

She was among the vulnerable now, the questionable fringe of society whose reputations hung upon the kindness—or unkindness—of others. After a single Season in London, she was accustomed to being seen only as an accessory to Caroline. But when she was singled out... well, that she was *not* accustomed to.

She realized she was still holding her violets in a tight grip, crushing the slim stems together and bruising the blooms. No, she hadn't expected to be singled out by either Henry or Wadsworth. Perhaps the one had inspired the other.

After all, they both wanted Caroline. She was a means to an end for them both. For good or ill.

"Are you quite well? Mrs. Whittier?"

Frances blinked and pulled her thoughts back into the drawing room. Sir Bartlett was watching her with the type of solicitude a man might bestow upon an older sister. "You look rather pale, if you'll permit me to say so."

"I'm fine, thank you. You needn't worry about me." She made herself smile. "Do you wish to sit?"

The baronet looked sheepish. "I was hoping to speak with Caro."

"Ah. Yes, well, she's scheming. I'm not certain about what." Another smile, this one a little tighter. Henry and Caroline still spoke low, their golden heads visible over the back of the sofa.

At the other end of the room, Wadsworth was jawing out a footman and gesturing at the fallen sandwiches in the corner of the room. This was unfortunate for Caroline's footman, but at least Wadsworth's spleen had turned impersonal. It could now be quickly vented, quickly forgotten.

"She does enjoy her schemes," Sir Bartlett was saying, his quiet voice warm with amusement. "She's the one who got Hambleton and Crisp to dress identically. Did you know that?"

Frances discarded the thought of Wadsworth and gave a much more genuine smile. "That sly woman. I did *not* know that; I thought they'd always been in the habit. How ever did she do it?"

The baronet shrugged. "Some compliment on the clothing of one, then the other. And then I believe she said if *one* was so handsome, *two* such would be nigh irresistible."

With a quick hand to her mouth, Frances covered a laugh. "She seems to be resisting them quite well. Have they not noticed?"

Sir Bartlett grinned, looking more boyish than ever. "Maybe not. I'm guessing they get great enjoyment out of the effect. And now they have an excuse to talk about their clothing all the time with one another."

"A match made in heaven," Frances murmured.

"Something of the sort. I'll never complain, because the more she distracts her other suitors, the more time she has for—"

He cut himself off abruptly as Henry gave a final nod and stood from the sofa at last.

"Have Millie help you," Caroline said in a louder voice. "Now, if the moment suits you."

Henry nodded again, and his eyes met Frances's over the back of the sofa. He gave her a wink.

She instantly turned into a Christmas pudding, all soft and overheated.

Stupid of her. It wasn't even remotely the right time of year for pudding.

"Thank you, Caro," Henry said, again focusing on the countess. "The evidence of one's own eyes is always the best sort of proof. Surely you agree with me." He grinned down at Caroline, a conspiratorial sort of expression.

You like proof, facts, evidence.

So Frances had written in her first letter, before she

knew it would be credited to another. Caroline had never read that one.

From behind, Frances could see Caroline's shoulders lift. "If one is a doubting sort. Actually, I…"

Frances gave a very unladylike cough.

"I am just that sort," Caroline finished smoothly. "Full of doubts. Very reliant on evidence. Yes, I've said something to that effect, but I suppose I forgot I'd mentioned it to you." She gave a shimmery laugh. "My memory is a sieve, you know. My head is too full of frills and fribbles. I am completely without Frannie's gifts of recall."

Now Frances rolled her eyes elaborately.

But Henry didn't notice, he only took his leave. As soon as he'd exited the drawing room, Caroline turned on the sofa. "Dear Frannie, what a terrible cough you have. Come and pour out a little tea, won't you? And, Bart, you must come and sit by me."

Thus summoned, the two moved around the sofa and seated themselves to either side of Caroline. As Frances smoothed her skirts into place, she hissed, "You'll ruin the whole secret if you're so obvious about every little bobble you make."

Caroline smiled. "Yes, Frannie, I'd adore some tea. Thank you." Much lower, she murmured, "I can't be expected to know when he's referring to something I'm meant to have written. I *didn't write it*, you know."

"You *can* be expected to be subtle, though."

Caroline waved a hand. "Subtlety is utter bosh. Confidence is what one needs."

"Hmmm." Frances couldn't quite bring herself to

say what she thought—namely, that those sounded like Henry's words.

"If you're only going to sit there and hum, you might as well pour out at once." Caroline gestured toward the tea tray. "You can serenade us all quite as well while you tip that teapot on end."

She sat up and extended her cup, and the commotion across the room finally caught her eye. "Good lord, what has Wadsworth done with all the sandwiches? Did he stumble?"

"It *was* a stumble of sorts." Frances sat herself primly on the sofa next to Caroline. As she filled teacups and measured out careful slivers of lemon and lumps of sugar, she felt her poise return.

Perhaps her life would always be portioned out by teaspoons and hours for callers and the occasional bunch of violets. It was not much to be proud of, but she was useful in her way.

And life could hold its tiny triumphs nonetheless.

Across the room, she caught Wadsworth's eye, and she raised her teacup to him for the sheer pleasure of watching him glare.

Thirteen

THE CALLERS HAD ALL GONE AT LAST; THE SANDWICHES had been tidied from the floor by a maid. The carpet and Wadsworth's dignity had been restored to order with equal skill—one with a few well-placed whisks of a rag, the other with a few well-chosen words from Caroline.

"Why bother appeasing him?" Frances said when she and Caroline were finally alone in the drawing room. "I know you don't care for him."

Caroline shrugged. "Not particularly. But why antagonize him? He might have his uses one day."

"He could be good for sharpening your claws on, I suppose."

Caroline laughed and agreed. "Now go have a rest. You look dreadful, and I mean that in the kindest way possible."

So Frances went to her bedchamber as bid. It was usually a quiet haven, a long, narrow room with walls the color of a new leaf and light pinstriped curtains.

With the help of Millie, Caroline's lady's maid, she shed the rustling bronze-green silk, which had won

entirely the wrong kind of notice today. Instead, she
donned a soft blue linen day dress that made her feel
much more like herself.

Not precisely at ease, though. The peaceful
surroundings had little effect on her turbulent thoughts
today. As soon as Millie had left, Frances folded herself
onto the wide-planked wooden floor, leaning against
the side of her bed.

She did feel tired, just as Caroline had suggested—
tired of lying, even through omission. Maybe it was
time she came face-to-face with a few truths. Namely
this: if Caroline was everything Henry wanted,
Frances had only herself to blame.

That was the case with her whole life, wasn't it?
Every turning was of her own choosing, every pursuit,
every inevitable fall.

She lifted the white swagged bedding that draped
nearly to the floor, then reached under the high bed.
Her fingers found the sturdy square of a rosewood
box, pulled it forward, and hefted it into her lap.

It was a fair size, a foot square, but it felt as light in
Frances's hands as if it held nothing of consequence.
It seemed as though it ought to feel heavy with
portent. *Here lies everything left of the first twenty-three
years of your life.*

She ran her fingers over the lid and rubbed its orna-
mental brass plate. Elegant and cold, engraved with the
ornate capitals *IMW*. Irene Malverne Ward. This had
once been her mother's jewel case. Lady Ward had
been gone for a long time, and Frances had only this
legacy with which to remember her mother.

Frances had given up everything else for Charles

Whittier, but she'd never regretted it. Not when her family's anger separated her from her childhood home, not even when Charles's disappointment separated her from himself. She had always assumed their separation would be only temporary, but war had made it permanent. When he died, she had been even more glad for her deception and disobedience, for their brief marriage.

She had given herself away too cheaply, she now thought. Now she was left with only this box, a compact reminder of what she'd tossed away for love.

A reminder not to be an idiot, really.

She was beginning to think she needed that reminder again. For the second time in her life, she was allowing herself to become fascinated with a man who was too young and too good-looking. She was losing track of what was right, tricking him to keep him close. That had not ended well the first time; there was no reason to think the second would be different.

She lifted the lid of the box, and the papers within it whispered faintly. A faint floral scent wafted from the dark wood.

There were a few letters from Charles, delivered to her with titillating secrecy while they were courting by moonlight. Charles was not well educated, though he had been bright and witty, with the finest mind for figures Frances had ever encountered. As an innkeeper's son, he had little call to practice a flowing hand, and the letters were scrawled untidily. She had never seen a worse hand from an adult, now that she thought it over—except from Henry.

Two soldiers, two casualties of war. Two, two,

two. Yet they were nothing alike, except that she cared for them both.

Though even that was not the same. Charles had been the love of her youth, her feelings so ferocious that they withstood even the certainty of his waning regard. Her love might have burned out in time, but it had been snuffed by his death before that could happen. And so it lingered like smoke, pervading the very air of her world. The loss had choked her, until after long months and years, it began to dissipate, and she could breathe again.

What she felt for Henry was different. She *knew* him from the first time she saw him—his hidden wounds, concealed under a role. She wanted to tease out his every secret, to gain the right to bring down his guard.

Through the letters, she had come to understand Henry's mind; now she hungered for his body. She was beginning to think she would not be satisfied until she had captured his heart, though she had no stratagem for doing so.

She was always out of step. She had grown up in wealth but married a workingman. Now she served as a companion, yet she raised her eyes to the son of an earl. She did not know for which world she was better suited. At times, both lives chafed, as though she lived in a garment cut wrongly and fitted for another's body.

She sifted through the papers in her rosewood box, looking for her drawing of Charles. Though she wasn't much of an artist, the likeness had been passable. No still image could have captured the things she loved best about him: the quirk of his brow when he was surprised, the slight pout of his lips when he tried to suppress a smile. He had been roguish and fun, and he had been proud of Frances, his highborn lover, once upon a time.

Of course, it was easier to be proud when one had enough to live on. It was easier to be in love too. In the end, Frances had managed it, but Charles had not.

Her fingers touched the bottom of the box. She had turned all the papers, and the drawing was not here.

She set the box on the floor and bent down again to peer under the bed. No, it had not fluttered out.

Strange. Very strange.

She straightened up and looked around her bedchamber. The only thing out of place was the box itself, where she had just set it down. She sat on the floor, leaning her head against the bed.

It was not as if she could not bring his face to mind without the picture. He had arched brows, warm eyes. His nose had been… straight, she supposed. His mouth…

She could not recall it, not right now. She could recall only the mouth that had kissed hers in the Blue Room.

She closed her eyes and pressed at them with the heels of her hands, wondering if shutting them would help her mind's eye to open. Her fine memory was failing her. The lineaments of Charles's face were blurring into those of Henry.

The faint old sketch was nothing but lines of carbon on paper, but she needed them. Now that she could not trust her memory to hold him safe, she had to find her drawing. It reminded her of more than Charles;

it reminded her of the choices she'd made and how they'd transformed her.

Possibly one of the maids had taken the drawing for some reason, though she could not imagine what. "Millie," she called, not caring that her voice rang at a very unladylike volume.

The lady's maid peeped into Frances's room within seconds, bobbing her head, her eyes wide at the sight of her mistress's companion sitting on the floor. "Mum? Is everything all right?"

No. "Yes, Millie. I didn't mean to alarm you. I just need to know if you've seen a picture in here. A sketch."

"A sketch, mum? No, I haven't. I could check with Pollitt. He'd know if one of the other maids had found something. Ah… what sketch would it be, mum?"

Frances hauled herself into a chair. "It was a drawing of Mr. Whittier. You understand why I wish to locate it."

"Yes, mum. Right away, mum." Millie looked sympathetic as she dipped into her curtsy and went to question Caroline's butler.

So, even the servants pitied her. Millie had a young man who always took her out on her half day off. The butler, Pollitt, who seemed never to feel emotion at all, had won a woman's lifelong devotion at some point in the unimaginable past, for he was married to Caroline's cook.

Feeling no emotion at all. That sounded wonderful.

Frances made herself stand, twisting to remove stiffness from her back. Her body felt tired and overfull of old secrets she would have gladly discarded.

She might as well see if there was some way to

distract herself. Maybe Caroline needed some letters—
some *real* letters—written. If not, she could find herself
a book to read.

She'd tried to face the truth, but it was too much,
now that Charles's face was turning into Henry's.

On her way to the morning room, she padded down
the corridor past the drawing room and heard a low
voice inside. A man's voice. Caroline was not alone.

Frances had a suspicion whom she would find even
before she peeked through the doorway.

"Henry." She slung a sloppy smile across her face.
"I thought you had left."

From his seat next to Caroline on the sofa, he
snapped to attention with the speed and grace of a
bone-deep soldier. "Only for a short while. Frances, I
didn't realize—"

"You were supposed to go to sleep, Frannie,"
Caroline interrupted. "Go away at once, and come
back in half an hour."

Frances could not have gone more numb if she'd
been plunged into ice water. "Of course," she said in
a toneless voice, and turned her back on the pair. Half
an hour, they wanted. She could easily imagine why.

"Wait, please," Henry called before she could take a
step away. Lower, he said, "Caro, I can show her now.
It won't harm anything."

Frances turned slowly on the balls of her feet.
"Show me what?" Her eyes hunted jewelry, a hand
clasp, some sign that Caroline had succumbed to
Henry's scheme for all that he insisted it was *not at all
improper*. Henry wanted to spare Frances a half hour
of suspense; he must feel he owed her that much after

their interlude in the Blue Room. A half-dozen kisses and a bit of illicit groping won her the right to be told in person that he had chosen another.

Caroline shrugged. "Fine, Henry. It's *your* secret plot." She drew an old-looking piece of paper from behind an embroidered cushion.

Henry began to fidget; he stood, cleared his throat, motioned for Frances to come in and seat herself, then cleared his throat again.

"You're fidgeting," Frances noted, feeling no less confused as she perched on a low-back Windsor chair. "The last time I saw you so restless, you, ah, asked me for help." Help composing a reply to a letter he thought he had received from Caroline.

Henry's face turned red under its sun-brown. "And you granted it very kindly. But I'm not asking you for help this time. I've made you a present."

"You made me a present."

Caroline blew a breath out between thinned lips. "In case we haven't said it often enough, yes, Frannie, he made you a present. Only it's not really ready yet, but since you wouldn't sleep and you wouldn't leave, now you're going to look at it." She slapped her hands onto her thighs. "I believe I've summarized the essentials of the situation."

"Oh." Frances's mind seemed to have been wiped as blank as the accounting slates Charles and his father used to keep at their inn. "I didn't realize."

"Obviously not," Caroline said crisply. "So. This belongs to you." She held the old paper out to Frances.

Even before Frances had unfolded it along its worn creases, she knew what it was. "Charles."

"You once mentioned having a sketch of your late husband." Henry's voice was quiet as he sank back onto the sofa next to Caroline. "Your cousin helped me figure out how to abstract it earlier. I hope you do not mind."

Frances unfolded the paper. There was her missing drawing: Charles Whittier at the age of twenty-one, as lifelike as a pencil and Frances's limited talent could make him. There was his clean jaw, the cleft in his chin, the twist of his smile. The shape of the mouth she had adored for years, had so often kissed—but had not, only a short while ago, been able to recall.

"Why did you take it?" She sounded peppery as she folded up the paper again, impatient with their teasing little plot. As though she was their pet, to be tricked and played with.

"He made you a present," Caroline chanted. "Good heavens, Henry, show it to her so she'll quit asking about it."

Frances watched, still feeling left behind, as Henry retrieved a leather case from behind another cushion.

"I shall have to remember to look under every one of your cushions, Caroline," Frances said. "You've been hiding things."

Caroline flapped a hand to shush her. "You're going to love this, I know."

Henry stood and handed the folded leather to Frances. When she didn't open it right away, he retreated again to the sofa and sat by Caroline. The two of them peered at her, eager for her reaction.

Despite herself, she smiled. They obviously meant well, and it was becoming just as obvious that they really *hadn't* gotten up to anything improper—beyond sneaking Frances's possessions, that is.

She unfolded the butter-soft leather and found within an ivory oval. The outline of a young man was drawn on it, his coat tinted a rich blue not much darker than Henry's eyes. The lines of the man's face were shaky and vague, but recognizably those of Charles.

Henry cleared his throat. "I colored the coat over the last few days, but I have not had time today to do more than copy his face in pencils. Maybe it's for the best that you learn of the portrait now, as I need to know his coloring before I can finish."

"Brown," Frances said quietly, still staring at the picture. "His hair light, his eyes dark." She stretched out a finger to touch the ivory surface, then thought better of it. She should not smudge the lines Henry had carefully marked out.

With his left hand, he had done this. It was not a great work of art by any means, but it was almost as clear as the drawing she had made with the living man before her.

She looked up at Henry's face again, her mind locked. "I don't understand. Why have you done this?"

His eyes were the painful blue of sapphires worn by a rival. "I wanted to give you a gift. To thank you for your friendship. Caro thought this was something you might like."

"A new picture of my dead husband that you created by stealing the old from me. That's what Caroline thought I would like."

"Well, yes." Caroline's voice was higher than usual. "I thought you'd prefer something more meaningful than a book, and it wouldn't be right for him to give a gift of clothing, you know."

"I do not understand why you need give me anything at all."

Henry looked embarrassed. His gaze flicked just to the left of Frances's, and his mouth tugged into a dent at one corner. "There was no need, but I *wanted* to give you something."

"Why?"

His voice grew quieter, not much more than a whisper—as if he feared having Caroline hear him. "Because of the ball. The way you... when we..." His eyes slid to Caroline before finding Frances again. "Thank you for helping me."

Help. Her every kiss and touch—he thought she had meant it as *help*. The summer heat was almost suffocating, yet Frances prickled with cold. It was just as she feared. She had drawn him aside, placed herself in his way until he could not ignore her attentions.

"You are too generous," she said in a faint voice.

She had led him with letters and with her own body, but by leading him, she had no idea where he truly wished to go.

Frances swallowed a sigh and looked into his beautiful eyes again. "Thank you, Henry," she said, managing the calm companion's voice he was used to. "It was not necessary, but it was very kind of you. And Caroline."

Henry looked relieved. "She thinks the world of you."

And what do you think? Of me? Of her?

Better not to ask any questions if she did not want to hear the answers.

"She knows that," Caroline said, sounding breezy again. "At least, she ought to. I'm horribly reliant on her."

Frances made the shape of a smile as she folded Charles back into his leather case. "Likewise, Caroline." She stood, and Henry at once matched her movement. "Here, Henry. You must have the chance to finish. If you want to."

He took the case from her. "I do. I've enjoyed working in watercolors; they're easier for me to blend than oils. And if you think you'll like having the miniature, that makes it all the better."

She could only nod. What could she say? That he and Caroline clearly thought the only man she needed was a dead one, three inches high, composed of pencil and watercolor and an oval chopped from an elephant's tusk?

That they were wholly wrong about that?

Charles belonged in a box of keepsakes now, even as his bones lay somewhere in the Netherlands. She had loved him and grieved him, and for several years that life had been adequate. But it didn't satisfy anymore.

"I could do with a sherry," Caroline murmured, standing and fanning herself with the inevitable ivory accessory. "Or something stronger. What would be cooling in this wretched heat?"

"Lemonade," Frances said. "With brandy in it." How easily she slipped into her role as Caroline's advisor.

"That sounds odd," Caroline said. "Let's give it a try, shall we? Henry, will you have one?"

"I think I've overstayed my welcome," he said with a rueful smile. "But I hope to see you again soon." He waved his hand, still gripping the small leather case, and made his farewells to Caroline and France.

Frances watched the empty doorway, listening as his boots thumped down the carpeted corridor and rang on the stairs down to the front door.

She heard the murmur of a servant, the thick rustle of a liveried footman retrieving Henry's hat. The front door opened silently, but she knew he was gone when the street clatter of hooves and carriage wheels spilled into the house, then was shut out again.

Silently, she turned back to face Caroline. The countess had folded her hands behind her back; her brows were puckered under her blonde coronet of hair.

"That didn't go at all as I'd planned," Caroline said. "I rather wish you'd stayed in your room."

"It doesn't matter. I'd feel the same about the miniature no matter when I saw it." She tried to force a smile, but it felt more like a grimace.

Caroline looked skeptical. "I think," the countess granted at last, "we've both earned a brandy by now. Don't you? We needn't bother with the lemonade."

She rang for a servant, but when the snifters arrived, Frances pleaded long-deferred fatigue and took her brandy with her. Rather than heading to her bedchamber for a rest, though, she went to her writing desk in the morning room. The letter from Henry still lay where she'd tossed it earlier today, after Caroline had discarded it.

Before she could change her mind, she gulped down the brandy. It burned her throat, fired her resolve. She found a pen and tugged her inkwell toward her.

The miniature had startled her out of her submission, such as it had been. She couldn't live in her rosewood box; she couldn't torment herself with Charles anymore. Not when her life had begun to offer new torments instead.

There would be just one more letter to Henry, and it would be their triumph. *Frances's* triumph. She would tell him everything she felt, everything she wanted, even knowing he would credit it to another woman.

He wanted the lie, she reminded herself.

Her fingers wrapped tightly around the quill, the feathered barb teasing her skin, and she began to write.

Fourteen

My dear Henry,

How glad I was to see you earlier today. How glad I am too that you have continued painting. You must see now that you have lost nothing of permanence. Anything can be regained, given time enough and desire enough.

I must ask you now to dwell on desire along with me, for it is often on my mind. It has been a long time since I've been with a man, but I have not hungered overmuch for a man's touch until recent days. As you and I spend more time together, my long solitude is a weight on my heart, and the days since my widowhood stretch out long and gray.

What have I lost? How can I bear it with so many years left ahead of me? Yet my loss, like yours, need not have permanence.

I have come to value your friendship greatly, yet it leaves me unsatisfied. Much as I enjoy every word we share, conversation is not enough. I think sometimes the truest, wisest, wildest, and deepest

*thoughts and emotions can be communicated only
with the press of hand on hand, mouth on mouth,
body on body.*

*How I should love to communicate with you ever
further. I have pressed your hand in mine. But have
I truly reached your heart? Do you understand me,
and I you?*

*Let us give it time if you desire it. Heaven
knows that I do.*

I am yours, as always.

Henry had to sit on the floor of his bedchamber while
he read this latest letter.

Even so, he still felt too unsettled. Too unprepared
to take it all in. So he stretched out on his bed, flat on
his back, and read it again as his body grew molten.

Ah, God. It was amazing. It was the type of letter a
man fantasized about getting when he was young. The
type an older man probably fantasized about getting
too, for that matter, especially if the sender were
young and beautiful.

The sender… that was the only part that troubled
Henry. Cheerful friendliness still marked his every
interaction with Caro outside of the letters; he had no
idea she had grown ready for a deeper intimacy.

He held up the creamy paper again, studying the
boldly incised words. They didn't seem to suit Caro,
but perhaps this was part of one of her own stratagems.
Do you understand me? the letter asked. No, he really
didn't. And he rather thought that was the way she
preferred it, despite the heat of her letter.

A few weeks earlier, he would have snapped up her offer regardless of his opinion. Any connection with the much-desired Lady Stratton would have been proof to the *ton* that he could conquer the polite world, even though the French had sent him home in pieces.

Now he knew the polite world had changed, just as he had. He needn't be so eager to fit himself into his old life; it had moved on just as he had.

Frances had been the first to point that out, with her terrifyingly clear vision.

Pillowy damask cushioned him, a luxurious coverlet on a soft bed in his brother's house. He fisted the rich fabric in his left hand, wanting to wrinkle it, to make some mark. Leave some sign of his presence.

No, he wanted more than that. He wanted happiness, intangible and maybe unattainable. Just as Jem had advised, he wanted to be with a woman who made him feel at ease. Comfortable even in his own wounded skin.

When he thought about it that way, the choice became clear. He didn't want to spend his life looking backward, pretending three years of his life had never happened and the loss of an arm changed him not at all.

He had once hoped desperately that would be the case. But he was no longer so desperate that he couldn't see the truth. There were some things he could never get back, and there were some things he was no longer suited to pursue.

One of those was a romance with a woman who seemed to have time for everyone but true interest in no one.

Only in Caro's letters did Henry see glimpses of a deeper self: what she cared for, what bothered her. But what if they married? Would anything change? He couldn't write letters to his wife for the rest of his life, then spend his days sitting aside while she enchanted others. And he couldn't ask her to change to suit him.

Not when there was someone else who already suited him.

Henry let out a shuddering sigh. His shoulders sank deep into the mattress, his booted feet dangling from the edge of the bed. After years of training, it was impossible to be careless, to let his dirty boots touch the coverlet.

A small matter, but out of these small matters, life was built. Frances understood that. She always had.

When he first met Frances, he had seen her as only a means to an end. With a speculator's view to the main chance, he'd asked her for help, laying his schemes on her shoulders. Oh, with an artist's eye, he'd admired her beauty too. Muted, yet striking in its own way.

But in the Blue Room, artist and speculator had vanished, and he was nothing more or less than a man. And *that*, more than anything else since he'd returned to London, had shown him that he might be able to rebuild his life after all.

He'd stepped so wrongly with the portrait of Frances's late husband. In trying to give her something that would *matter* to her, he'd only raised old ghosts—at least, that was what he guessed when he saw that haunted look on her face.

Such longing for a lost one was familiar. He'd been competing with the ghost of his old self since he'd come back to London, hadn't he? But there was nothing to be gained by chasing spirits. The joy of the pursuit turned hopeless as soon as they vanished.

He hoped he could convince Frances of this. But first, he needed to convince himself.

Heavy red wax from the letter's seal softened under his fingertips. Henry lowered the letter to his side and flexed his feet in his boots, his shoulders against the yielding surface of the mattress.

He would never have to sleep on the ground again. He would never have to march for miles under a sun baked hot enough to leach the color from his uniform. And yet... he'd never really be free of the war if he always held the secret of Quatre Bras inside him.

He owed Caro an explanation first of all. And then—then he owed Frances the full truth. He must build his new life on a sturdy foundation, or it would all be flimsy and fragile.

Each society ball would be a building block, each call at Albemarle Street the mortar. If Caro had given Henry the determination to stay in London, to make something of himself again, Frances had inspired him to consider *how* he might do that. How a man with one arm could take hold in high society again. How someone who had seen the horrors of war could understand how to live in peace.

He didn't have all the answers yet, but he knew how to find them. Starting tomorrow.

Hand on hand, mouth on mouth, body on body. Someday he might even experience that again if all went well.

He pressed the letter closed and let it flutter to his chest, let his hand wander downward.

He could not seize happiness alone, but as he thought of Frances, he came as close as he could.

Fifteen

"HENRY, WELCOME. I'VE BEEN EXPECTING YOU TO CALL."

Caro's butler had shown Henry into the drawing room, where Caro met him after only a few minutes' wait. Caro stretched out her hand in greeting with queenly grace, as though it was perfectly normal for Henry to call at noon—an hour when the polite world was often still abed and certainly was not badgering its neighbors with surprise visits.

This ruler of fashion looked as stylish in her Pomona green silks as any portrait of the late Duchess of Devonshire, her fan hanging carelessly from a silk ribbon at her wrist. Breezy and confident, she could have passed no such fraught night as he had.

"You surprise me," Henry admitted, surrendering his hand into hers for a tense second. "I wasn't sure after the exchange of the miniature when I might call again."

"Or whether you ought to call at all," Caro added smoothly. She gave him a knowing smile that made him wonder just how much she *did* know.

She sank onto the long sofa from which she'd surely

hold court in a few hours. With a lift of her brows, she asked, "Clearly you have something on your mind. Will tea do for coaxing it out, or should we ring for something more bracing?"

"Nothing right now, thank you." He found a fussy cabriole-legged chair and dragged it near her, then settled himself on the brocade seat.

"As you wish." Nestled against the cushions littering her sofa, Caro looked completely at her ease. "To what do I owe the honor of this visit? I have a guess, but I won't say in case I'm wrong, and I do hate to be wrong."

Henry's shoulders were knotted, his spine a brittle ramrod. "In that, you resemble your cousin greatly."

Caro arranged a fold of her gown into a more graceful drape. "Yes, I suppose so. Frannie and I both tend to confine our opinion to areas in which we feel ourselves on solid ground."

Her bright eyes flicked up, caught his. "Which, right now, I suppose I do."

This was getting more awkward by the second. "I'm aware that this appears to my disadvantage, calling on you at such an unusual hour, but—"

"Actually," Caro countered, "it appears to my advantage, not to your disadvantage. My neighbors will think I've made another conquest."

She plucked at a tassel on one of her embroidered cushions, studying it with deliberate attention as Henry's thoughts unspooled in a giant loop of *oh, damn*. "But never mind that, Henry. Why not tell me why you're really here?"

She surprised him again; he didn't perceive the

slightest bit of flirtation in her tone. If anything, she seemed... businesslike? The tone combed his thoughts into a sensible order.

"All right." He collected his right arm into his left hand, took a deep breath, and plunged in. "I wanted to thank you for the very great honor of your letters, and also let you know that I think it prudent to put an end to the correspondence."

She smoothed the cushion she'd been toying with and looked at him with those startling Paris Green eyes. A small smile bent her lips. "I'm not usually concerned with what's prudent, Henry, but in this case I think I can divine what you're too polite to say. You are interested in another lady, are you not?"

Henry wracked his brain for a proper response. Caro was awfully cheerful considering the bent of their conversation. Not that he had particularly wanted tears or a tantrum, but this blithe unconcern—he felt he saw only a mirror. She reflected what those around her wanted to see, but who was she really? The uncertainty made him uneasy.

And that, more than anything else, was reason enough to stop writing the letters. He needn't stop them for Frances's sake. He would stop them for his own. "My feelings for any other lady don't affect my decision, Caro. I'm truly sorry if it causes you pain."

To his surprise, she smiled again, wide and lovely. "You have nothing to apologize for, Henry. You needed something for a short time, and I was happy to be a part of it. Now you find you need something else. Who can fault you for that? Your life has been unmade, and you are remaking it."

Henry's mouth opened, but he could think of nothing that he ought to make it say. Finally, he managed, "You are very perceptive."

"I am indeed." She settled back against her long sofa again. "More than the world realizes, Henry. For example, this lady for whom you will not admit your regard. It's Frannie, yes?"

He flailed for the cool dignity he'd often sported as Captain Middlebrook of the First Foot Guards. "I'd prefer to discuss my feelings for Frances with Frances herself."

"So you *do* have feelings for Frannie."

Well, there was no point in denying it now. "Yes. I hope you are not offended."

"Offended?" She propped herself up on one elbow. "I am the farthest from offended that you can possibly imagine. I am more offended that you are the first man since we came to London a year ago to see Frannie's worth."

Her lithe figure stretched beneath the sleek fabric of her gown, and Henry again thought what a wonderful subject she would make for a portraitist. Other than an artist's admiration, her beauty roused him not at all.

She subsided onto the sofa again and shook her fan from the ribbon around her wrist. Turning it between her hands, she said, "This is Frannie's fan." She flipped it open and displayed the painted surface.

Henry recognized it at once as a fair copy of Primaticcio's *Odysseus and Penelope*. The old soldier, bearded and gruff, caressed the chin of his pale and proud wife as they sat entwined in postcoital sheets, recounting their adventures to one another—passionate, like-minded.

Without thinking, he tried to reach out for the painting, but his shoulder only flexed, his right arm immobile in the grasp of his left.

Caroline flipped the fan closed, then open again, and turned the painted face toward her own countenance. "Frannie admired this painting very much. She always wanted to think that some soldiers came home and found happiness again."

With a quick snap, she closed the fan a final time. "She gave this to me after I carelessly broke my own fan. I've forgotten to give it back to her, or maybe I just didn't want to." Her forefinger traced the ivory guard. "That is as good a summary of Frannie's character, and mine, as any I could imagine. And that is why you are much better off choosing her."

Henry made himself smile, knowing that she expected him to feel relief and certainty. But doubt shadowed his thoughts: *Even if I choose her, she might not choose me.*

As a younger son rather than an heir, Henry had never commanded the money or influence that Jem held in an effortless grip. He had little enough responsibility either, until he went into the army. Even there, for too long, he'd made his way on charm and his brother's connections. Now he must make his way on his own, just as he was. No secrets; no hiding.

The thought terrified him, perhaps even more than pity did.

"Don't you agree?" Caro prodded. "I assume you do, or you wouldn't have come here today."

"I'm sorry, I didn't follow." Henry frowned, distracted by his own confusion.

A carefully arched brow lifted. "I wondered if you agreed that Frannie was eminently worth the pursuit. I considered it merely a rhetorical question, but then you worried me with your lack of response."

"Again, then, I must apologize." Henry rolled his shoulders, trying to relieve the tension that yanked at them. "Your cousin's appeal could never be in doubt. I'm only wondering about my own."

"That's for her to decide, isn't it?" She smiled, superior and sly as the *Mona Lisa*. Then a thought seemed to strike her, and her expression turned sharp. "You're not asking for my blessing, are you?"

Henry considered. "Not exactly. I'm asking for your understanding. And for a bit of solitude with the lady. There's rather a lot that I need to explain."

This was, apparently, the right thing to say, for Caro beamed at him. "That, you may have. I don't have the right to give you my blessing. But if you're ready to speak with Frannie now, we can see what she has to say."

"Yes," Henry said. He nodded to underscore his words. To give the appearance of a courage that was lacking.

Oh, he was certain of Frances, of her worthiness of his trust. But was he ready to repose it? To reveal his secrets, his shame, his weaknesses old and new?

He must, or he could never be sure of her. He would not court under false pretenses again.

"Yes," he said again. "Thank you, Caro."

"You are very welcome." She rose to her feet, and

he stood too. "Let us go find her. She'll probably be in the morning room."

❧

After Caroline left Henry at the doorway of the morning room, she mounted the steps to her bedchamber. This was her haven, quiet and luxurious in its dark woods, delicate plasterwork, green damask.

She invited men to share her bed sometimes, but just now, she was happy to be alone.

If a month ago, someone had told her she would be delighted to hear that a man had no interest in her, she would have been surprised.

If a month ago, though, someone had revealed that Caroline would soon engage in an elaborate plot to marry off her cousin, that would have surprised her less.

The man who could choose Frances over Caroline was a man who could see all the way to their hearts. The *ton* was quite sure that Caroline had none; perhaps that was why it had taken to her so well this season. She was blithe and careless and amusing, and as long as she was very amusing, very blithe, and very, very expensive—that was all most men in London were looking for.

It was enough for Caroline for now. She had nine years of marriage, of quiet patience and solitary nursemaiding, to put behind her. The chaotic, empty amusements of London were exactly what she wanted.

But they were not enough for Frances. They were not enough for Henry. Thus the secret letters.

The letters had been hazardous to begin with; secret

correspondences simply weren't *done* by ladies of quality. They'd become still more dangerous once Frances confided that Henry thought they were from Caro.

It had seemed ridiculous to Caroline at first, because she knew quite well she could never ensnare anyone with words on a page. Her weapons were flicking fans and practiced smiles. Eventually, Caro was sure, Henry would figure out the truth: that it was Frances's vivid soul to which he responded.

Caro had always muted her own reactions to Henry; she made sure to give him as many hints as she could without spoiling her cousin's secret. Talked with him alone only when he wanted to fashion a gift for Frannie, and even then only within a room full of people. Hoped that the deception would be at an end, and Frances would find her way to happiness as Caro had not.

Maybe Frances would; maybe even today. Maybe even now happiness had marched into the morning room, all abashed pride, and laid itself at her feet.

The idea of such devotion was as bewitching and unlikely as borrowing the Crown jewels for a breakfast at home.

As Caroline stretched out on her bed and let the cool solitude soothe her, she could almost feel that she really was happy for her cousin and not envious at all.

Sixteen

"Come in," Frances said in response to Henry's knock at the half-open morning room door. "I can't think what I did with your mistress's bill. Do you have a copy with you?"

Her back was to Henry as she shuffled through a stack of papers atop a small saber-legged mahogany writing desk. Against the background of the rich orpiment-yellow walls, her coiled hair shone with the dark luster of Van Dyke brown pigment.

The sight of her heartened him, banishing a little of his apprehension. "Yes, mum. Seven hundred yards of silk and five thousand buttons," he said in a nasal impression of a clerk.

Frances froze, then turned slowly to face him. "Good lord," she said. "You've billed me for goods enough to dress every maiden making her come-out this year."

"I take it you were expecting someone else?"

Her cheeks bled warm, and she hastily turned and shoved her papers beneath a blotter before facing him again. "Well, yes. Caroline's modiste made her a very

special gown for Lady Applewood's next ball. I know
it's unfashionable to pay one's bills promptly, but I
think it the right thing to do. Only you are clearly not
a modiste's assistant."

"Clearly not."

She looked rather at a loss. "Ah… did you come
to see Caro?"

"I've seen her already."

Now she looked still more confused. "Do you
need something from me, then? Tea or secret advice
or… something I'm apparently not thinking of?" She
trailed off, then crossed her arms as though warding
off a chill.

Her gown was an unadorned Prussian blue, spare
and dark. It reminded him of the Blue Room, of the
quiet freedom therein. Maybe he could recapture that
feeling with her.

Of course, no capture was ever easy or without casualty.

"I only need a listening ear," he answered. "If you've
the time."

Lips parted, she stared at him for several seconds.
"Yes. Certainly. Do come in."

Frances spun the chair at the writing desk to face
him and perched upon the end, watching him warily.
And why shouldn't she be wary of him? He walked
through the doorway only to prowl around the furniture with the nervous energy of weeks of pent-up
secrets, years away from intimacy with a woman.

Finally he sat on a sofa, a green scroll-armed affair
that Bart would probably deem *all the crack*. "Look." He
stood, then sat down at the other end so he'd be closer
to Frances. "Look, there's something very particular I

need to tell you, and I'm anxious that I not be interrupted. Would you be willing to lock the door?"

Her brows knit, but she nodded. Retrieving the key from a compartment in her littered desk, she went to do as he'd asked.

"You sound rather dire, Henry." She reseated herself on the sofa with him rather than her chair, a small gesture of closeness that heartened him. "Is everything all right?"

"As much as it was the last time we saw one another."

"That's cryptic and not especially comforting," she said.

He managed a smile. "I'm not here to comfort you. Nor to be cryptic. I need to tell you the truth about me."

She blanched, the sickly pale of bismuth white pigment when exposed to sulfur. "The truth."

This was not a good beginning; he hadn't even told her anything yet and she looked horrified. "Yes, the truth. Perhaps you've heard of it," he said a little more sharply than he'd meant to.

"Yes." Her chin lifted, her shoulders pulled stiffly back. "Of course. I'm just surprised by the need for secrecy."

"Ah." His left hand found the cuff of his right sleeve and picked at the hem. "Well, I actually mean to do away with secrecy, at least with you."

He pulled in a deep breath, feeling his chest expand within the binding layers of shirt, waistcoat, coat. "You once asked me if I wished to discuss the injury to my right arm. I think it's time I do. You see, if you don't know the truth about me, we'll always be separated by it."

This was rather a bold statement, which he amended when her eyes widened. "Everyone, I mean. I'll be separated from everyone. Secrets separate everyone." He pressed his lips together so he'd stop blurting things out.

She watched him with her Bossu-Wood eyes, all green and brown and still so wary. Her spine was straight as a tree, and her fingers were as tightly laced together as twigs in a nest. "Yes, I suppose you're right," she said at last. "If you feel you must tell me something, I'll be honored by the confidence."

"You're very kind," he murmured.

"Not really." She managed the first real grin he'd seen since he entered the room, and her poker-stiff shoulders relaxed a bit. "Just dreadfully curious. Ah... did you already tell... whatever you're going to tell... to Caroline?"

"No." His head snapped back. "*No*." There was no place for Caroline in this room; he'd locked the door against her. Against the rest of the world. "I want to tell *you*. You have a gift for taking me as I am. That's more important than anything Caro could write in a letter."

Her cheeks flushed rosy, her lips parted. "You— choose me? Not the letters?"

"Not the letters," he confirmed. "I've already explained things to Caro."

Frances's eyes widened; she looked as flushed and glowing as though she'd just been tumbled. A shaft of desire speared through the coils of tension, of worry, of lasting shame that kept Henry tightly wound. In the Blue Room, he'd touched her; he'd brought her close. Thus alone, maybe he could do that again.

Of course, that all depended on what she thought of him when he was done. But he knew it was time to tell her. It was a certainty in his gut, like knowing the right instant to pull the trigger on a pistol.

"And now I need to explain things to you." He took a deep breath. "At Quatre Bras. That's where my arm was hurt." No, no sense in cloaking the truth in smooth words. "That's where I lost the use of my arm. I won't ever get it back."

He studied the back of his left hand, still sun-browned from months campaigning across the Continent. Frances's pale fingers reached for his and interlaced with them. "I know," she said. "It doesn't matter to me."

"It might when I tell you how it happened. You know I was a captain at the time."

"Yes."

"A privilege of being an earl's son. I was able to buy my way into the army and take a position of leadership much more quickly than if I'd been poor."

"The son of an innkeeper, for example," she said. "Such as my first husband. That's no matter either, Henry. Your rank is your good fortune."

"Your first husband was a—" He cut himself off at the sight of her startled face, returning his gaze to the slender anchors of her fingers.

He hadn't known that about her, that she had married far below her birth. It seemed he wasn't the only one with secrets, though judging from the expression on her face, she hadn't meant to reveal hers.

He had vowed to bare his today; maybe in time she would return the favor.

"Well." He cleared his throat. "As you said, my rank was my good fortune. My father died when I was just a boy, but he left money for me to purchase a commission, though my mother would not permit it while she was alive. Jem didn't want me to go to war either, which only made me more determined. I was stubborn. I wanted to make my own way."

He laughed, a bitter, hoarse sound. "As if being gifted with thousands of pounds to buy a lieutenancy is making one's own way. And Jem's connections ensured that I was promoted to captain as soon as humanly possible. I made my own way, all right."

Frances's hand shifted in his. "You cannot be blamed for taking advantage of... well, of your advantage. I am sure the army benefited from your good leadership."

"You're sure about that, are you?" Henry made himself look at her face. Her expression was worried, but her fingers tightened in his. A reassurance: she wasn't going anywhere.

Yet.

He shook his head at her. "I had only the best of the army. The First Foot Guards. Very prestigious, you know. A fitting place for the son of an earl. We held the blockade at Bayonne for months. Over time, I earned the trust of the men who fought under me."

He'd worked harder to earn that trust than he ever had for anything else. Despite his youth and inexperience, he had at least seen the need for that. Thus his trick of sprawling on the ground, as if nothing could scare him.

He was usually too exhausted to think of elegant

phrases to inspire his men, and so he spoke plainly to them. He gave them his honesty and his own trust, and it had worked much better than if he had puffed himself off as the son of an earl. There would have been no point to such arrogance; a blue-blooded man could be killed just as easily as a red-blooded one.

Blood would tell, though. Henry's certainly had.

A sigh tried to escape, but he swallowed it. "I did my best to deserve that trust for a time. But after Bonaparte abdicated, I grew soft during months of relative ease. I began to think there was nothing left of war but being feted and looking at art."

"That was a wonderful time," Frances murmured. "The festivities here went on for weeks. We never imagined Bonaparte would escape and rebuild his army."

"None of us did either," Henry said. He might have been able to return to England during those buoyant months of peace had he wanted to. Wellington had come back to London for a time, and honors had been heaped upon the great general. But Henry had preferred a Continental billeting. He'd been unsatisfied, feeling as though he hadn't truly made his own way yet, and he wanted to explore further. Become an artist or a soldier or both.

Instead, he had become neither.

"Much of the cream of European society found one another during the months of Bonaparte's exile," Henry continued. "It was rather like the London season, only the balls were held in palazzos and châteaux instead of crowded Town mansions. I saw paintings I'd never dreamed I'd be able to view in person. I was sure once I returned to London—someday, whenever I wanted to be—I would be reborn as a painter, mysteriously able to recreate life in oils as they had."

"Oh." Frances pressed a hand to her mouth. *Pity*.

His fingers flexed in her other hand, wanting suddenly to escape. But he would finish, no matter how her expression changed. "'The best-laid schemes o' mice an' men gang aft agley.' Isn't that how the poet Burns described our efforts? We tried to recreate the polite world in Europe, and it was our undoing. Perhaps you have heard of the ball thrown by the Duchess of Richmond?"

Frances shook her head. "It was very grand, I suppose?"

"Very grand, indeed. The duchess's ballroom was long and low ceilinged, but you can imagine nothing loftier. All the best people were there. Wellington and nearly all of his officers. Several foreign princes. The pinnacle of the Belgian aristocracy. We waltzed and supped. I danced twice with Lady Georgiana, Richmond's daughter, and she teased me about causing a scandal. It was a very great joke. By this time, I had almost forgotten what war was like."

Henry could almost hear the duchess's merry orchestra inviting him to dance. Strings, dainty and vibrant, and layered over them, the shouts of the lancers slaughtering his men. Only a few hours apart, he could never separate them now.

It was hard to believe it had taken place mere months before. It seemed ten years ago—or only a night.

He worked his fingers free from Frances's hand and rose to pace around the room. "As the evening turned into night, we received the sudden news that Bonaparte was mustering for battle again. We left the ball at once and prepared to fight. Wellington chose to head the French off at Quatre Bras. I would have thought it a picturesque little country crossroads, I am sure, had I not been awake all night and marched twenty miles to reach it. At least I had put my boots on. Some men still wore their dancing pumps."

"Good lord," Frances breathed. "I am sorry."

Henry trailed his fingers over the smooth plaster of the wall, rubbed the heavy patterned velvet of the window draperies between his fingertips.

"Do not be sorry for me, please." *Please*. "It was no more than I signed on for and no more than anyone else would have been expected to do. But I had enjoyed the softness of peace, and I wasn't ready to return to war. My head had been turned and my eyes were tired. I should have noticed what I'd been trained for three years to notice: tall crops that could hide enemy soldiers, tall old trees that could hide still more. I noticed none of that, and so I led my men into a trap."

"What happened?"

He stared at a painting on the wall. A hunting scene. The men wore bright red coats, the color Henry's uniform coat had been before the sun faded it to the color of a bloody brick. They wielded guns they looked delighted to use. They held the reins of sleek horses with bobbed tails, ready to spring over walls in pursuit of a small fox. Oh, what fun, to go hunting.

He turned, impatient with himself. "I didn't see the lancers. There were so many; I don't know how I could have missed them. I must have thought I was home again in England. I ordered my men forward as if we were marching in a parade, and they marched right into lancers instead." He shut his eyes, but too well did they remember the sight of man after man, skewered. Horrible.

"I myself was fortunate," he said with dark irony. "I was able to dodge them and take a few down before several Frenchmen ripped my musket from my hands while I tried to reload. The wrong choice again. I should have drawn my sword. They dislocated my shoulder; I must have looked dead as I fell. I might as well have been. I was not much of a threat to them after that. Nor was I any help, as my men died in the woods. We lost hundreds. Those that survived went on to fight at Waterloo. They were very brave."

"As were you," Frances said. Henry could not see her face; his eyes were fixed on the polish of his top boots. Not Hessians. He would never wear tasseled Hessians now, like a dandy pretending to be a soldier.

"I was passable at best. A dislocated shoulder is nothing out of the common way. But I was too tired to bear the pain until a surgeon came, so I asked one of my soldiers to fix it. He was more tired than I, poor fellow, and he pulled wrongly, and far too hard. I don't know what happened. I only know it hurt terribly, as though my arm was being ripped off, and then it went numb. And it's been numb ever since."

How he would have loved to come home whole, covered in glory. But he had not. For a long time, he hadn't even been sure whether he had really come home.

"You were at war, Henry," Frances said at last. "Your soldiers knew the risks just as you did."

Henry pressed on. "But they trusted me."

"Then you must have been a good captain to them."

Henry looked up at her, and she managed a little smile. "Henry, we can never know how our actions will turn out. We can only guess."

"But I made such terrible mistakes," he faltered. She could not have understood the significance of what he told her.

"We all make mistakes, Henry," she said quietly, her eyes downcast. The thumb of one hand rubbed over the third finger of the other, precisely where she would wear a wedding ring. "If you knew my own past errors—well, I hope you know that I'd never think less of you for what you see as your faults."

"But my arm…" He stepped close to her again, within reach, but he did not touch her.

"Yes, your arm," she repeated. Her eyes flicked up and met his, suddenly hard. "What of it? If you could have waited in agony for heaven knows how long on the chance a surgeon would turn up, then your arm might be fine today. Or maybe it would not."

He stared at her, stony. She didn't understand; he'd disappointed himself. The army was *his*, not his brother's. Not anyone else's. His captaincy was his responsibility alone, and he had ended his stint in failure. His arm was a daily reminder of that.

Maybe that was why he'd been so determined to make a success of his life in London. He needed something to make him feel whole again.

"Well," he said quietly. "Thank you for listening to my sordid little tale. I do appreciate your time." At least she hadn't been horrified. Only pitying.

Though maybe that was worse.

He turned toward the doorway, ready to leave.

"Henry, wait. Please."

Reluctantly, he pivoted toward her. Her olive-tinted face was pale, her cheeks a hectic pink. Those lips, the dark rose of a madder pigment he could never again mix and mill with ease, were slightly curved. The expression looked sad somehow.

"Please, listen to me, Henry. I don't mean to belittle your loss. Only to say—such things happen during war. Terrible things happen to good men, and there's not always any way to prevent them. Even Wellington lost soldiers. It's not right, and it's not easy. It just… *is*."

"Yes," he said dully. "I know all of that. But don't you see, it wasn't chance. It was because of my own carelessness that they were killed. It was *my fault*."

"So you've said. If you'd noticed the lancers and called for your men to retreat, don't you think the French would have pursued?"

He stilled. The stone block of his body began to soften, deep inside. "I don't know. I suppose… they might have."

She nodded. "They might have. We can't know. Or if you hadn't gone to the ball, maybe things wouldn't have gone differently after all. Maybe the lancers were very well hidden. Or maybe you did the best you could with the orders you were given. Maybe if *Wellington* hadn't gone to the ball and danced his feet off, he would have found a stronger place to make a stand than Quatre Bras."

Maybe. Maybe. Something inside the stone-Henry

crumbled at the sound of that word. It was a possibility word; a possibility that simple accident, simple bad luck, had killed his men. He would give his right arm to think that was true, that their deaths weren't his fault.

He had already given his right arm—another accident, more bad luck. Maybe… it was nothing worse than that. The loss would be bearable if it was not a reminder of lives thrown away, if it was his loss alone to bear and overcome.

Frances spoke on, her voice as quiet as a morning birdsong. "All through the war, Henry, terrible things happened, and lives were lost or saved on the slimmest of chances. Maybe if my late husband, Charles, had simply been able to slog through a swamp day after summer day without coming down with Walcheren fever, he would never have sickened and died. Or a bullet might have killed him instead. Or if I had been different myself, he need never have left me at all. He would never have wanted to."

She turned her face toward the window, as though the outside world held some answers for all her unknowns. The high-slanting remnants of morning sun found her profile, gilded her skin, and picked out bright tints in her hair. Henry forgot to think in colors; he only let himself look at her—proud as ever, and limned like an earthy angel.

Somehow, it lessened his pain to know he wasn't the only one who hurt.

Inappropriately, this talk of her long-dead husband made him want to touch her, stroke her, kiss her until she forgot the man.

He settled for a bit of comfort. "You cannot think that your husband went to war because he did not love you enough to stay."

"Maybe." That word again. Frances's mouth twisted up at one corner, though it was not a smile. "No, I suppose he went because he felt he had to. Because we are all human, and we must all eat and drink and have the means to live. And we cannot live in agony."

With a swift, decisive shake of her skirts, she stood and grasped both of his hands across the swooping back of the sofa. "Henry, you enjoyed the familiar pleasure of a ball during war. This does not mean you should never have pleasure again. And you asked the soldier to help with your arm because you could not imagine living in pain."

She rubbed her fingers over his right hand, and he almost thought he could feel it, so starved was he for touch. "I'm glad you did. I could not wish for you to live in pain either."

"And I would not wish it for you," he said hoarsely.

"So we do the best with what we have," she said. "We carry on even though our lives alter."

"Simple as that," he murmured.

"Oh, there's nothing simple about it." She dropped his hands and pressed hers together tightly in front of her chest. "Sometimes it seems like the hardest thing in the world. But what else is there to do?"

Now it was her turn to move about the room, fidgeting with the blotter on the desk, giving vases of flowers a little twist so the brightest blooms would face forward.

Just think of who makes you happy.

That's what there was to do.

Two steps brought him behind her, only a breath away from her tall body. She faced the orpiment-yellow wall, seemingly studying the painting of the hunting scene, but she knew he had drawn close. He could tell by the way her shoulders tensed, her head turned a fraction to the side.

"Frances." His voice still sounded hoarse, as though the name itself was weighty on his lips. A few loose strands of her hair danced in the heat of his exhale. He rested his left hand on the wall, circling her as much as he could with his body.

His right arm hung motionless, of course; he couldn't encircle her completely. She could escape if she wished.

But she didn't even try. She simply turned around and tilted her face up to him, so they were almost nose-to-nose. "Henry."

The movement of her lips as she spoke his name, the quick sweep of her lashes as she blinked only inches away—these were bits of everyday magic, wrapping him in a spell of peace. The whisper of her breath was warm on his face, the slight movement of air a promise. A beginning.

It was easy, within the spell, to lower his head, to brush her lips with his own. It was a gentle question.

Her answer was immediate. Her mouth was hot on his, her hands swift as they slid up his chest and gripped his shoulders.

"*Mmmm.*" A sudden nervous laugh tried to escape his throat, and he lifted his mouth from hers.

He breathed deeply, trying to banish the sudden

weakness in his knees. She fidgeted, so he slid his left hand to her upper arm and rested his forehead atop her dark hair.

Inhaling the clean scent of her hair, all sweet citrus and soap, and the warmer smell of a woman's skin. One breath at a time.

"What is it?" She wiggled her head so she could fix him with those clear eyes, so true and honest. He would not hurt her with an excuse, making her feel as if she were not good enough.

"I'm afraid," he whispered.

She didn't press him further; she only nodded and ran her thumb along his jawline. "I am too."

"What do you have to be afraid of?"

She gave her own little *mmm* of a suppressed laugh. "You are golden," she said. "You are young and noble. I do not know why you should choose me for your company and your confidence." Her hand slipped over his body from jaw to neck to chest, and it felt like a blessing.

"You truly think that of me."

"I do."

I do. She spoke the words from the deepest of vows. She wanted him when he thought he would never be wanted again.

He chuckled at the marvel of it. "I think you do not see me accurately, but I cannot wish you to be less generous than you are." Again, that startled warmth within his body of frozen stone. She had taken hold of his heart with her words. How glad he was that it still beat, that it still yearned for a women's passion and thudded in response to her touch.

Her hands were roaming now, pressing the planes of his chest, sliding beneath the heavy superfine of his coat, tugging at the fabric until they found their way beneath the barrier of his clothing. Ten fingers—beautiful fingers, *Frances's* fingers—touched his sides, slid up his ribs until his close-fitting waist-coat stopped her.

They stood face to face, her hands halted. She raised her eyebrows, wicked and gleeful, asking.

The worry vanished from his body, burned off in a swift fire of hunger. He wasn't stone anymore, but skin and bone and muscle and sinew, all eager man. Her wanted her hands moving over his body; he wanted her body moving over his. He wanted to touch and wake her most secret places, now that he'd told her his most secret truths.

"Yes," he said, in answer to the words she hadn't said. "God, yes." His thumb traced the straight, sweet line of her jaw.

"Then we are agreed," she said with a smile. "How glad I am that you asked me to lock the door."

Seventeen

It took both of them to shrug Henry free from his coat, to coax the tight-fitting sleeve down the unbending length of his right arm.

Miraculously, this didn't bother Henry in the slightest.

It was as though the soldier part of his brain that worried and analyzed had been shut off; now the artist part could take the lead. The artist part with every sense alive, that could savor the whisper of the still, warm air through the thin linen of his shirtsleeves, that could notice the spreading flush on Frances's skin as her eyes roved over his body—face to chest to groin to feet, and back up again.

He hardened. How could he not?

"I could positively eat you," she murmured. "It's simply not fair that you look so good."

Henry shivered and shut his eyes for a brief moment. "That is a matter of opinion," he said with a choked laugh. "I'm of the opinion that you'll look good enough to eat once we take off a few of your clothes."

She raised her eyebrows. "All in good time."

With a wicked smile, she faced him, her nimble

fingers teasing at the knots of his cravat. She stood closer than close, so close that his vision went hazy and she was just a blur of darks and roses and the blue of her gown, the press of her long, soft body against his hardness. He tilted his head as the tugs and pulls pressed at his neck, scratched starched linen against his skin.

Any more of these tiny ecstasies and he would embarrass himself. He took a half step back, away from the tantalizing pressure of her body, and studied her face as she picked apart the mathematical folds of his cravat. She was biting her bottom lip, concentrating on her work. Her cheeks were the loveliest tint of rose, and her thick dark hair was springing from its pins.

He could never capture life in oils again; he knew that now. He hoped only that if he looked his fill, he would remember it indelibly. This sparkling moment when a woman had chosen him, and he had chosen her.

The cravat fell open, and Frances ran cool fingers over his throat. The light scrape of her nails on long-untouched skin woke nerves throughout his body, and he had to shut his eyes against the bright shock of it.

Amazing. As she drew gentle fingers over his neck, he let himself feel. Let his body wake and remember.

It had been years since Henry had been with a woman. He'd never been a rake about Town, never sought the company of whores or willing widows while in the army. When he'd taken a lover to his bed, it had always meant something.

This time, it meant everything. It meant everything

to be home again, to be honest. To be naked, yet still to be wanted.

His throat closed, and he caught Frances's hand, interlacing their fingers.

"Are you all right?" she asked. Her eyes were clear as a mirror. In them, he could bear to look at himself again.

Yes. Yes, he was all right. He nodded and coaxed her mouth to his again.

She fit against him like the piece he had been missing. Her lips parted for his kiss, her belly brushing against his as he gathered her tight in the cradle of his arm. They were body against body, heat against heat, and even through layers of fabric, Henry could feel her form—the soft press of her breasts, flat against his chest; her fingers gripping his shoulders, tighter with every kiss.

He could have kissed her for hours, sinking into the wonder of it. The magic of human hands, of mouth on mouth. The way lips fit together, nipped and pulled. Such small gestures that could wake such tremendous needs. This time, his need came not from starvation but from fullness. He was brimming with awe, sipping gingerly at the pleasure of her touch, then drinking it in greedily.

Frances tugged her hand free from his and slid her arms around the middle of his back, encircling him and pressing their chests more tightly together. She wiggled her hips, her breasts, and the friction buried Henry under a torrent of sensation. The whisper of linen over his skin. Her heat against his hardness.

All right, enough kissing. He had to get her clothes off.

Her mouth clung to his and opened, licking him with tiny flames, and he felt as if he must swallow all of her. He fumbled for the buttons of her gown, but even if he had two hands, they would have been shaky with need.

He finally eased a button free at the back of her bodice. Then another and another, more quickly. As soon as the bodice was loosened, Frances pulled and tugged, and her clothes began to slide to the floor. Her gown was first, and he saw the stays he'd imagined in the Blue Room, the stays that had so frustrated him. Her breasts were lifted high, separated, two gifts in a fine linen wrap. He ran his hand up her arm, savoring the warm pliancy of it, then slipped a finger inside the top of the stays. He stroked the soft skin, finding the edge of her nipple, but he could do no more than torment them both.

"Help me," she gasped, and she turned to present him with the back of her stays.

A foot or more of tight lacing, and he with one hand.

Well, if there was anything to motivate a man to new feats of dexterity, it was the promise of seeing the naked body of a woman. Henry went to work, tugging at each loop with a swift dexterity that surprised him.

"My goodness," Frances breathed as the fabric parted and fell, leaving her only in a thin linen chemise. "I do believe not even a lady's maid could have done that so quickly."

"A lady's maid has not my incentive," Henry said low into her ear. She still faced away from him, her head turned roguishly over one shoulder. He placed his mouth at the curve where her neck met her shoulder, slid his lips over its softness and licked it with the tip of his tongue. Her skin was damp and faintly salty from the heat. She smelled of oranges, sweet and tangy.

He liked the taste of her, the scent of her. He licked her again, then blew on the moistened spot. She shivered and laughed, and the sound of her delight was a victory.

He was pleasing her. Thank God, because he could not keep his mouth from her now. He lipped at the curve of her neck, sucked at it, bit it gently until her head began to sag and she made a low sound of need.

His hand roved over her unseen breasts. They were soft and full, with hard little gems at their tips. His fingers caught and plucked at her stiffened nipples, rubbing the light fabric of her chemise over them. She gasped and staggered at the touch. "Yes."

Yes. That just might be his favorite word. There was such pleasure in hearing that *yes*.

Henry fit himself more closely behind her. He rubbed himself against her soft bottom, dipped his hand inside her chemise and found her nipple with his bare fingers. Frances's skin was sleeker than satin, her puckered nipples enticingly taut. She filled his every sense: the little gasps she gave as he palmed and stroked her breasts; the light citrus smell of her, growing heavier with the musk of desire. The warm taste and smooth glide of her skin. Her dark hair, fair face.

He wanted to know her every intimate secret. Whether her body was a different color in her most private places. What shade her nipples were. Whether she would flush when she came.

She fit so tightly, so rightly against him. And she was gasping, leaning into his hand. He could take his time; he would do this well. She should climax before she saw him. She'd be kinder, more generous, looking at his maimed body through a haze of bliss.

Many times every day, Henry wished for two arms that obeyed his command. Right now would be an ideal time. He wanted one to flick at her nipples, one to titillate her moist center. An assault of pleasure on two fronts, so to speak. The idea made him smile.

"You're smiling," Frances said. Her voice sounded thick and honeyed.

"How could you tell?"

"I feel your lips curving against my neck."

That made sense. He nipped her neck, pressed one more kiss to it, and rested his head against hers.

"Are we going to finish undressing you now, Henry?"

He couldn't keep himself from flinching. "I wanted you to finish first."

She plucked his hand away from her breast, pulled it free from her chemise. "Nonsense. We're doing this together."

Two arms gave her an advantage over him. She could pinion his arm in her grasp while pushing at him with her other arm, pressing him backward until his calves found the edge of the room's long sofa and he could back up no more.

"Stop," he said. "I'm—"

She pressed him in the center of his chest, shifting him off balance. He sat down heavily on the sofa.

"Do you truly want me to stop?" She still held his left hand. She was looking down at him with curiosity. Hope. Hunger.

Delicious.

He'd wanted to delay his own pleasure, but maybe a change of plans was in order. All the sensation in his body seemed to be in his twined hand and in his cock, so hard and constrained that it was almost painful. He was taut as the wires of a pianoforte. He wanted release.

"Don't stop." He had become the vulnerable one again.

But as he looked up at her, saw her warm eyes crinkle and her delighted grin, it didn't matter how nakedly he pleaded. As she'd said, they were doing this together.

She sank to her knees on the floor before him, and he could only hope that he didn't gulp. The front of his breeches was tented, obvious. *Touch me.* He wished, hoped, feared.

Instead she tugged, far more prosaically, at his boots. He watched her round arms flex and pull, her breasts press and bob under the frail cover of her chemise. The translucent fabric offered tantalizing hints of her form.

"Damn these boots," she muttered, pulling with both hands, and Henry laughed. Ah, it felt good to laugh and smooth away a little of the tightness inside him. He might not shatter with embarrassing speed.

With a final heave, she pulled the second boot free, rocking back onto her heels. Then she slid her hands up his legs—just as she had in the Blue Room, only this time he would not stop her.

The rest of the world could be damned for all he cared, for he was alone with her in heaven as she gripped the muscles of his thighs, then slid her hands up further to swiftly unbutton his waistcoat, slip the braces from his shoulders, tug at the waistband of his breeches until they slid down his hips.

He felt distant, amazed, as this bright and lovely woman freed him from his clothing. He quaked like the ground during a deadly fusillade of cannon fire. His vision was clouded; his muscles trembled. He did not know whether he felt terror or ecstasy. His clothes were his armor, his uniform; they made him resemble everyone else. But each layer was a false skin that separated them.

Then she grazed his length with her hand, and he was drawn back to the present with aching force.

"God," he gasped.

She knelt before him again, still wearing her chemise. "Do you want to take your shirt off, or would you rather leave it on?"

Another gift. She offered him herself, and the chance to hide his weakness. She would be joined to him either way.

But no. If he truly trusted her, he had to show her his very worst. He had already told her so much; showing her his body was not much more to do.

Right. If only it felt that way.

He clamped down ruthlessly on that doubt. "I will be naked if you will."

She grinned. "That sounds fair to me." In an instant, her chemise was a white fabric puddle on the floor.

Oh, he should never have made that promise.

Every shade and shadow of her body was lovelier than he could have imagined. Her breasts were round and heavy for his hand, tipped with nipples the pink-red of a damask rose. Her skin was cream and *verdaccio*, the warm color Italian painters used to tint flesh. She was art come to life, her waist and hips a gentle dip and flare. And between her legs... his mouth grew dry. Perfect. She was strong and whole in her nakedness, and he could only repay her with the broken proof of his own folly.

But he *had* promised. He owed her something in exchange for such beauty, even if he could only give far less than she deserved.

"Can you..." He shut his eyes again, not able to watch her face, and jerked his head to the right. He couldn't pull his long sleeve over his wasted arm. He had trouble enough just gathering the full linen shirt and lifting it over his head.

He couldn't do it alone. They had to do it together.

His eyes still closed, his skin seemed to come alive. The fine woven cloth glided up his chest, bunched over his head, slipped down his arm. A sickening instant of suffocation, then he was free.

So. She saw him bare, and she had neither gasped nor groaned nor left him. Instead, hands stroked down each side of his face, neck, shoulder. It was there all feeling disappeared on the right, but on the left, her hand continued down, down, until it clasped his.

He opened his eyes and saw Frances crouching before him once more. Her hands were holding his. Both of them.

His right hand looked disproportionately large,

wrenched oddly at the end of his stiff and wasted arm. The biceps of the arm were flat, the bones prominent. Too still for life, too warm for death, and far too thin for a man's body after weeks of disuse.

"I'm sorry. It's not…" He choked. "It's not what I would wish for you."

"It's not what I would wish for *you*," she replied, her eyes fixed on his. "But for myself, I would wish for you to be nothing other than what you are."

She slid her hands back up to his shoulders and pulled herself onto the sofa, straddling his legs. He held her close with his arm, a firm embrace, and breathed in her warm scent. Sweet oranges and the tartness of desire. He would remember it forever.

Her breasts were right before his face, nipples pressing out, wanting to be tasted.

And so he tasted, sucked, tugged, nipped at the hard little tips. Frances gasped and quivered and writhed as if he was drawing all control out of her body, as if the sensations were unbearable, but she could not bear for him to stop. He cupped her bottom, pulling her closer. She nestled her hips against his, tipping his erection vertical, and she rocked and rubbed his hardness between their bodies while he kneaded her skin, feasting on her.

Yet he felt tight with unsatisfied hunger. Tasting her, touching her, was not enough. She filled his senses; he wanted to fill her too. He squeezed her rear, then allowed one finger to slip forward to pluck at her.

She was ready, to her very core. Damp, hot, enticing. It was all real, her desire. He rubbed her until she moaned; he wanted her to ask for more.

"Now," she said. "Please."

Thank God. He could not have borne the wait much longer; he would have burst or broken or been destroyed.

Instead, he was remade anew, thrusting up and into her waiting body with a groan. The sensation was instantly familiar—a slick tightness as smooth as putting on a glove, as welcome as taking her hand. They fit; they belonged. Together, even if nowhere else in the world, and that was all that mattered in this cleansing wash of pleasure.

He was as deep within her as the ocean, and they moved like the tide, back and forth in waves, lapping, pounding. They were one vessel, one craft, borne ever higher on the surge. Together they crested, breaking and exploding like water dashed against rocks, and he cried out as if he was drowning—or maybe being saved.

She clung to him afterward, shivering as if she was chilled through, and he shuddered with the slow ebb of a wave going back to sea.

She had taken him, all of him. She had let him empty himself into her.

For the first time since Quatre Bras, the hollow inside him began to fill.

Eighteen

THE SUN WAS FAR TOO BRIGHT.

Frances pressed her hands to her eyes as she lay in bed the following morning. The thin fabric of her chemise grazed her nipples, still sensitive from unaccustomed play. Henry had devoured her body as if he had hungered for her, just as she had for him.

She sat up and wrapped her arms around her chest, willing the flare of remembered lust to vanish. She had no patience for it right now.

Nighttime breezes had left her room chilly, but before long, the summer heat would force its way into the house and turn her bedchamber into a wood-floored oven. It would be best to get dressed now, to act as if this were a normal day, with nothing to do but help Caroline divide and conquer the men of the *ton*. The day before already seemed a vivid dream, and it might be better if it had been. Real-life passion had never ended well for Frances.

She hadn't expected to tumble into Henry's arms after his confession. She hadn't known whether she was reassuring him or distracting herself. So much truth, he gave her. All she had given him in return was her body.

She had tricked him with the letters, confused him and caught him under false pretenses. She had done so to Charles too, and in the end he had slipped away from her. What, then, could she expect from Henry?

She rose from her bed and tied a dressing gown tightly around herself with impatient gestures. She had already won more from Henry than she had expected: his professed devotion, his trust. He'd stripped himself bare for her, in more than one way. She hoped he would not notice that she did not give him so much in return. One day, when it was too late for him to pull away from her, she would trust him with the full truth.

Or maybe she would not. Charles had proved this much to her: it was never too late for a man to pull away.

⤋

Henry's newfound buoyancy lasted all night and through the endless early day, until the reluctant clocks in Tallant House struck through the morning hours and told him he could call on Frances again.

Not that he needed to stand on ceremony. But he wanted to do everything right. He would court her honorably.

Such was the power of happiness, to make the commonplace seem delightful. No wonder Jem had fallen for Emily and her sense of joy. Henry felt a positive slave to Frances, who had heard him, accepted him, taken him in.

Just as he was.

This time, when he knocked at the door of the Albemarle Street house, the flowers he fumbled with were for Frances. He had chosen damask roses, taking his time to find blossoms the same lush pink as her nipples. Pink for *perfect happiness*. With a flourish, he would hand them to her. Maybe drop to one knee to make her laugh. He loved her throaty laugh. Or he would whisper in her ear the significance of the color and watch her blush. He loved her blush too.

As soon as the butler admitted him, he saw Frances lurking at the top of the stairs from the ground floor. She paced back and forth before the drawing room door, which was flanked by life-sized statues of Mars and Venus.

The troubled lovers. How apt, considering how much of love and how much of war took place in Caro's drawing room. For Henry's part, he was done with the latter and ready for the former. So, so ready.

Frances's warm eyes widened at the sight of him; her lips parted. Her hair was not confined primly, but had been allowed to spring into curls the color of coffee. Altogether, she looked as though she had been kissed thoroughly and wanted to be kissed again.

In that, he could oblige her. "These are for you," he said as he bounded up the stairs and thrust the bouquet toward Frances, utterly failing to make a grand gesture or even say something romantic. He wanted the flowers out of his hand, out of his way. They were petals and sticks, nothing compared to the feel of a human body in his grasp.

She scooted back out of his reach. Her soft slippers shushed on the polished marble floor.

"You shouldn't have," she said quietly. She smiled, but her eyes darted to the drawing room door, which was resting slightly ajar. She looked... well, a little guilty, if he was reading her expression correctly.

"I should have, indeed. I don't even mind that you don't have any flowers for me," he teased. Lowering his voice to a whisper, he said, "Shall I tell you why I chose the color? It reminded me of the shade of your—"

"Thank you, I think I can guess." Her cheeks grew as bright as those of a girl meeting her lover behind a stable for a grope. She shuffled her feet and looked toward the drawing room door again, as though she didn't know what to do next. The blooms lay awkwardly in her arms.

"Why are you standing out here? Is something happening?"

"I was waiting for you," she said, and he felt light again, flying foolishly high. Surely he had the right to be a little foolish today.

How love makes young men thrall and old men dote;
How love is wise in folly, foolish-witty...

Something like that. Shakespeare. Henry had not read literature for years, but he knew England's greatest poets and scholars had long ago agreed that foolishness and love were irrevocably and inevitably intertwined. This was a good time to be a fool, to tell Frances of his wish to court her honorably, while he was in her thrall and the memory of their folly was sweet on his skin.

"There's something I must tell you," he said. His voice sounded raspy, abraded.

She laid her roses at the feet of Mars and took Henry's hand. "Then come upstairs with me," she said, looking relieved, "for there's something I must tell you too."

෬‍ᴓ

The last time she'd said such a thing to Henry, Frances had pulled him to the Blue Room, pinned under an eagle's stare. She'd been unsure of what to say; she only knew that she needed to give him comfort and comfort herself.

She was slightly better off this time. She knew what she needed to say. It was just so damnably difficult.

It should be·easy. Quick. *Henry, I wrote the letters.* But she did not want to say the words. She couldn't take the risk.

So she brought him to her bedchamber instead.

"It's private here," she excused herself. "I thought we would be able to say whatever we needed to one another without being disturbed."

Henry booted the door shut behind him with his heel. His mouth was grave, but his eyes were wicked and merry. "Very private, indeed. I shall do my best not to disturb you if that is what you wish."

Frances watched his lips move, but she barely heard his words. She could think only of how they had pressed at her mouth, her neck, her breasts.

Henry suddenly seemed very tall and the room very small. There was nowhere to sit where she would not be close to him, nowhere to stand where she would not be within his reach. Nowhere in the world she could go and not remember his body within hers, filling her, joining with her, making her realize how alone she had become.

"It does not matter what I wish," she said faintly, pressing her knees together. "Would you care for a chair?"

"I'll sit on the bed," he said cheerfully, and sank onto the coverlet, his long legs stretched out before him. "Would you care to join me?"

"I would," Frances said, enjoying the way his eyebrows shot up. "But I think it best we say what we need to first." How admirable. How wholly against her inclination.

"Fine. I'll speak, then." Henry cleared his throat. "Ah—I wanted to tell you that I'd like to court you."

Oh.

It was everything she had longed for. Yet rather than glee, the statement evoked a sick feeling of guilt. "You... want to court me."

"Yes." He hitched one foot across the other thigh, and Frances drank in the long lines of his body. "Maybe it seems a little anticlimactic after we—well."

"'After we—well?'" Frances teased, stalling. "I think that was quite climactic. Twice climactic, wasn't it?"

He grinned. "You're trying to terrify me again."

"I never have managed to terrify you yet." She gave in and sat next to him on the bed. "So, you want to court me."

"Yes, and not just because of the sex." His voice fell on the last word, and his high cheekbones flushed darker.

"You are completely darling." Frances ran a finger down his profile, letting him nip at her fingertip play- fully. God, she wanted this man. Already, desire was wide-awake and thrumming hotly through her blood, despite the nagging awareness of secrets untold.

"*Darling*?" Henry sounded incredulous. "What a dishwater endearment. I'm going to assume that's the current London cant for virile and masculine and overpoweringly passionate."

"Of course. That's exactly what I meant. It's all those things."

He shot her a sideways look. "I'm glad you agree. So, will you allow me to court you?"

A blush of shame heated her, and she looked at her lap as she replied, "I'll allow anything from you, Henry. Anything at all."

He choked. "That's a statement full of intriguing possibility if I ever heard one."

She could feel him relax, the mattress shifting as he leaned back on one elbow, started to swing his booted feet up onto the bed before thinking better of it. Up his legs swung, then down, and he was left at an odd angle with his torso twisted to one side behind her, supported on his left arm. His right arm subsided onto the bed, out of the way.

"Does this mean you agree to my suit?" he pressed.

"So it's become a suit already, rather than a court-ship. Much more formal, isn't that?" Frances curled her toes in her slippers. The big toe on her left foot snagged on a hole in her stocking. If this were a dream, surely her stockings would be perfectly darned.

And surely he would allow her to stall, to find a way to draw out their pleasure again, instead of watching her with those bright blue eyes and waiting for her to reply.

"All right, yes. I agree to your suit." She felt somehow dimmed as she replied, her words casting a shadow over the room that only she could see. "I'm honored, Henry. I care for you greatly."

This was the truth cut down to its very heart, though she was beginning to think she felt far more than she dared admit. This man who judged his own courage so harshly, yet interpreted her every kindness so generously.

She could become very, very foolish about him, indeed.

Instead of saying more, she busied her hands. With no quills to trim, nothing to sew, she twined her fingers in Henry's hair, rubbed his scalp, tugged at the roots. His short-cropped hair was a metalworker's ecstasy of bronze and gold and copper, but fine and smooth as embroidery floss. She liked the look and feel of it.

He leaned his head into her hand and closed his eyes. "I am very glad you said that. You've no idea how uncertain I was."

"About asking to court me?"

He opened his clear eyes. "No. About what you would say in return."

Frances stilled her hand on his head. Silly of her. It was not as if he could read her thoughts through her fingertips. "You must have known how I felt about you."

"I hoped. But I wasn't certain."

"You weren't certain." She could almost laugh. "Well, it seems I am good at keeping secrets." How close she skated to the edge of disaster. He had no idea.

In one fluid movement, he sat upright. The ropes

under the mattress creaked a faint protest. "You are, Frances. I've known that about you ever since we met. You kept a smile on your face though your toes hurt; you handed over your fan to Caro; you let a complete stranger bother you with impertinent requests."

"Oh. Well. That was—"

"That was Applewood House, the day we met. You show a pleasant face to the world because you feel that's your duty."

Frances shoved herself against the headboard and wrapped her arms around her folded knees. "I've never been pleasant to you out of a feeling of duty." She frowned. "Actually, I haven't even always been pleasant to you. I was quite horrible about that fireplace screen you painted."

"No more horrible than the screen itself." He shrugged, his expression rueful. "But never mind that. I love your teasing, your wicked humor. That's how you show me who you really are."

"Of course," she said faintly, wishing she could wad herself up more tightly. *Love*, he'd said. Not *I love you*, but *I love something about you*. It was close—dangerously close. And farther than he knew, for how could he love anything about her when she hadn't told him everything?

He looked at her with eyes of trust, and his words stacked upon her like stones.

She could not take that trust from him. She could not take away his hope, and hers, for the slightest possibility that he would change his mind. She wanted him too badly to betray his trust by letting him know it had already been betrayed.

And surely it was a very small matter to have sent a few letters under someone else's name. Or to have lived a different life once, which had by now been left quite behind.

Surely that was so.

"What did you want to tell me when we came in here?" Henry's voice was gentle. His fingers roamed the curves of her face, exploring her contours with an artist's worshipful attention. Each faint touch plucked a cord of wistful desire, resonating through her whole body.

She ran a thumb over his mouth, silencing him. He caught it between his lips and grazed it with his teeth. The pull of his mouth on the sensitive pad of her finger squeezed her insides, sent a bolt of heat to her center.

The war had walled him off, divided him, more than he even knew. The past had divided Frances as well, from many people.

But she need not let it divide her from Henry. Even the walls of Jericho had fallen, given enough faith and the work of a fine soldier. Had not she and Henry agreed to be soldiers together?

Besides, she never had cared about walls between her and her desire. She rushed headlong, willing to be crushed. She grazed his earlobe with her teeth and murmured, "Let's do it again."

His whole body jolted, galvanized, and his face turned wondering and wicked at once.

It was easier to tumble into his physical thrall and ensnare him the same way.

So she'd thought. But as she held his face in her

hands, kissed his mouth, murmured she knew not what into his ears, she could have cried with loneliness even as she turned for him to slip her dress from her body.

Nineteen

A FINGER TRACED THE LINE OF HENRY'S CHEEKBONE, then drew along his jaw. His skin prickled and woke at the touch.

He was not asleep, but drifting as he lay. His body was full and satisfied. His thoughts sank under a glossy foam of sensation.

He would never get tired of the way Frances touched him. Her fingers, slim and strong, skated over his skin with gentle certainty. It felt as if she knew what she wanted, and the knowledge was precious to her. *He* was.

Thank God.

He'd had much to be thankful for in recent weeks. More than he had expected, certainly, when he'd taken on a rash quest for a noble wife who would serve as a prize of war, proving that he was still whole and unchanged.

He wasn't, though. He'd been broken apart in a storm, but the pieces of him that survived were the strongest.

And now he had everything he wanted, did he not?

It was difficult to credit. Yet he lay in Frances's bed; she was curled against his side, and her fingers mapped the contours of his body, tracing his boundaries, seeking another adventure.

He turned his head away. "I owe you everything," he murmured into the soft press of her down pillow, letting the feathers smother his words. He wasn't sure he wanted her to hear him. His debt was shamefully great.

The questing finger traced down his neck; then the whole hand splayed over his chest, and Frances pulled herself more closely to him. "What was that?"

Um. "I said, 'I'll go this evening.'" How was he to think properly with her touching him?

She stroked his chest, nails raking lightly through the dusting of hair. "And what does that mean? You'll stay in my bed all day?"

"That plan suits me if it does you."

"Certainly." Her hand slid down his chest and stomach, found his already-waking shaft. His hips jerked at the touch. "Before you *go* this evening, would you like to *come* this afternoon?"

Henry groaned. "Brilliant and witty. There is no matching you."

"I think we match rather well." Her mouth began to wander downward, curious and hot, and his toes clenched.

"I will agree with anything you say when you— oh, God. Yes. *God.* I do believe I've died and gone to heaven."

She lifted her head and gave her kiss-swollen lips a lick. Henry shivered. "You seem so perfectly correct all the time, Frances. No one knows what wicked depths you have, do they?"

Her smile tipped sideways. "No. No one knows." She slid up the bed and nestled behind him again, her body a comma against his. Her voice was muffled against the damp skin of his back. "I was still correct, though, wasn't I?"

"You have no idea how much. But it's my turn to correct you now, I think." It was difficult to turn on the narrow confines of the bed without pinning his nerveless arm at an awkward angle. He could hardly tell when it was trapped beneath him.

But all things seemed possible now. He pushed himself upright and looked at his lady, tangled in the sheets.

There were deep shadows under her eyes, fragile and ashy as ground peach-black. He had not noticed this earlier. Obviously his vision had been too fogged by lust.

"Are you all right?"

She turned onto her back and looked up at him. "I'm fine. Why?"

"You look tired."

Her mouth quirked. "That's hardly complimentary."

Henry bent his head to her neck, noticing that her eyes closed as soon as he pressed his mouth to her skin. "I mean," he said between kisses, "only that"—he caught the sheet in his teeth and tugged it downward—"you do not look as if you want to be importuned again."

Frances smiled. "What a way to describe our lovemaking. Have I importuned you, then?"

"Of course not." He stared shamelessly at her breasts. "Men are always willing to take more than women want to give. It's not fair, but it's the way of the world." He wondered if she was too tired to let him taste her.

Her eyes opened at his words, glassy and distant. He had never seen such an expression on her face before. "That is not always the way of the world."

He did not know what she meant, but it was hard to think too deeply. She had not covered herself, and as he watched, her nipples tightened into hard points. His mouth felt dry. He wanted to drink her in.

He turned on the bed, slid off the end and kneeled on the floor. With a quick tug on the sheet, he laid Frances completely bare.

She raised herself onto her elbows. "What are you doing?"

"Whatever you'll let me do."

Her cheeks blushed the dark, warm red of minium. Her lips were red too, from kisses, caresses. With her hair tousled, her skin flushed, her body laid out before him like a banquet of sensation, she looked magnificent. He wished he had a way to capture this moment forever. This was erotic and spiritual together. This was *right*.

Frances shut her eyes for a moment, looking as though she were trying to persuade herself into something. Then she opened them, a self-conscious smile on her face. "All right. I'll let you do anything."

"Really?" His cock grew fully hard.

"Oh, yes. Anything. Are you feeling creative? You may cut my hair, choose my clothes, bathe me in bergamot—*ulp*."

Henry had tugged at her leg until she slid farther down the bed toward him.

"Those are all fascinating offers," he said. "But not precisely what I had in mind right now."

With his elbow, he nudged her knees apart. "Damned useful things, elbows," he murmured, and Frances let out a shaky laugh.

He slid a finger within her, then another, and she sank back onto the bed, already trembling. One lick where she was slickest, and the tremors turned to shudders.

"Henry, please, please." Her voice was faint, as though she wanted something she was afraid to ask for.

He could well guess what she wanted. His fingers moved within her, and she moaned. Surely she would fly apart at any second. Then he would slide within her, feel her inner muscles clenching at him. To give her pleasure was as sweet as finding his own.

He tongued her, drew on her, worked his fingers in her, waiting for her to crest so they could be joined.

But she slipped down instead, her body stilling under his touch. He tried to pull her up again, working his fingers and mouth harder—no, she gave a gasp, but her sleek wetness was drying up. He withdrew his fingers, plucked at her sensitive bud with them. Too late somehow. She was already paling and subsiding, her swollen flesh losing its arousal.

He could not bring her back to the peak, and he began to feel foolish trying. He sat back in a squat, realizing how much his knees hurt from kneeling on the wood floor.

Frances sat up, looked down at him from the edge of the bed. "I'm sorry."

Her face looked pale. Her eyes and cheekbones were shadowed. Or perhaps it was only the angle at which she watched him, the light from the window striking her from above.

Henry clutched at the tangled bed sheet and pulled it around himself. This left no cover for Frances, but he didn't care right now. Something had gone wrong, and likely it was his fault, and he didn't want to face that reckoning with a bare arse.

He shut his eyes and thought of the most un-arousing things possible. Pus. Brussels sprouts and goat brains. Lord Wadsworth's sneer.

That did it. His too-eager body succumbed to his control again, and he mustered a reasonable amount of calm as he creaked from the floor to his feet and sat next to Frances on the bed. Again, he asked, "Are you all right?"

"Yes." She crossed her arms across her chest, covering as much of her nakedness as she could. She rubbed at her upper arms with her hands. "Well, not exactly. I suppose I am a bit distracted."

"Distracted." Was she, now? When she'd stroked him to life, opened herself to his mouth and his most intimate touch.

Frances unfolded her arms, began gathering and twisting her hair from where it had spilled over her shoulders and down her back. Pins had scattered everywhere, and she slid from the bed to search out the small metal wires on the floor with one hand as she held her hair in a loose coil with the other.

So they were done, then. "Are you going to tell me what was distracting you?"

She kept picking up pins from the floor. Her hair was already restrained, a ludicrous pairing with her lush nudity. "It was nothing serious," she said in a tight voice. "I was—"

A scratch at the door cut her off. "Mrs. Whittier?" a young-sounding female called.

Frances stood up as quickly as if she had a spring within her. "Yes, Millie?" She shot a warning look at Henry, and he felt a contrary urge to announce himself to their interrupter. *Come back later, Millie. Madam and I are trying to fornicate.*

Trying and failing. He clamped his mouth shut and looked at the wall as Frances began to pace around. Thick billowing sounds told him she was snapping out her rumpled clothes. She'd need help putting on her stays. Well, much luck to her.

The unseen Millie spoke through the closed door. "Excuse me, mum. But Lady Stratton says as she needs you right away. His lordship the ferrety-looking man seems likely to pop the question in front of everyone."

"Wadsworth," Frances said. "The man ruins everything."

Was it Henry's imagination, or did she not sound as disappointed as she ought?

"Please, mum," Millie said, her slightly muffled voice now sounding panicked through the door. "Do come· right away. Lady Stratton says you're ever so good at keeping the man in line."

Henry relented before the servant had an apoplexy in the corridor. "Help me get dressed," he whispered, catching Frances's eye. "Then I'll send the maid in to you."

Frances nodded at Henry, then called back through

the door, "Of course, Millie. Tell her I'll be there directly. And then come back to me, for I'll need your help dressing."

❧

Considering how debauched they'd been this morning, Henry thought they looked respectable enough right now. Frances had donned a demure gown of blue serge—there was simply no hope for this morning's gown, so crushed had it been by Henry's fingers and their tangled bodies.

She might wear prim clothing, but he knew the truth.

As Henry had dressed, his light mood had returned. The world had opened for him in the last twenty-four hours, and only he knew its secrets. He knew what fires lay beneath Frances's cool exterior. He knew how her lips parted when she reached her peak, how she gasped his name as if it were a prayer or a plea.

So he had not been able to bring her to climax with his mouth. What of it? They would have all their lives to try other things. He would make it his mission to find what brought her to ecstasy. He had never had such pleasurable orders before; it would be a delight to carry them out.

There was no one to see his wolfish grin. Frances was marching ahead down the stairs to the first floor and the drawing room. Her shoulders were straight and drawn slightly back, as if her heart was presenting a target. *Do your worst, world.*

He really felt as if the world could, and he would not be a bit bothered.

"Frances," he said as they reached a landing. He had

to stop her. One more turn of the staircase and they would reenter the public world. She would become a companion again, and as far as anyone knew, he'd be just another caller for Caro.

Surely they could not transform so easily. Had they not shared something irrevocable? Could they not promise the same?

She faced him, looking solemn. Those peach-black shadows still darkened her eyes.

"Frances, let us announce our betrothal today. Right now, even. In the drawing room."

"Our betrothal? Are we betrothed?" She gave him a teasing smile. "You have never asked me to marry you."

A finger of unease poked Henry's spine. "Please, be serious. I'm in earnest, Frances. You must have known we'd never"—he lowered his voice—"never do such intimate things without being bound to each other."

Her smile sank down into a crooked, twisted thing. "It's not wise to take anything for granted."

The words were a swift jab in the gut, not at all the response he'd expected. Henry could only gape.

You really are *terrifying*. For the first time, he thought so—because she batted his offer away as though it meant nothing.

He must have shown his shock, for she softened at once. "But you are right. I consider myself bound to you, quite tightly."

It seemed she was going to say more, but a shout from the drawing room below interrupted her. There was a crash of something heavy being broken, like a china ornament or a vase thrown against the stone of the hearth. Or against Wadsworth's head if Henry was lucky.

"Good Lord." Frances sounded worried. "Wadsworth must have proposed already. He'll be in an almighty rage. Quick, Henry, go downstairs and find your flowers. Be ready to give them to Caroline, as if you're calling on her. Hurry. No one must suspect anything about us."

She shoved at his chest, then pressed herself against the landing wall, as if her dark blue dress could possibly vanish into the green and white plasterwork on the landing.

Henry planted his feet. "What is wrong? There's no need to lie, is there?"

"It's just for today," she said in a ragged whisper. "Please. I don't want Wadsworth to say anything to you."

"Wait." He shook his head. "Why? Do you think he will insult you?"

"Probably, but I don't care about that."

"Then you think he will insult me. Frances, I don't care about that either. But if you do, let's go back upstairs until he leaves."

"I have to go in. I'm sorry. Caroline has asked for me; she will need me." Her eyes met Henry's, wide and panicky.

Not what one expected to see when a woman agreed to marriage.

So. She *was* ashamed of him. And this was what happened when one showed a woman one's every weakness: it became magnified. Now it was seen by two, not just one.

Henry had seen a hot air balloon launched in France. It had been punctured by a vandal after its thrilling flight. The hollow bag writhed and twisted as the heated air escaped, and it was left a sad ruin of fabric on the ground, unwieldy and useless.

It just came to mind, all of a sudden.

"If you think it best," he said over a roaring in his ears as loud as a balloon turning itself inside out. "We won't make an announcement until you're ready."

"It will be soon, I hope." Her hands knotted together. A foolish use for fingers when one had ten at one's command.

"You don't know, though?" Henry's near-sleepless night suddenly weighed on him. "Frances. Do you regret it?" *Me?*

"No!" Her eyes flew wide open, and she reached a hand toward him. "Oh, he is coming."

She pushed past Henry and fled down the stairs toward the drawing room. Heavy footsteps pounded within the room, and the door slammed open just before Frances reached for its handle.

Wadsworth flung himself through the doorway and almost walked into Frances. He caught himself in midstride just outside of the drawing room and stared at her, dumbfounded.

She froze, blinking back at him.

Henry must have made a noise, for the viscount's eyes flicked up toward the stairway. Henry realized at once that he had blundered; he should either have drawn back out of sight or followed immediately behind Frances as if he'd just come to call. Instead, it was abundantly clear that he'd been admitted into the personal apartments.

Damn it. This was exactly the type of "announcement" Frances wanted to avoid.

Wadsworth's face was red over the high starched points of his cravat. His eyes narrowed, flicking from Henry back to Frances, and Henry recognized the signs of a baited animal ready to lash out.

He was more than willing to lash back right now. Spoiling for it, actually. Too little rest and too much uncertainty would roughen any man's edges, and it hadn't been long since Henry had stopped fighting for his life.

He knew just how to get the fight he wanted from Wadsworth.

He imagined that he was strolling down Piccadilly, a malacca cane in his hand, as his feet found the stairs and carried him to the doorway of the drawing room to stand at Frances's side. He assumed an expression of delight, as of one old friend encountering another in an unexpected place. Such nonchalance would infuriate Wadsworth.

"Wadsworth," he said as smoothly as if they were meeting at the counter of a tobacconist's. "Good afternoon to you. And how go your affairs today?"

Twenty

HENRY WAS NOT WRONG IN COMPARING WADSWORTH to a wounded animal. The man's nostrils were flaring. He looked like a beast that had lost a very hard race—and a bit of blood too.

"Eavesdropping, Middlebrook? Perhaps all those years in the army stripped you of your good breeding."

Henry ignored this clumsy sally and replied with maddening cheer. "Oh, you *do* recognize good breeding when you see it? Judging by your own actions, I didn't realize that about you."

"I suspect there's much you don't realize about good society." Wadsworth's eyes narrowed. "For example, you must not know that a gentleman doesn't accompany a lady upstairs into her private apartments." His breathing still came a bit fast, but save for the dishevelment of his carefully pomaded hair, he was shrugging back into his sharp, ambiguous urbanity. "Unless you *do* know that, and you are not a gentleman. Or this *person* is not a lady. Which is it?"

Frances lifted her chin and glared at Wadsworth, looking as though she was preparing to stomp on a rodent.

What a tableau they must make, the three of them standing in the doorway of the drawing room. If Wadsworth would but put a shawl over his head, they could perform an amateur theatrical for the other... Henry counted... seven men, plus Caro, who were watching them, transfixed.

They were all getting a dramatic performance today, though they had probably expected nothing but the usual pleasantries and flowers and dainty sandwiches. Already they had seen a vase thrown. Shards of majolica and scattered daisies lay before the drawing room's marble fireplace, and the carpet was dark with water.

Henry was very aware of the stillness of his right arm—the arm that ought to draw Frances within its cradle, the arm that made Wadsworth think him weak. But he could fight with society's tiny, barbed sentences as well as he had once handled a bayonet. "I'm unsure who you would call a lady or gentleman, Wadsworth. For your own sake, I hope you define a gentleman by blood rather than behavior. Otherwise, by all rights, you ought to relinquish your title to someone more deserving."

He raised an eyebrow, calculating just the right insouciant lift as a spring within him began to coil up tight and tense. Eager energy began to flood him— the desire to fight and wound, to vanquish, to prove himself. Frances was unsure of him for some unknown reason. She need not be. He'd prove it.

"And how do *you* define a gentleman, Middlebrook?" Wadsworth's face had turned a dark violet. "I should say it was one who knew his betters."

Whispers broke out in the drawing room, nothing

but a distant buzz in Henry's ears. He peered closely at Wadsworth's face, then tilted his head and stepped back. With a nod, he held his thumb up to the side of the viscount's face.

"What?" Wadsworth's livid color had begun to drain, and his lips looked oddly bloodless. "You have no reply?"

"Oh, don't." Henry let his posture sag, his face transform into a portrait of misery. "Don't let yourself calm down, please. Why, you had turned the exact shade of Tyrian purple; it was a marvelous effect. That's the color that used to be worn by all the Caesars of Rome. Ah, there you go—you've taken on that rare shade again. Hambleton? Crisp? Have you seen Wadsworth's face? You ought to have waistcoats made in this color."

Wadsworth's brows yanked into an angry vee. When he opened his mouth to speak, Henry smiled pleasantly. "Since Tyrian purple used to be saved for royalty, Wadsworth, I suppose you'd consider it an appropriate shade for yourself. Did you know the dye comes from the mucous of snails?" He turned from the sputtering Wadsworth to Frances. "Did *you* know that? You do know the oddest things about people."

Her eyes caught his, and she managed a faint smile. "I did not know that, Mr. Middlebrook. But I admit that nothing you tell me about Lord Wadsworth would surprise me."

"The kitten has claws," Wadsworth murmured.

"Heaven save us from such manners." A woman's voice. Through the drawing room doorway, Henry saw Caro stand from her flower-caged seat and thread through the room toward them. "You three are excellent at attempting courtesy without succeeding at it. But I suggest you either come in to the drawing room and be genuinely polite or take a little time to drown your prickly tempers in a brandy bottle."

To Henry's surprise, Wadsworth shot Caroline a cool look. "And who are you, madam, to dictate my behavior? Naught but the daughter of a vicar, aren't you?"

Clearly some wall of courtesy had been broken along with the majolica, but Wadsworth was no tactician. This was fratricide: hurting one's own allies.

Caroline straightened her shoulders. "I am the widow of an earl and the owner of this house. You can't possibly require any further authority. But if you are so presumptuous as to request more, I will remind you that I am the woman who has refused your suit, and I can't see what further we have to say to one another."

"Look, Frances," Henry said ruthlessly. "Wadsworth has turned the color of snail mucous again."

He probably shouldn't have said that. It was not the act of a gentleman to heap further humiliation on a man who'd just been publicly chastised.

But since he *had* said it, he probably should have expected the punch.

Thud. A perfect, whole, five-fingered fist hit Henry just below the ridge of his left cheekbone. The shock snapped his head back, echoed through the bones of his skull. The dull sound of it seemed still to be ringing in his ears when the pain hit his face in a sudden, hot wash.

His first emotion was surprise; the viscount had more spine than Henry had credited him with.

His second was a desperate calm, the calm of a man

scrabbling to hold together his fortune during a deep gamble. Frances was ashamed of him, and now she'd seen Wadsworth strike him. A *roomful* of people had seen that. The pain in his face was nothing compared to that agony of humiliation.

He lifted his hand to his aching cheek and pivoted toward Frances as deliberately as he could, as though he had all the time and self-control in the world. The coiled spring within him wound ever tighter. "I believe I've just been batted by an insect," he said in what he hoped was a tone of calculated wonder. "I didn't realize they flew in the better households. Did you see it? Was it hideous?"

"Don't." Her voice was barely more than a whisper, her eyes fixed on his. The ring of green around the edge of her irises looked particularly bright. "Don't make it worse."

For an instant, Henry was back in her bed, sliding skin over sweat-slick skin, making her cry out. *We saw each other naked; we shared each other's bodies.* How had they left that intimacy behind so quickly? It was not a mere flight of stairs away, but the unbridgeable distance of her unspoken regret.

"There's no way to make it better," he said.

He could see now, no woman would protect him against men such as Wadsworth. Not even Caroline, with all her money and influence, could keep the golden muzzles of London society tied on tightly enough. If Henry was to emerge victorious, he would have to fight his own battles.

He turned to Wadsworth, standing almost nose-to-nose with the viscount, close enough to smell the starch of his clothes and the sharp, oily bergamot with which he scented himself.

He was the cleanest foe Henry had faced in several years, that was certain.

"You've struck me," Henry said as though reading a mildly interesting article out of a newspaper. "I wonder what you think will happen next. Do you think I can possibly let that pass?"

Wadsworth swiped his mouth with the back of his hand. "I think you'll take it." Again, he launched a fist at Henry.

With a quick snap, Henry caught the viscount's forearm and warded off this second blow. He held the arm tight, pushing it back from his face, letting it struggle and flex inside its carefully tailored sleeve.

He stared into Wadsworth's eyes and saw his own face reflected in their gray gloss.

There was his greatest foe; there. And he *was* strong enough.

"Name your second, Wadsworth," he said. "And choose your weapon."

At these words, the drawing room exploded with the din and chaos of canister shot.

Henry smiled. Yes, London was full of its own little wars. And he was determined to win.

Twenty-One

"YOU HAVE TO BE PLAYING A JOKE ON ME," JEM SAID. His light eyes were open so wide, they appeared to be trying to escape his head. "That's what this is. A joke? You're very funny, Hal. Very funny."

The earl sat heavily in the chair at his study's desk, breathing hard. His cravat was starched and tied high and tight as fashion dictated, and he tugged at it fruitlessly with a forefinger. "God, Hal. An excellent joke. But you must not say it in that serious way. I almost believed you for a second."

Once again, Henry faced his brother across the massive desk in Jem's study, but this time he needed no advice. He had made his decision; now he needed only the blessed, unthinking relief of action.

"It's true," Henry said. "I challenged Wadsworth to a duel. We'll meet tomorrow at dawn."

Which was just the way Henry wanted it. He was spoiling for a fight, for the chance to prove something, anything. He must win. His letters had not been enough, a minuet had not been enough, his body had not been enough. He was not sure how much of his heart had been ventured. Too much for comfort's sake.

He smiled, knowing the expression must look gruesome.

Jem unsnarled the end of his cravat from its elaborate folds and coaxed the long starched rectangle away from his throat. "Good God, Hal. I can't credit it, even from your own lips. *You* issued the challenge. For a *duel*."

"He struck me, Jem. I couldn't let that pass."

"He struck you?" Jem blinked, then shook his head, loosening the cravat further. "No, no. That can't be overlooked. But how did it ever come to that, Hal? Wadsworth outranks you. He should never have struck you in public."

"Apparently he disagrees." Henry shrugged. "I suppose I baited him. I meant to."

Jem rubbed a hand over his eyes and pressed at his temples with long fingers. "You baited him in Caro's house, before an audience? He could hardly ignore the humiliation you caused him."

"Just as I could hardly ignore his own insults."

"But a *duel*. Damn it, Hal." Jem fixed him with bright blue eyes. "Maybe the situation can yet be smoothed over if you both send apologies. Who is your second?"

Henry had expected this part to be difficult. "Well." He crossed his left arm over his chest, gathering his thin right arm into his grasp. "Well, I hoped you would do it."

Jem sat up straight in his chair. "Did you, now? Me, your second to a duel."

Henry nodded. "I couldn't ask Bart to do it. He'd

never have the stomach for it. Also, he's leaving London any day for the country. I don't want to ask him to postpone his journey for—"

"An illegal and quite possibly fatal duel," Jem interrupted. "No, of course not. No one should regard that with any degree of seriousness. It's only a *duel. Hal.*"

This last word was groaned, as Jem rose from his chair again and grabbed a brandy decanter from a sideboard. He splashed brandy into two generously sized snifters and shoved one across the desk to Henry.

"No, thank you," Henry said. He felt remarkably calm now. The die had been cast, and he had only to do what came next, and next, and next. No more choices until the duel was over. By then, everything else might work out.

Many more impossible dreams than this had come true. For others.

Jem shrugged and drained one snifter, then the other. With a cough, he sat back down and began fussing with the items on his desk. A ledger, an inkwell, a fistful of quills. A quizzing glass. A watercolor miniature of Emily that Henry had painted long ago.

Jem had never wanted to snap the tiny portrait away inside a watchcase as Henry had intended. He said he wanted to look at the miniature always because it would remind him of his wife and his brother, two of the people he loved best in the world.

Henry sighed. "I should have brought you an ice from Gunter's," he muttered. He should have done a lot of things. He should have tried harder to make his brother happy, time and again. Happiness was all Jem had ever wanted for him, and this was how Henry repaid him.

No wonder Jem had had to loosen his cravat. It was a wonder his head hadn't blown apart, like a kettle with no outlet for steam. But it was too late to go back now, and Henry would not change the path he was walking even if it were possible.

Jem lined all the quills up into a neat row, and Henry remembered Frances teaching him how to hold a quill in his left hand. A quiet day in this very house. He'd had such hope then, but already the two women—Caro and Frances—had begun to mix and muddle in his mind, and he did not know exactly for what he ought to be hoping.

"Those are taken from the left wing of the goose," Henry said stupidly.

Jem looked up. "These are from a swan." He stretched his mouth into a tight shape that approximated a smile.

He looked calmer now, as if the ritual of shuffling the objects on his desk—not to mention gulping two snifters of brandy—had soothed him.

"So you want me to be your second," Jem said again. He leaned back in his chair again and spun one of his long swan quills between his fingers. The feathery barb tapped against his thumb, over and over, and Henry began to wonder what his brother was thinking. It was rare that he ever had to speculate. Usually the expression on Jem's face was as easy to read as a printed page.

"That's a hell of a thing for you to ask of your brother, you know," Jem said mildly, still spinning the quill.

"I don't have anyone else to ask."

"That's a hell of a way to be." Jem set the quill down on his desk and nudged it into a neat row with its fellows. "But I suppose it makes sense. A man with many friends doesn't find himself getting snared in a duel in the first place."

"Anyone could get into a duel with Wadsworth," Henry said. "You'd have challenged him too if he'd insulted you in front of Emily the way he insulted me before—" He cut himself off just in time. Frances did not want anyone to know about their relationship. He wanted to give her all that was honorable: his name and everything he owned on earth. But in her shame for him, all she wanted was secrecy, so he could at least give her that.

"Your lady," Jem finished, and Henry nodded his gratitude. Jem's mouth curved again, and this time it seemed a real smile. It was only a shadow of his brother's usual buoyant grin, but it would do for a start. "Yes, I suppose I can understand that. I'd have wanted to kill him with my bare hands."

"You wouldn't have," Henry protested.

"I'm not saying I would have *succeeded*. But I would have *wanted* to. Why are you belittling my skill, though? You want me as your second, don't you?"

"You'll do it?" Henry didn't know why he was holding his breath, as if everything rode on this. He didn't *have* to have a second.

"Ah, Hal." Jem raked his hands through his hair. It was still the rich dark of lamp-black, but Henry noticed that it was beginning to gray at the temples. He had a sinking, shuddering feeling of having been gone for an unutterably long time, of having missed an unfathomable amount.

Jem, it seemed, agreed with him. "Hal, the war is over. Our society rests on peace now, and we must keep peace amongst each other. You can't threaten people and challenge them to duels. You especially can't challenge a peer. We don't kill here. The whole world knows that."

"Bollocks," said Henry. He disliked the idea of *the whole world* facing him down, telling him where he'd gone wrong.

"What does it do to your lady's reputation if it becomes known that you are going to fight a duel on her behalf? Are you going to offer for Lady Stratton?"

Henry stared at him. "No, indeed. And I'm sure she wouldn't have me if I did. I'm fighting for myself, not for her."

Jem drew in his chin until it was hidden amidst the loosened points of his cravat. He peered at Henry with what was apparently intended to be a terrifying stare. "Not Lady Stratton after all. So who is your lady, then?"

Henry suddenly felt ashamed. His left hand grasped his wasted right arm more tightly, reminding him. "Mrs. Whittier. Or...I thought she was."

"Mrs. Whittier." Jem tilted his head. "Is she, now? That's an interesting choice, Hal. I like the woman myself. But what do you know of her family? You'll be opening yourself up to a lot of talk if you court a lady's companion."

Henry's fingers gripped his right arm so hard that it would have gone numb if it was not already. "She's the daughter of a baronet. And she's cousin to a countess, so that ought to be a lofty enough connection for any of the gossips."

Jem drummed his fingers on his desk, once, twice, then nodded his agreement.

"Such questions don't matter," Henry said. "As I told you, I'm fighting this duel for my own reasons."

Jem leaned forward, propping his elbows on his desk, then gave up on trying to look terrifying. He folded his arms on the desktop and sunk his chin onto them. He looked tired, as tired as Henry felt inside.

"All right, then. I'll be your second," Jem said quietly. "Oh, Hal. I'll do what I can for you. I'll help you go through with it and hide the scandal however I can, or if you want to call it off, I can try to negotiate with Wadsworth's second." He lifted his head up, hope sparking in his blue eyes. "What d'you say? There's no shame at all in that. Calling it off. I'm sure I can get some sort of apology from Wadsworth if you'll offer one of your own."

Henry appeared to consider this. He gave it his best, dropping his right arm and stroking his chin in an expression of thought, though he knew it was impossible. An apology would not protect Henry. He needed the certainty of having defended himself. Of having fought and won at last.

Before he could demur, the door flew open. "Jemmy!"

Emily bustled into the room in a whirl of poppy-red muslin and a cloud of rose perfume, waving a note. "Jemmy, you will not believe what Caro told me. Only listen! Oh, Hal, hullo. Er…" She looked uncertain, and her hand with the note in it dropped to her side.

Jem sat up straighter. "Em, this isn't a good time. We're discussing… well, men's business." He tried to compose his face into a stern expression.

"Fiddle," Emily said. She sat on the edge of Jem's desk, twisting her torso so she could glare at both brothers at once. "If you're discussing what I think you're discussing, then you both ought to be ashamed of yourselves."

"What do you think we're discussing?" Jem was tugging at his cravat again.

"One of you has done something very stupid." Emily waved the note again. "Maybe both of you have. Hal, you young idiot, Caro has told me everything, and I simply can't believe you would let yourself be—"

Henry could not be seeing right. He snatched at the paper. "This is from Caro?"

"Yes, and as I was saying, she told me all about the challenge you issued. Jem, you must make this tangle go away. You can't permit—"

Henry cut her off again. "This note. This one in my hand. This is from Caro."

Emily rolled her eyes. "*Yes.*"

She kept talking; Henry heard the smooth flow of her words, lifting every once in a while for emphasis. Sometimes Jem's low voice would answer. But Henry had no idea what they said. He just stared and stared at the paper in his hand.

It was wrong. Something was very wrong.

He knew this paper well, the heavy, cloth-like feel

of it. He knew the seal pressed into the thick splotch of red wax. But he had never seen this handwriting before in his life. It was a careless thread of nearly illegible loops, not the angular, confident script he knew as Caro's.

Yes, Henry had done something very stupid, though he did not know what. And someone else had done something stupid too. He felt as if he were stumbling through the Bossu Wood again, seeing nothing that was important.

"This note was written by Lady Stratton?" he demanded through the clutter of voices. One last time, to be absolutely sure.

Emily and Jem fell silent, and Emily looked more worried than Henry had ever seen her. "Yes," she confirmed. "But if you don't tell me what's going on, I'm going to clout you with a poker."

"I don't know what's going on," Henry said. "Excuse me, I have to go. Emily, if you need to clout someone, Jem will have to stay behind and serve the purpose."

He took the note with him, and he left.

Twenty-Two

"HENRY, THANK GOD YOU'RE HERE."

Caro rushed forward across her morning room to meet Henry. Her eyes were wide, her full lips parted, eager as Venus riding to shore on a shell. A lamp made a halo of her Indian yellow hair, ruddy gold in the dim room.

Indian yellow. Henry remembered now, the pigment was made from the urine of starving cattle. It was precious, but it was foul. One could not trust in the true nature of anything that appeared to be beautiful.

The room was close and poorly lit, not meant to be used at this late hour. The walls that looked so sunny in morning were now a drab, dirty mustard. Frances's dark gown and hair blended into the nubby forest-green upholstery of the sofa on which she sat.

How many secrets had been told in the privacy of this morning room, he could not say. He had told all of his own. But someone else had not.

He drew back his shoulders. "Lady Stratton. This is yours, I believe." He thrust forward the note he'd taken from Emily.

"Yes, I suppose it is." Her voice was hesitant. "Yes. This is the note I sent to your sister a little while ago. Did you read it?"

"I didn't have to read it," he said. "I only had to look at the form of the handwriting. So it *is* from you. It's written in your hand."

Henry looked up at Caro, ignoring Frances. Her presence prickled at his skin, though, like the itch of a wool coat on a hot day. He did not want to be aware that she was but three feet away. That her citrus perfume had been rubbed off by his body that morning. That she had gasped when he handed the note to Caro.

That he was right, then, about the letter. All the letters. Damn it. He had hoped even against hope that he was wrong, and that everything was just as it had seemed for the past several weeks.

"Ah. So you know at last," Caro said. "What a relief."

"Not *precisely* the word I would use, my lady," Henry said in his sunniest voice, his own smile a dead thing. "Would you be so good as to allow me a few moments alone with your companion?"

He could not keep his fist from tapping a jittery tattoo against his thigh as the countess's smile slipped. She nodded, laid a quick encouraging hand on Frances's shoulder, and left the room, shutting the door behind her.

Now they were alone.

Frances spoke first. "I'm sorry you found out this way, Henry. But I'm glad you've figured everything out."

She tried a smile, probably hoping it would help, but there was no help for it. He stalked away from her to the far side of the room and found himself staring at the framed hunting scene, as he had only the day before.

The poor fox was just going about his business. He had no idea what awaited him.

"I don't think," Henry finally said in a clipped voice, "that I have figured everything out at all. I have not figured out why these letters were sent to me, or why I was led to believe they were from Lady Stratton. The only thing I have figured out, Mrs. Whittier, is that you and your lovely employer have been lying to me since almost the first moment we met."

He whirled, facing her. Wondering if she dared face him.

She dared. She straightened her back and stared him straight in the eyes. "I didn't lie to you, Henry." She stopped when he snorted, a sharp exhale of disbelief. "Fine, I did lie. But only by omission, and only because you wanted it."

"I—" This was too much. He could only sputter.

She was all shadows and darks, her eyes fathomless pools as she picked up the thread of his sentence. "Did anyone sign the first letter you received, Henry? No—it was sent from *a friend*. I didn't think it proper to sign my name on a letter to a bachelor, but I assumed my identity would be clear to you, considering we'd teased one another about forming an alliance. And considering," she finished in an acid tone, "that you scarcely exchanged a dozen words with Caroline when you called."

Henry's head felt as though it were full of black powder; his thoughts shifting and incendiary, ready to explode with just a spark. So this whole tangle had begun as his mistake?

"Impossible," he said in a cracked voice.

"It's not impossible," Frances said. The rustle of her gown told him she was fidgeting, though she sounded fiercely calm. "I recall the situation perfectly. You summoned me to Tallant House through your sister; I assumed it was because you wished to tell me what you thought of my letter, for good or ill. But no, in your *infatuation with Caroline*"—she spoke louder to cover Henry's bark of protest—"you saw what you wished for. A letter from a woman who could give you everything you wanted. I tried to correct you, but you wouldn't hear it, so I let it pass. Can you blame me for wishing to spare us both the humiliation?"

This, he could seize upon. "Yes. I do blame you. If you lacked the will to end the deception then, you could have signed your own name to the next letter. Instead, you chose to continue lying to me."

He started to pace. The beat of his feet fell into the perfect regularity of ordinary march time: seventy-five paces to the minute. Fast as a heartbeat.

Too fast. His steps ate the length of the room in a few seconds. He forced himself to slow down, turn back to her. "It would have been a small matter, surely, for you to tell me one truth of your own amidst so many of my revelations. 'I wrote Caro's letters.' There, it took me only four words."

"For me to tell, yes. But how long for you to accept after hearing the truth?"

Henry's mouth pinched into a tight line, and his gaze dropped to the floor. He watched his feet tread on the carpet, elaborately patterned with squares and vines. The movement was dizzying and he stopped. Stood still. He had to think.

"I don't know if I *can* accept it. But it is always better to know the truth than let a lie fester."

"Yes." She sighed, an exhalation as long and sad as an echo. "I've known that for a long time."

Henry froze. Whether he had received a blow or had been given the chance to deliver one, he did not know. "Explain yourself."

Her hands fluttered through the air. "I lied to Charles so he'd marry me. He found out. He went to war. He died. It's a simple story." She lowered her eyes. "I suppose ours is too. Two people who meant well. A friendly misunderstanding. An act of love that makes it all unbearable. The end."

She laced her fingers in her lap so tightly they looked bloodless.

It was a magnificent speech. Every word perfect. The quaver in her voice when she'd said "love" gave just the right ring of authenticity.

His whole self had been naked before her inside and out, in this very room. She had seen his every weakness. He had suspected it was too much for one person to bear, yet he told her all the same, hoping to tie her to himself. But now he was the one who could not bear it, and the ties between them felt like bindings against which he struggled.

"I trusted you." It was an accusation, as much toward himself as her. Stupid, to trust so much and so soon.

"And I was grateful for that trust. I always have been."

"But you did not repay it."

"No." The word fell heavily into the silent room and rippled for long seconds. "No. I regret that very much. When I admitted I was afraid of losing you, I was telling you a deeper truth than you knew."

Oh, his ribs would surely crack if his heart thudded with any more force. For his sake, she had lied. For want of him, she had lied. She meant well—but. She. Had. Lied.

"I don't know who you are. Who you ever were."

Frances shook her head. "You know me better than you ever realized. You have seen letters written from my very heart."

"Heart. Ha." He turned his head away to stare at the hunting scene again. Red coats and snug trousers. Guns and horses. Bright, glossy. Gentlemen playing at war.

"Henry, that heart seemed real enough to you when you thought the letters were from Caroline. You all but told me once that you would never have stayed in London if she had not asked you."

There was a snip in her voice now, a chill to the words. She was getting annoyed. Apologize and be apologized to in return; she must have thought it that simple.

Well, Henry wasn't going to let Frances wriggle out of the situation; he'd show her no more quarter than he'd given Wadsworth earlier that day. They thought they knew his limits. They thought they could bend him, even break him. Wrong.

It was dim in the room, fast-darkening outside. He prowled around the edges of the room, making his way by feeling. Running fingers over the filigree of plasterwork, the frames of paintings, the molding of the dado. These were the contours of London life. For the first time, they felt fussy and alien under his touch.

He stalked to a carved giltwood chair. Its legs lurched and stuck in the thick carpet pile as he shoved the chair closer to the sofa on which Frances was seated.

Her brows lifted in surprise when he sat down, not in the chair, but on the floor in front of it. It slid as he rested against its fragile frame, and he tensed, catching his weight on his good arm.

"Tell me, madam," he said lightly, already feeling clearer-headed. "Something changed in you this morning, and you seemed to feel shame. Was it after I told you the truth of what happened to my arm, or only after you saw it, that you felt the full measure of scorn for me?"

She batted his question aside with a wave of her hand, as if it were an annoying insect. "Don't be an idiot, Henry. This has nothing to do with your arm, and I never scorned you. What shame I felt was only for myself because I knew I owed you more truth than I'd given you."

"A sudden attack of conscience? How delightful for you. And just what truths do you owe me? Should I expect more surprises?"

Her slippered feet pulled back as if seeking protection under the hem of her gown. "You should if it surprises you to hear a few facts. Namely, I cannot undo my life. Not the choices I made ten years ago, nor the ones I've made since meeting you."

"That is all obvious," Henry said. "You're not telling me anything of real worth."

She gave a little sigh. "All right, then what of this? I lost everything once before. If I lose you now, I know I can bear it. But I would prefer not to. Is that plain enough for you?"

He shook his head. *She* did not understand. She had helped him skate over the surface of society for a while. But he had given her something much deeper.

"Tell me, Henry," went on Frances's relentless voice, seemingly from far away. "Did you ever care for me, even a little? Or was I always a happenstance? Was it a relief to salve your pride with a woman who was desperate for you?"

He stared at her, stunned at the gall of her questions. She had warned him at their first meeting that she could be terrifying. Her frankness was as terrible a weapon as her unforgiving recall.

This—much more than learning she wrote Caro's letters—made him feel as if she had stood at his side only to pierce his heart more easily.

The silence stretched long and brittle as a strand of glass. "Well. There's my answer, I suppose," Frances said at last.

"No, it's not. You are not permitted to think yourself wronged by me," Henry said sharply. "I've never done anything I thought might wound you."

Except use you to court another woman.

Oh, damn it.

He shook feeling into his legs and lifted himself into the dainty chair he'd been trying to lean against. There. He was face to face with Frances. Her gaze followed him as he rose, wondering what he would do.

He did not know. It was harder to be face to face

with himself. He needed no glass for it, only courage in the twilight.

Were kind lies worse than unkind truths? He had begun with the hope of Caro, the woman everyone wanted. He wanted the triumph of it. Frances had been a means to an end.

In truth, Caro had been a means to an end too: the respect he wanted, the ease he sought. Instead, he'd found them in Frances, and he'd found the beginnings in himself.

But if he and Frances had built their relationship on a foundation of sand, nothing had remained safe. Not even himself. So how could he ever find his way home?

He could not ask Frances any more than himself. Neither of them had the answers.

"Yet you are willing to wound yourself. Even die," she said after a long silence. "The Henry I thought I knew was painfully aware of the value of life."

"If I don't risk this, my life won't be worth living." He sounded pompous even to his own ears, yet it was not untrue.

"Not everything must balance on a single knife blade, Henry," she pleaded. "You needn't duel to prove I didn't hurt your pride. Life is worth more than honor."

"I'm not dueling for you," he said. He pushed himself to his feet with a swiftness that made Frances blink.

"Oh. No." She seemed to sag as she looked up at him. "No, I know that."

She drew in a halting breath, as though it was an effort. "I hope you will allow yourself to understand my intention. And I hope you won't duel." She turned her head away from him.

Stark lamplight limned her profile: the straight line of her nose, its rounded end. Her high forehead and arching brow. Her jaw set, and her mouth inflexible.

No. Her mouth was quivering at the corner.

He wanted to sigh, to stroke his thumb over the indentation at the corner of her mouth. To tell her he didn't *know*, he didn't understand what it all meant. What it would mean if he forgave her. If he could forgive himself for being a fool.

But he had a duel at dawn. That much he understood. So he inclined his head in a silent farewell and left her, and they were both alone again.

He stepped out onto a street that was silent under a brown sky.

Just brown. Dull and ashy, from nighttime and coal dust. No artist's pigments came to mind. Nothing exotic, nothing pleasurable to look on. It seemed all the color had bled from the world tonight.

He pulled himself up straight and wrapped the tattered shreds of his pride around him like a cloak. It was all he had left, much good might it do him.

∞

After Henry left, Frances collapsed back on the sofa and allowed tears to leak from her eyes for precisely two minutes. Then she shut them off and dried her face.

She'd cared enough to lie to him. It would take more than that—all her courage, even *love*—to give him the truth he deserved.

And she did love him. The idea of losing him

was so painful as to convince her of that. She'd been tumbling inevitably down that slope since the night of Lady Applewood's ball, when he'd first sat next to her and asked for her help. It was irresistible, to be sought and needed. And he had been irresistible as well. If he hadn't so much dignity and pride, she wouldn't love him so well.

Oh, this curse of love.

For love, she would tell him all her secrets. For love, she would admit her failings. She would do this to help him understand her, even knowing that it might kill his regard for her.

If he lived through the duel, he deserved the chance to decide for himself. He'd already given her that chance.

She pressed her fingers against her eyes for a long moment. Then she stood, picked up a lamp, and carried it to the writing desk at which she so often worked.

It was likely that he would live. Most duels were settled bloodlessly, with a symbolic shot into the ground. But she couldn't be sure; both Henry and Wadsworth were in deadly earnest about proving their honor.

All she could do was wait, and write, and hope that the truth would help Henry find her again someday.

She pulled paper, pen, and inkwell close to her. Tapping the quill on the blank sheet, she thought for a minute, then plunged in. She wrote for hours, her hand traveling over page after page, until her fingers ached from holding the pen and her eyes felt crammed with sand.

When she finished, she signed the letter, at last, with her own name.

By that time, the sun was already clawing faint

scratches in the night sky. Frances found a tired-eyed maid just beginning her morning rounds. She had a footman woken, had the letter taken to Tallant House.

She did not know if it would arrive soon enough to reach Henry before the duel. Or if he would read it. Or if it would make any difference.

For that, it might have been too late before she wrote a single word.

Twenty-Three

THE BLACKNESS JUST BEFORE DAWN WAS A BEAUTIFUL time of day.

This in-between time lingered only a sliver of an hour, yet Henry knew it well from his years in the army, from early rising to ready for battle or siege, or simply preparing for another long slogging march. It was a time of exhaustion, when it seemed the night would never end. But it was a time of promise too, just before everything changed, before the sun washed away the darkness and made the impossible seem possible. This darkness felt different from that of the grimy night.

Chalk Farm was stark and silent in the dim. Henry was unfamiliar with the field at the edge of Town, but Jem had assured him that Wadsworth chose the location well. More isolated than Hyde Park, it was deserted at this hour. Not even animals lowed. Only a breeze whispered through the chilly damp.

As Henry stepped out of Jem's carriage, he could vaguely make out the shapes of trees studding the field, of men with covered lanterns milling around. He'd been sure he would beat Wadsworth to the dueling ground, but he had underestimated the viscount's courage.

He wouldn't do so again.

His boots rustled through the grass, eating up distance with great speed. He was ready. More than ready. A little *too* ready. A cool head was a necessary asset during battle, but Henry had too little sleep and too much to prove to feel cool-headed right now.

A hand seized his arm, jerking him to a halt in midstep.

Jem, of course. Henry squinted at his brother in the faint light cast by Jem's carriage lanterns. "What? Let's get started. Everyone else is already here."

Jem's head turned in the direction of the shadowy figures beneath the trees, but there was not enough light for Henry to see his expression. "Hal. Please think again. Reconsider this duel. If you would only apologize to Wadsworth, we could settle this whole affair and neither one of you need risk your life."

Henry shook his arm free. "I'm not going to apologize."

Jem sighed. "Hal, you must see reason. You could be killed. Wadsworth will shoot you—or even if he doesn't, you won't be able to fire back at him without your right hand."

"You should have more faith in your own brother, Jem. Perhaps I'll shoot him instead." A jittery bubble of mirth rose up in his chest and tried to force its way out.

"No. No, you mustn't do that. I don't much like the man, Hal. But please, think of the scandal of it. The coroner. I might be tried along with you, you know, if he dies. For my sake, reconsider, if not for your own." Jem's voice grew quieter as he spoke. "For my sake, Hal. Don't do this. Please. Don't do this to yourself."

Jem turned his face back to Henry, and the glow from the carriage lanterns etched deep lines in his face. He looked as though he had lost all hope.

Henry was breaking his unbreakable brother. The look on Jem's face, more than anything else Henry had seen or thought in the last twenty-four hours, shamed him.

And that was a day that included a failed attempt to seduce Frances, a botched proposal, his public argument with Wadsworth, his challenge to a duel, and the revelation about the letters. Frances's trickery. The betrayal of his trust. The betrayal of… himself, really.

It was a day that had unmade Henry in every way, but not until this moment had he felt himself crumble.

He and Jem were separated by nearly a decade, by a title, by years apart. By temperament. By certainty. Jem was certain Henry was going to die or be disgraced, and he was certain there was nothing he could do about it. And he could not bear it.

It was a brother's love, pure and simple, and as painful and fruitless as any other type of love.

Henry could not please his brother now. He had meant what he had said to Jem the day before; he was doing this for himself. If he backed down now, he would know that he had failed himself: that he could not let the war end, and that the French would never stop defeating him, and he would never truly come home. He could not let that happen.

It was fitting, somehow, that one last battle would allow him to begin a life of peace.

Besides, he had weapons Jem knew not of. He had stayed awake for long hours after leaving Frances the night before. He had taken a full inventory of himself. He knew exactly what was in his possession now and what was not.

"Trust me, Jem." He offered his brother a smile, but he did not know if the faint sun-red beginning to creep over the horizon revealed his face to his brother.

Trust me. It was all he wanted. All he asked of those he loved.

He suppressed the thought. Time enough to think of that later. Of Frances. Caro. The snarl of his life. He would comb it out smooth this morning or simply cut the Gordian knot.

"Very well," Jem said after a long pause. Abruptly, he strode toward the trees and the waiting opponents, and Henry followed, falling into step at his side.

As they walked, Jem recited the procedure in a flat voice. "Lord Carlson is serving as Wadsworth's second, and he and I have worked out the terms. You will duel with pistols, as you know. Carlson is bringing a set. You will step out twenty paces, turn, and fire. Because you issued the challenge, Wadsworth will fire first. I was able to persuade him down to one shot for each of you. Carlson has arranged for a surgeon to be present." Jem halted once more. "It will all be done as quickly as possible. I thought that might be easiest."

For most of them, it might. But to Henry it mattered not at all. He was beginning to feel quite calm. His jumpiness, his too-eagerness, was smothered under sharp awareness as the moment for action drew near. It was as if the slowly brightening sky was sinking into him, burning off everything but the present moment as surely as it sipped the dew from the grass.

"Don't worry about me, Jem," Henry said as they began to walk again. "Wadsworth might not find this as easy as he expects. Which makes it all the easier for me."

He could see the grass beneath his feet now, still shadowed black under the faintly red light of the peeping sun. Dark as atramentum, ruddy as dragon's blood. All the beauty of art was before him again this morning. Henry did not know whether it would turn still lovelier or if it would all turn ugly.

It was time for something to turn, either way.

It seemed only a second before his feet brought him to the three men who stood beneath the sheltering trees in the field. Wadsworth, pale but composed. Carlson, a stout young lord whom Henry knew only slightly, held a rectangular walnut pistol case with all the pomp of a man proud of what has been entrusted to him. The thin man standing to one side, clutching his hat in one hand and a leather instrument bag in the other, was surely the surgeon.

"Good morning," said Henry in the most jovial tone he could manage.

"Save your greetings, Middlebrook," said Wadsworth. "The only thing I want from you is an apology."

"You shan't get it," said Henry. "Even if you offer one first." He smiled beatifically. "Lord Carlson. Always a pleasure."

Wadsworth swung an arm in a sharp gesture of impatience and turned away, pacing in a line of five steps, back and forth.

"There is no reasoning with my brother," Jem said with exasperated apology. "I assure you I've tried. Let's get this done quickly. May I see the pistols, Carlson?"

The lord nodded and opened the case. "As you see, Tallant. There are seconds' pistols as well."

Jem blinked. "Ah… I'm sure we won't be needing those, Carlson. Hal? Care to take a look?"

Henry peered into the case. They were lovely weapons. Gentlemen's toys, all glossy walnut stock and smooth steel bore, with engraved trigger guards.

"They'll do. See to their loading, please, Jem." Henry noted how Carlson's eyes narrowed and swept over his right arm. Henry could not hold the pistol, pour in powder from a horn, and add shot. That took two hands. But loading the pistol was not the object of the duel.

Henry watched Wadsworth pace back and forth, back and forth, as Carlson and Jem prepared the small guns. By now, Wadsworth had surely paced off a furlong. He probably wanted to walk away; only his pride was holding him here.

Damned pride. Henry felt a flash of unwilling affinity.

He walked over to Wadsworth and stood in his path. The viscount immediately stopped stalking back and forth. His foxy face went up, as if he'd scented something that startled him.

"It's difficult, isn't it?" Henry offered.

"What?" Wadsworth looked suspicious.

"The waiting."

Wadsworth's mouth tightened. "I can handle it. See to yourself if you're so worried. I don't know how you'll shoot without the use of your right arm."

A cornered animal again. "Your concern is most edifying. I, however, am more concerned for you."

Wadsworth turned on his heel and resumed pacing his path. Five steps away from the trees, five steps back. His shoulders were held too high, almost hunched, and he avoided looking at Henry.

"I'm no pheasant, you know, Wadsworth. No partridge. No fox. Have you ever pointed a gun at a human being before?"

A slight hitch in the viscount's stride, but he made no reply.

Henry continued in a conversational tone. "War hands glory to few but gives almost everyone the chance to handle a weapon. I've pointed a gun at many a man before, though never on the dueling field. I imagine it's much the same, though, don't you think? The weapons may be prettier, but the act is not."

Wadsworth was pacing back to the tree now. His gray eyes flicked to Henry's. In the slow red light, his face looked flushed. "How do you mean, Middlebrook?"

Henry shrugged. "No matter how many statements of honor you wrap it in, it's still life and death. It's an ugly thing to risk."

"Yet you are determined to risk it." Wadsworth's chin tilted down and to the side. His eyes roved over Henry's face. Hunting. Always hunting. Looking for weaknesses.

"I have nothing else to risk. It's time." Henry drew a breath. "I am not sorry for my challenge. But I'm sorry that it was necessary. For both our sakes."

There, Jem. It was almost an apology. That was the best he could do.

Wadsworth narrowed his eyes. "You're a cur, Middlebrook."

Henry turned away, took a pistol from his brother. "Then you must do your best to shoot me down like a dog."

He faced Wadsworth one more time, holding the pistol lightly in his left hand. "It's not as easy as you think, Wadsworth. To shoot a man or lance him or bayonet him. To see his blood pour out and know you're the one who stole his life away."

He raised his eyebrows as the viscount's mouth grew taut. "But I suppose you have your own version of such an injury," he said in a voice as low as a lullaby. "You know how to bleed someone dry with words as surely as a bullet could. It just takes a bit longer. Less so, of course, if you choose only the weak. But perhaps you do not always know who the weak truly are."

Henry turned his head to the lanky surgeon, who stood nearby. Hat discarded on the ground, he gripped his bag of instruments in white-knuckled hands. "Do you know how to remove a bullet, Dr.—?"

"Smythe. Yes, sir, I do, should that be necessary." Henry had expected the tall man's voice to be reedy and quavering, but he spoke with quiet dignity. A good choice for a duel.

"Would you say a bullet wound is more painful than a dislocation, or less so? I have suffered one but not the other."

"I'm told a bullet wound is very painful, sir, though the severity of the wound depends on the location. A dislocation can be just as painful, though as you know, it is not fatal."

"Not usually," Henry said. "Well, I suppose it does

not matter. Wadsworth, you look a bit overset. Are you taking ill?"

The viscount had been passing his pistol gingerly from hand to hand. He stilled, scowled. "I'm fine. Are you finished with your stalling?"

Henry bobbed his head. "Take your weapon to hand, Wadsworth. I am ready when you are."

With a nod from the seconds, they saluted, turned, and paced off the distance. Twenty steps each, a matter of only fifteen seconds or so.

Henry pivoted and waited for Wadsworth to take the first shot.

He could see no more than a silhouette in the reddish light. The man had decent form; Henry granted him that. He turned sideways; his right arm and hand rose in a straight line, disappearing against the shadow of his body. Hidden within that shadow was a gun. Wadsworth could fire it at the ground or send a bullet into Henry's heart. All Henry could do was stand there, a target, waiting.

This is stupid. The idea flashed suddenly into Henry's head. *Stupid, stupid.*

Not stupid to stand up for himself; that was one of the brightest things he'd done lately. No, he'd been stupid to let it escalate to the point of life and death. Stupid to think he needed to win over all of London when winning one worthy heart was enough.

How stupid of Wadsworth too, to fight when he did not need to.

The shadow-Wadsworth was taking forever to fire. Henry saw the silhouette of his arm waggle, shake free from the line of his body. At last he pulled the trigger, and the shot went staggeringly wide, the bullet burying itself in the trunk of a tree ten yards away from Henry.

Done, then. It was done.

Henry wanted to jump, cry out, shake Jem's hand.

But he still had his part to get through. There was only one performance of this show, and it must be quite theatrical if it was to have the desired effect.

He took his stance, pivoted to the side. His left arm stretched out straight and true. His arm, the gun, the form of the shadow-Wadsworth, were all in a perfect line. His hand did not shake as he aimed.

And then he wheeled, and in one swift motion he took sight and fired at the same tree Wadsworth had hit.

Smoke rose like a faint morning mist, and a flutter of applause signaled that the seconds considered the duel at an end. The surgeon would not be needed; nor would the seconds' pistols.

Henry tramped the forty paces to Wadsworth and stood at his side. "That was not a bad shot," he said. "We ought to be within a few inches of one another. Unfortunate for the tree, but I'm sure it'll survive this morning's work."

The viscount gaped, quick breaths hitching his chest. "How…"

"If you are satisfied this morning, I am," Henry added calmly.

"You… your arm…" Wadsworth reached for Henry's coat sleeve, then drew his hand back as if singed.

"You see, Wadsworth, that I can defend myself. I always will. But I would much rather sleep in of a morning than come back to Chalk Farm. Wouldn't you?"

The man looked at the gun in his own hand, then in Henry's. His cool eyes narrowed, and his mouth twitched. "Indeed."

With a curt nod, Henry walked away. He heard grass rustling a few seconds later and knew Wadsworth was trailing a few yards behind him.

His ears were open to every sound—the high buzzing call of a starling, the crackle of a breeze blowing the drying green leaves of late summer. The sky was the color of mosaic gold and ruby-clear realgar.

The air smelled faintly of powder, but the scent did not tighten his chest, pull him back in talons to the Bossu Wood. It was just a smell. Less pleasant than, say, vanilla. More pleasant than the filthy streets of Whitechapel. It was… fine.

But the world was more than that. It was *fine*. Not in the sense of acceptable. In the sense of excellent. It was a *fine* morning.

He met Jem under the tree he and Wadsworth had shot. Poor tree. It had performed a good service.

Jem poked his forefinger into a hole in the bark. "Not three inches between your bullets," he said in a wondering voice.

Henry handed him the pistol. "Thank you for being my second, Jem. It means more to me than I can ever tell you."

"You could try to tell me a few things," Jem said. "For one, how did you make that shot? Was it luck?"

"No."

Jem darted a sideways glance at him. "How'd you do it, Hal? I was sure you'd be killed."

Henry couldn't blame his brother for his lack of

confidence. He'd never told Jem the truth, though it was simple. "I may not have known how to write or paint with my left hand when I came back to London, but I knew how to shoot with it."

Jem was still staring at him, agog, as if Henry had asked him for help trimming a bonnet.

Henry grinned. "There's no call to practice art or penmanship during war, but a man never knows when he'll be in a tight corner and will need to fire well with both hands. I simply practiced. I practiced a long time ago."

He patted Jem on the shoulder, prodding him into a march toward Carlson and the waiting pistol case. Jem's blue eyes were narrowed for once, not wide, and he seemed to be searching Henry's countenance in the brightening dawn.

"Well done, Hal," he said. "Well done. If you had to have a duel, this was the way to do it. I oughtn't to say I'm proud of you, of course. Not for dueling."

"Of course."

Jem sighed. "Oh, Hal. It was hell, wasn't it? The war, I mean. I hated seeing you with a gun in your hand this morning, but you must have had one in your hand every morning for years. I just didn't see it happen. I didn't realize what it meant."

"It's all right, Jem."

"No, it's not." Jem shook his head, squinting into the distance. "If I'd been a better brother to you, it would never have come to this point."

Henry put his hand on his brother's arm, stopped him. "Jem. It was never your fault I had a gun in my hand."

Jem twisted away, shaking his head. Henry tried again. "Jem. Listen to me. I know you think you control the world, but you don't."

Jem's eyes flew wide and startled. He stared at Henry. Uncertain.

And then he laughed.

Shakily at first, then strong enough to bring a smile to Henry's face and allow him to continue. "None of it was ever your fault, Jem. I did what I thought best, and you were the best brother imaginable for letting me go against your will. You could have prevented me, you know. You're wealthy and influential. Instead, you let me make my own way."

It had taken Henry a while, but he'd finally done it. The whole of his experience as a soldier could not, should not, be reduced to one day, one arm, one failure. For three years, he had done his best to be a good soldier, a good leader. He'd tried all his life to be a good man.

Quatre Bras had been a disaster. But he would not allow anyone to blame him for it again. He had already blamed himself enough.

It was done.

He chuckled, the sound surprising him. "I suppose that's worth an arm, after all."

"What will you do now?" Jem asked. "Are you going to leave London for Winter Cottage?"

"I don't know," Henry said.

That was fact: he *didn't* know. He had finished one battle this morning. He'd conquered many demons. Hell, he'd even reassured his brother, who had never been in need of reassurance in Henry's memory.

But he'd left carnage behind him last night—a brutal fight with Frances—and he did not know if the wounds they'd inflicted could be healed.

For now, though, the sun was up, and the air was sweet in his lungs.

For now, it was enough.

Twenty-Four

HENRY CAME HOME TO A STACK OF LETTERS HIGHER than his fist.

Sowerberry handed over the sheaf of correspondence with a sniff, telling Henry the notes had been piling up since dawn.

Henry had not realized the City awoke so early, but London was a gossipy village that just happened to have hundreds of thousands of inhabitants. There were invitations to breakfasts, Sowerberry said. Calls. Boxing, fencing, riding, hunting. All manner of manly sports.

It seemed it took a duel—one of the worst trespasses against mannerly society—to bring Henry back fully into its fold.

There was no letter on heavy paper sealed with red wax, though. Henry shuffled the notes twice to check.

Well. Why should there be?

Next to Henry, Jem yawned. "Anything for breakfast yet, Sowerberry? I could do with a pot of tea. No, chocolate."

"My lord, her ladyship has requested that you attend her at once upon your return."

Almost before the butler could finish his sentence, Emily pounded down the stairs and threw herself into her husband's arms. "Jemmy, Jemmy, thank God you're safe."

Her auburn hair was tumbled down her back, and she was engulfed from neck to ankles in a quilted dressing gown of Jem's. It was frayed at the hem, and there were damp spots on one sleeve that looked like stains from tears hastily wiped away.

She looked frightful. Henry had never seen her so... undone.

Poor Emily, waiting at home this morning. Hoping for the return of both brothers, fearing only one might come back, or none.

Poor Emily. It was probably the first time in the decade he'd known her that Henry had thought that phrase. It was certainly the first time he'd seen her look frightful.

Jem patted his wife's back with a tentative hand. "Now, now, Em. We're fine. Everybody's just fine."

"I was sure you would both be shot." She took a deep breath, straightened, and smoothed Jem's coat where her embrace had wrinkled the fabric. "You haven't killed Wadsworth, have you?"

"Nobody got killed this morning. Except possibly a tree," Henry said.

"Good." Emily took a deep breath, nodding. "That's good."

Then she spun to face Henry, glaring. Once, twice, she struck him hard in the chest. "You *idiot*. You damned, foolish, stupid, careless—"

Jem's head snapped back. "I say, Em. Such language."

"—ballroom-leaving, card-cheating, paintbrush-dropping *idiot*." The invective poured out of her in one breath. She struck Henry again before pulling him into a hug that crushed the breath from his body.

"I'm glad to see you too, Emily," Henry said with the scrap of air left to him.

She sniffled as she pulled away, her eyes red. "I was so worried, Hal. I didn't want to say anything to the boys last night. I just prayed you'd both be home safe this morning." She folded her arms tight across her chest and shrugged. "So, now I can get angry in peace. But I suppose you might as well have some breakfast while I yell at you."

"That hardly sounds conducive to digestion," Henry said with a smile. It didn't bother him at all. Not the hitting, not the cursing, not the threats of more yelling. He understood the hidden meaning there. It all meant *I love you*, as surely as Jem had when he had begged Henry not to duel.

Every time they called him Hal, they told him so. *I love you.*

How could he repay the constancy of his family? He'd tried to make amends to Jem this morning, but how could he make amends to Emily?

He'd start with an apology. Henry caught her on one shoulder as they filed in to breakfast, his fingers snarling, clumsy, in her tangled hair. "I'm sorry, Emily. The waiting must have been awful."

She looked up at him, blinking with a force that belied the dryness of her eyes. "It was. But I'm sure you didn't have the best morning of your life, either."

"I don't know." Henry considered. "I might have,

at that." Emily narrowed her eyes, and he shrugged. "Hit me again if you need to. I'm sure I deserve it."

"You do. But I'll save it till you've got a few kippers in you."

Her hands whisked down the length of her borrowed dressing gown, and a look of chagrin crossed her face. "I suppose I ought to get dressed first. The food's ready, though. I had it laid out not half an hour ago."

"You look lovely, Em," Jem said. He kissed his wife on the nose, then moved to the sideboard and began lifting dish covers. "Even wearing my dressing gown. You're the loveliest thing I've seen all day, and I've already been up for a couple of hours."

Emily laughed shakily. "Since you've only seen a passel of men, Jemmy, that's not much of a compliment."

"Sure it is." Jem began serving eggs onto a plate. "I saw Hal duel and not get himself killed. That's something."

Behind Jem's back, Henry's eyes found Emily's. She offered him a watery smile as Jem talked on, heedless of the compliment he'd just paid both his wife and brother.

"Gad, you can't believe how he can shoot. Em, it was amazing. He just waited, cool as any of Gunter's ices, then took his shot. Deloped, really. Hal, I don't think Wadsworth will ever be the same. Nor the tree, for that matter."

He chuckled, turning with his filled plate. "Oh. But I'm not proud of you. Not for dueling."

"Of course not," Henry and Emily said in unison. *Proud*, Jem kept saying. It didn't matter that it was prefaced with the word "not." Henry could tell what he meant. Jem never was good at hiding his feelings, even behind disclaiming words.

This type of pride was very different from the precarious feeling that had hacked at Henry's peace of mind since he returned to London. There was *pride*, and there was *proud of*. He'd had a bitter surfeit of the former. The latter was sweet, much more to his taste.

Jem seated himself, but before he could draw in his chair, Emily perched on his lap. Jem's light eyes flew wide open. "I say, Em. Ah… are you all right?"

She laid her head on her husband's shoulder. "Not yet," she said, tugging at his lapels. "But I will be. Now tell me everything that happened. And if you leave anything out, I'll rub bacon grease all over your coat."

Jem needed no further encouragement to begin, forking up eggs with his right hand as his left held his wife tight. After a few seconds, Henry began to feel distinctly superfluous.

It wasn't that he was embarrassed watching Jem and Emily cuddle and talk; it was comforting to know that a husband and wife could still care for each other so much after ten years of marriage. No, it was more as though his part was over. He'd played it this morning at Chalk Farm. For an encore, he'd allowed Emily to batter him, and he'd given her an apology.

And now there was nothing to do but leave the stage. Perhaps he *had* better go to Winter Cottage. There would be no shame in it now. It might even be peaceful.

But regret twanged through him. All the letters that had poured in this morning, just because Henry had acted like a damned fool—or maybe like a man who'd come to his senses after long insanity. It was a small comfort to know that he could move easily through polite society again.

Only a small comfort, though. The letter he most wanted he had not received. And the woman who might have written it didn't exist.

No sense in filling a plate with unwanted food, listening to Jem hash over the morning. Henry had little appetite for any of it.

He started to move toward the door of the dining room, but Emily called him back.

"Wait, Hal." She patted at the bulky dressing gown, finding a pocket and pulling forth a folded square of paper.

As she held it out, Henry's fingers began to tingle. He felt more shaky and uncertain than he had when waiting for Wadsworth to take his shot.

"This came by runner this morning, just like all the other letters. It arrived about a quarter hour after you left." Her mouth curved, her smile knowing but tired. "I set it aside. This one's special."

Henry reached across the burnished wood table and took the square. There was no seal on the wax; it was just a heavy blob of red.

He knew who it was from, though. He knew from the feel of the paper, the heft of the letter in his hand. Even before he cracked the seal, he knew.

What it said, though, he could not imagine.

Only one way to find out. "Excuse me," he said, and hurried up to his bedchamber as if carrying a forbidden treasure.

The letter was thick, several sheets folded together.

Page after page of Caro's heavy paper. Line after line in Frances's hand. She'd falsified its form, he realized, when she showed him her handwriting during their writing lesson. She'd hidden her true self, but here it was.

He took a deep breath and found a chair. None of this sitting on the ground nonsense.

And he read his letter.

Twenty-Five

Dear Henry,

If you're reading this, you are alive, and you aren't so angry with me that you threw the letter in the fire at once. I suppose that's a reasonable starting point.

I regret the way we parted earlier, though it was probably inevitable. I delayed so long in telling you the truth about the letters—my letters—because I knew you would be disappointed.

And you might still be, after you read this letter, but you deserve to know everything about my past. First, because it returns the favor of your confidence in kind; second, because I hope it will help you understand why I wrote you the first letter, and why I kept sending more though I knew you thought them from Caroline.

I was the much-loved only child of a Sussex baronet. As you know, Caroline is my cousin. She is the daughter of my father's younger brother, a clergyman who held a prosperous living a half-day's drive away from my father's home. As we grew up,

I was the privileged one, with a rich dowry, though Caroline's beauty was always thought to be dowry in itself—dazzling enough for the clergyman's daughter to have a season of her own. But I was the one on whom my parents pinned the hopes of a good match. I was to advance us all.

This seemed a pleasant enough fate to me when I was young, and so I passed my weeks and months and years in cursory good works, waiting to turn nineteen and travel to London for my season. Because my damnable memory ensures that I always have dates and names at ready recall, I often gave lessons to children in the nearby village; at least, I did so when it suited me. I really do enjoy teaching, as you know, because it allows me to be right and to give advice. An irresistible combination.

In the course of one of my lessons—a botanical walk—I first crossed the path of Charles Whittier, the son of the local public house's owner. Charles was the handsomest man I'd ever seen, and I was fascinated by him at once. To catch his interest, I came to the village every day, walking past the Red Lion time and again, fabricating errands, taking on more pupils, hoping to impress him with my goodness and intelligence.

I needn't have tried so hard. He was ready enough to be impressed by the baronet's daughter. He must have thought I would be the making of him. And I was delighted to be needed—to be his savior, his everything. Since I knew my parents would never approve of my meeting Charles, much less pursuing him, we made arrangements to meet in secret. This allowed things to go farther than they might have otherwise. A parent's watchful eye does tend to slow the progress of a courtship.

I promised to marry him as soon as we were both of age. Under the terms of my parents' marriage settlement, I would have a dowry of twelve thousand pounds, enough to live modestly for a lifetime if we were careful. But Charles was not careful; he began borrowing against the expectation of it. Soon, everyone in the village was talking of the misalliance.

My father was livid when word reached his ears. He forbade me to see Charles again. So I told him it was possible that I was with child. This was not exactly a lie, though it was a trick. I did not truly think I was; in fact, I have never conceived and may be unable to. But it was possible, as I told my father. Anything under the sun is possible.

I can remember, even now, the look of horror on my father's face. He had never expected his only child to trespass against him. He told me I must go to London and catch a husband quickly, so that the truth might be concealed. If I were unable, I would return to the country and he would permit me to marry Charles by license. But he refused to turn over my dowry to, as he said, "such an upstart" as a workingman.

Now I learned something new from him: my dowry was contingent upon my marrying with my parents' permission. If I married against their wishes, the money would not be paid. This was a heavy blow, for on this sum I had pinned all the hopes and plans for my future life.

My father looked almost pleased as he rendered his verdict. I realize now, he was doing what he considered best. He must have hoped to bring me back to what he thought sense, but I was at least as stubborn as he, and much more devious. I told Charles only that my father agreed to let us marry by license. So you see, on my father, I played a trick. To Charles, I withheld a piece of the truth—as I did to you. I suppose there's no real difference between those and lies, except one of philology.

I did go to London for a while, and I loved the novelty of high society, the dances and colors and wealth. But I did not want to be courted, since I had left my heart at home.

"I'm not Honorable like you are, my dear," Caroline always teased me about my courtesy title. *But Caroline was honorable enough to fulfill our family's purpose in London. She made a brilliant match with an elderly earl. And once she married, I came home to Charles.*

When it became clear there was no babe on the way, my parents forbade me to see Charles. Perhaps they hoped eventually to marry me to some reclusive gentleman who would not ask too many questions about his wife's character. But I was stubborn. I kept meeting Charles in secret, and since he continued borrowing against his expectations, I never told him the truth about my dowry. I suspected, even then, that he loved my position at least as well as he loved me.

When he turned twenty-one, a few months after me, we were married. Soon enough, he figured out the truth about our financial situation. So did his creditors. Charles might, perhaps, have sued my father to try to recover the dowry on some niggling legal ground—but, of course, without the dowry, we had not the resources to take on a baronet.

It didn't matter to me; I didn't care for the money. I was too much in love to be anything but selfish. I would do nothing to risk losing Charles; yet I miscalculated and lost him all the same. When my dowry vanished, he did not love me enough to stay when Frances was all I could give him. I do not know if he would have married me, knowing the truth. But when he learned it, and learned that I had withheld it from him, our marriage was struck a mortal blow.

My parents refused to see us. Charles and I moved away to start a new life in a town where no one knew us, but there was never enough to live on. When the War of the Fifth Coalition began in 1809, a recruiting party came to our village, beating the drum for volunteers. They paid a small bounty to any man who enlisted. To Charles, the army seemed the solution to our problems. War held the promise of glory, of making something grand of himself. You know as well as I that the reality is much different. I talked to the recruiters. To soldiers' wives. To men who had come home from the war ill or injured. After doing so, I knew Charles would probably never come back to me. Still, I could not ask him to stay for my sake when he wanted so badly to go. It was my atonement.

There was no glory for him, of course. He died

ill and alone, far away on the Continent, and I thought I would die too from the sorrow of it. I felt guilty at first too, as if I had pushed him away to his fate. So deeply did I grieve him that it took me some months to realize how poor I was. But it was the same problem we had always had: there was not enough to live on. I began to sell off our possessions and take in sewing, but it was never enough.

This is when a letter came from Caroline. She took me into her home when my parents would not see me. She paid off my debts. She let me cry on the shoulder of her expensive silk gowns. I did not exaggerate when I said I owed her everything. She's the sister of my heart, always generous. Why, she even lent me her identity when I sent you letters and you wished them from her.

That's who I am, Henry: a devoted, devious fool for love.

Once again, I have done the wrong thing, but this time for the right reasons. I have been selfish in wanting to be with you, but I also wanted you to be happier. I wanted you to find again the things you had loved and thought lost. And when you began to, I was as delighted as if they were my own joys.

I've never lied to you except to keep you near—but you would never have stayed near if I had not lied. Do the ends justify the means? That is for you to decide, I suppose: whether what we have gained together is more than what you have lost.

I hope to see you again soon if you live and

forgive. Often, even, if you like—just as I told you in my first letter. My regard for you has always been true.

Please believe me to be,
Yours,
Frances

Twenty-Six

"FRANNIE, YOU MUST EAT SOMETHING." A HAND thrust a plate of watercress sandwiches into Frances's field of vision, covering the blank sheet of paper at which Frances had been staring for several hours.

Frances rubbed at her eyes. "Watercress? No. That's not even food."

The hand set down the plate. "Yes, it is," said Caroline's voice. "My callers eat these sandwiches every day. They positively gobble them down as if the bread is stuffed with ambrosia."

"That's because they're trying to impress you with their good manners." Frances lifted the plate from the top of her desk and tried to press it back into Caroline's hand.

"If they want to do *that*, they should eat a little less. But for your sake, I'm not at home to callers today. So you can eat the sandwiches instead."

Frances crossed her arms.

"That's all the response I am to get?" Caroline dropped into a crouch next to Frances's desk with a rustle of silk skirts. "Fine. I invoke my lofty rank and order you to choose between two options. You may eat something, or you may go to sleep. Or you could go have a bath. Three—three options. That's quite generous of me."

Frances stared at the blank paper as though a reply from Henry might materialize on it. She only had to concentrate hard enough, wish for it fervently enough. She was not sure she even remembered how to shut her eyes.

Caroline's fingers curled on the edge of the writing desk, and she rested her chin in her hands. "Frannnnie," she chanted.

All right, so Frances did remember how to shut her eyes. She covered them for good measure. "Stop it. Stop that lost-kitten face, Caroline. Stop."

"But I know you've been sitting here all night. One of the footmen told Millie."

Caroline sighed. "All right, uncover your eyes. The lost kitten is gone. I look perfectly blasé. But please, get up, Frannie. We can send for some newspapers, and we'll get all the scandal sheets this morning. Or I can send Pollitt to Boodle's to talk to the servants there. Someone will know what happened."

"Yes," Frances said. "But I'm afraid to find out."

Her joints felt numb from sitting in the same position for hours. The plate of uneaten sandwiches proved that this was far from a normal day, while the blank paper on the desk reminded her of the letter she'd sent.

As long as she sat at this desk, she was connected to him. As long as she stayed in this room, wore the clothes in which he'd last seen her, and did not learn the outcome of the duel. He would still be all right, as long as she didn't know he wasn't.

That was stupid, of course. Caroline was right. They might as well find out.

And she might as well stand up. She pushed back her chair, stretched, and realized she was sore in places she'd never noticed. The fronts of her shoulders. The base of her skull. The backs of her knees. And Lord, did she need a chamber pot.

"You look terrible," Caroline said helpfully.

"I ought to. I've given it a determined effort." Frances's elbows and knees popped as she shook out her skirts. She felt like the oldest woman in the world. "But it doesn't matter. Let's get those papers."

They had scarcely two minutes to wait before the lady's maid, Millie, scratched at the morning room door and entered with an armful of newsprint. "We've been out gathering these, my lady. Pollitt's just ironed them for you, but they don't have the news you'll be wanting. But *I* heard from John Coachman that *he* heard someone talking in the mews, and *they* said that they'd talked to a maid from Tallant House, and *she* said the duel's done finished already."

Caroline nodded her perfect understanding at this string of confidences. Thus did London's news circulate; thus did its gossiping heart beat. She shot a look at Frances as she accepted the newspapers from her lady's maid. "And? What happened?"

Frances couldn't speak a word. She just waited, rooted to the floor.

"Neither gentleman's been shot, my lady. And John Coachman says as he heard the earl's brother made a fine show of himself, for all that he's got only one arm what works proper."

Frances clutched at the back of her chair. She wouldn't sit down again; she'd break into pieces. But oh, thank God in heaven. Henry was safe. It was over.

"That's wonderful news, Millie. Thank you," Caroline said. "Here, take a watercress sandwich with you. Take one for John Coachman too."

Frances tightened her grip on the chair, not caring that she might split the fine old tapestry cover with her nails.

Henry might be feted all over the City this morning, but it was possible he'd gone back to Tallant House first. If he was, he'd have received her letter. Surely he would read it at once. Or he'd decide he didn't want to read it at all.

How long would she have to wait for an answer? Or how long before she knew silence was all she'd get as a reply?

Longer than she could wait in this room. She sighed. "Caroline, I'm going to have a bath."

Too many questions. Maybe hot water would wash them away.

❧

Caroline knocked while Frances was still soaking in the bathtub.

"Frannie?"

Frances's head jerked up, and she coughed and sputtered. She'd dozed off in the tub, and her chin had slid below the water's surface.

Excellent. While Henry survived a duel, Frances

would drown on a mouthful of stale, lukewarm bathwater. She rolled her eyes, lifted her hands. They looked soggy and wrinkled.

"Frannie, can I come in?" Caroline peeked in, then averted her eyes at once. "You are still in the bath? God heavens, Frannie, you'll turn into an old prune."

"At least I'm a clean prune."

"I suppose I ought to be pleased about that." Caroline rummaged through Frances's wardrobe and found a wrapper. She laid it out on the bed, carefully arranging and smoothing the garment with her back to the great copper tub. "Towel off and wrap up. A letter's been delivered for you."

Water splashed and flopped as Frances hoisted herself to a sitting position. With her back still turned, Caroline added, "It's not from him, Frannie. But you might as well come see. It's better than staying in the bath until you get as waterlogged as a dead fish."

"Old prune and dead fish. The absence of your suitors has inspired you with disgusting flights of creativity."

"Well, if you don't like it, you should come read your letter and let us both rejoin the social world."

With Millie's help, Frances was dried and dressed in less than ten minutes. Her hair fell loose down her back, leaving wet spots on her gown, but it was a sensible dark cotton day dress that wouldn't stain.

She found Caroline and the mysterious letter in the morning room. With a swift swipe of her thumb, she cracked the seal, eyes darting over the unfamiliar round handwriting in search of her correspondent's name.

Sir Bartlett; that is, Bart Crosby.

A letter for her, from Bart Crosby? How odd; he

was Caroline's admirer. Yet the letter was for Frances.
The salutation confirmed that.

> *Dear Mrs. Whittier,*
>
> *I thank you for standing as my friend during my
> calls on Lady Stratton.*
> *As you may know, I have a country estate,
> Beckworth, to which I customarily invite a party at
> the end of the season. I have recently learned that
> you are fond of country life.*
> *If you should ever take a fancy to escape the
> City, please know that you—and Lady Stratton,
> naturally—are always welcome at Beckworth. I
> plan to depart today, so if you wish to reply, you
> may direct your letter there.*
>
> *Yours truly,*
> *Sir Bartlett; that is, Bart Crosby.*

How distinctly odd. Decidedly strange. Indescribably
bizarre.

A letter from Bart Crosby.

The only person with whom Frances had recently
discussed country life was Henry. Had Henry told
Bart—and if so, to what purpose?

"What does it say?" Caroline asked, walking over
to peek at the paper in Frances's hand.

"Nothing much." Hastily, Frances folded it again
and pressed at the soft seal. Her own puzzled questions were enough to contend with; she didn't want
Caroline to start speculating as well.

Of course, when the second letter for Frances arrived only a few minutes later, Caroline could not help but speculate.

"Good heavens, Frannie. That looks like the Applewood seal. Can you think why they would be writing to you? I was sure we had behaved ourselves tolerably well at their ball a few weeks ago."

"I am sure we did." Frances's brows knit as she coaxed open this new seal. "They wouldn't care that you hit Lord Wadsworth with your fan. And I know we didn't spill lemonade on anyone."

"Then we behaved much better than Lady Applewood's eldest girl," Caroline said, but Frances was hardly listening.

> *Dear Mrs. Whittier,*
>
> *I am writing to ask you for a favor! Would you have guessed?*
> *At my recent ball, dear Lady Stratton told me you always make everything better and easier for her. I know there is only one of you!—but if you have a moment, I'd be delighted to have you pop over and advise me on some arrangements for our next ball. Someone with a fine memory and impeccable manners is just the sort of woman I want at hand. I hope to wrest Lady Stratton's receipt for lemon tarts from her clutches—and if I do, of course, we shall sample cakes and tarts aplenty.*
>
> *Kindest regards,*
> *Venetia Applewood*

"What does she want?" Caroline pressed. "Is it about spilled lemonade?"

"In a way," Frances said, handing her the letter. "It seems she wants a companion's aid. She offers cake as an incentive. Rather wise of her."

"Ah, this is my fault. I praised you to the heavens when I last spoke with her." Caroline looked self-conscious. "I might possibly have been feeling a bit envious of her elegant mansion, and I wanted to remind her that I had things she had not. Namely, the help of a Frannie."

"Ah. Well, you are very lucky in that regard. I can't deny that I'm a rare gem. Even Wadsworth once called me a jade."

Caroline ignored this mild attempt at humor and set the letter down carelessly on the edge of a table, from which it fluttered to the floor. The morning room was as untidy as Frances had ever seen it. Post and papers and periodicals littered the room; dried petals fallen from vases of wilting flowers were scattered over tabletops. Caroline had been warning the maids away for the past day—a negligence of great kindness.

"Frannie." Caroline drew a deep breath. "I did mean well, for both of you."

There was no sense in pretending not to understand. "I know. I meant well too. It doesn't matter, though. We'll be fine, just as we have for the past year in London. You can topple suitors like ninepins and throw roses in the privy."

Caroline's mouth pulled into an approximation of a smile, about as far from the real thing as an alleyway dolly-mop from a French courtesan. "It's a compelling picture. But I cannot really be as selfish as the world thinks me, because I've tried to give away my dearest friend in marriage."

Frances stifled a sigh and sank onto the sofa before remembering, *damn it*, this was the sofa on which everything had happened. The sex and the betrayals. It was a lot for one piece of furniture to hold up to.

She slid to the floor and leaned her head back onto the cushioned seat, studying the delicate plasterwork tracery of the room's ceiling. "I shan't marry again."

"Of *course* you won't." Out of the corner of her eye, Frances saw Caroline drop into a chair. The same one Henry had occupied the night before. "A man fought a duel for you, but he's not interested in marrying you."

"Men fight duels for stupid reasons all the time."

"True, but you are generally far from stupid. Besides, Wadsworth was not to be borne by anyone of good breeding. I was glad when Henry called him out. I ought to have done it myself, instead of throwing a vase at him."

"*You* threw the vase?" Frances's head snapped up.

"Certainly. You didn't think one of my puppies had done so, did you?"

"Yes, I did. I thought Wadsworth threw it after you refused him."

"Oh, no." Caroline studied the perfect pink and white moons of her fingernails. "I threw it at Wadsworth after he importuned me once too often. My aim was off, unfortunately."

Importuned. Frances snorted.

"It was a shame, for I liked that vase." Caroline pursed her lips. "Well, I don't suppose Wadsworth will be coming back, and that's worth the loss of a bit of porcelain. As for you—I cannot think of anything to counter my loss of you, even if it is for the happiest of reasons."

"Don't be silly, Caroline," Frances said. "I'm not going anywhere."

Before Frances could reply, Pollitt entered with a salver bearing another note.

"For me?" Caroline asked.

"For Mrs. Whittier." The butler bowed, holding forth the salver to Frances.

She thanked him and collected the note. "This is getting ridiculous."

At a glance, she could tell it was not from Henry. The writing was too clear and certain to have been scrawled by a right-handed man using his left hand.

Caroline seemed relieved to leave behind the heaviness of the previous minutes. "My goodness, Frannie. I haven't seen you get so much post in years."

"I haven't. Probably not in the past year put together." She slit the seal and glanced at the letter. "This one's from Lady Protheroe, inviting me to a small party tomorrow evening."

"Ah, excellent. I accepted last week before I realized she meant to keep the party small. I am glad she decided to include you."

"Why should she?"

Caroline drummed her nails on the giltwood arm of her chair. "You are notorious, my dear."

Frances snorted again. Words were wholly inadequate to capture the ludicrousness of that statement.

"You *are*," Caroline insisted. "Henry defended your honor in a *duel*. Now everyone wants a look at you."

"He did nothing of the kind. You know as well as I that the duel was not for my sake. Wadsworth simply provoked him beyond endurance." Frances drew her feet up, tucking herself into a ball.

"Ah, but you were standing at his side; he drew you in to the Fateful Encounter. I'm afraid the *ton* is not going to believe anything except that Henry is a man deeply in love. Which in itself is not notable, but we are all wrung for things to talk about at the end of the season. Unless Prinny gambles away a hundred thousand pounds, this duel will probably be the most interesting thing that happens this week."

"You could cause a scandal and draw all the gossips away," Frances suggested. "You're much more interesting than I."

"I have another idea," Caroline said, picking up a fallen issue of *Lady's Magazine* and snapping it open to a random page. "Why don't you try to enjoy the attention? For once, the *ton* is giving you the regard you were born to. Wadsworth might have done you a very good turn after all."

Frances only hunched her shoulders. Being noticed by the *ton* would have delighted her before she met Henry. She would have loved to feel as if she belonged again in the world she'd given up for Charles.

Now she would have loved… well, just to feel loved.

❧

Five dreary, stifling days passed. Days in which the city baked, and letter after letter came, inviting Frances to all manner of end-of-season festivities. But gossip began to dwindle as Frances stayed home, and Caroline went out and about as if nothing was out of the ordinary. She went to Lady Protheroe's supper party. She went to teas and breakfasts. Always, before she left, she cast Frances a wordless glance. It was easy to interpret.

Pity.

I'm sorry, Caroline's face said. Well, Frances was sorry too. Her faultless memory replayed the past weeks for her, wondering at what point everything had been knocked askew.

The puppies were not calling; that was a small blessing. Caroline had given Frances the gift of a peaceful house, which was as much as anyone could give right now.

Five days after the duel, Frances sat in the deserted drawing room, just as she had for the four days previous. Silence pressed so heavily at her ears that they rang, high and faint. The summer heat seemed to have wilted her within her gown, and she sprawled in a puddle on a tufted settee covered in drab-colored velvet.

A scratch at the door heralded the arrival of Pollitt, bearing a note on a salver. "For you, Mrs. Whittier."

In a hectic instant, Frances sat up straight. Somehow, her voice was calm as she scrabbled for the folded paper. "Thank you, Pollitt."

But even before the butler had bowed from the room, she knew this wasn't from Henry either. The writing was as smooth and feminine as she had once pretended hers was, when she falsified the form of it for Henry.

She sighed to herself. It was probably from some bored noblewoman who wanted her to plan a Venetian breakfast while wearing a courtesan's night rail. The polite world seemed determined to make a spectacle of her.

But this note was different.

Dear Mrs. Whittier,

Surely every runner in London has now been tired out on your behalf, and my brother's. Notes have been flying about the City faster than money changes hands at Devonshire House's gambling parties.

As you know, Henry is mindful of his handwriting, so I am bade to summon you. Won't you take pity on the poor runners and come to Tallant House?

Sincerely,
Emily Tallant

At last, at last.

The letter fluttered from Frances's hand. Before it reached the floor, she was calling for her gloves and spencer.

Twenty-Seven

FOR THE SECOND TIME IN RECENT WEEKS, LADY TALLANT shut Frances into the morning room. Henry let himself in not a minute later, knocking the door shut with his elbow. "What's this about, then?"

"Why, you summoned me." Frances had flown through the streets to Tallant House. Now the shortness of Henry's voice clipped her wings.

He shook his head. "Caroline sent me a note saying there was something you needed to discuss with me."

Frances's mind wobbled. "Caroline sent you a note?"

Henry nodded, his brows bronze slashes on a wary face.

Damn Caroline. Frances grimaced. "What a horrible thing for her to do. I'm sorry for the trick. I have come because Lady Tallant sent me a summons, I thought on your behalf. I have the letter here." She produced it from her reticule.

His eyes flicked over it in an instant, a corner of his mouth lifting. "It seems our relatives wanted their place in our correspondence after all."

He made a *hm* sound in his throat, as though noting something mildly interesting.

What was going on here? Henry didn't look angry. But he could not have wanted to see her, or he'd have written to her himself or paid her a call.

Frances had waited long enough for answers. "So Emily and Caroline have played a little trick on us. Now that we are together, do you have a reply to my letter from five days ago? Or am I to take your silence as reply?"

Amusement vanished from his face. "I have been waiting to reply until I knew exactly how."

"And have you decided?"

"Some of that depends on you."

She lifted her chin. "What more do you need from me? How much more frank could I have been with you?"

Henry's left hand fumbled with his right sleeve. His mouth was set in a grim line.

Apprehension clenched Frances's stomach. "What is it? Have you done something?"

"I… wrote a letter of my own. I'm not sure what you'll think of it." His lips flexed and pulled, as if he wanted to draw the words back.

Were their roles reversed, Frances would have thrown herself upon his body to make him forget she'd said anything. She'd done so twice. But Henry had more courage—or maybe just less desire.

"Tell me quickly," she demanded, "before I imagine that you've bought six harem girls and intend to turn Tallant House into a den of sin."

"Nothing of the kind, I assure you." He pulled a

folded paper from the tail pocket of his dark blue coat. The letter flapped loose, its seal already broken. "Here, you'd better read it."

Mystified, she took the missive from him.

> *Dear Mr. Middlebrook,*
>
> *Thank you for your recent correspondence regarding your attachment to my daughter. As you are no doubt aware, I have not been in communication with her for years.*
>
> *I am more delighted than I can express to know she is well, and that she has found a friend in yourself. I knew your late parents slightly. It is clear to me from your letter that you are honorable, just as they were.*
>
> *You need not have asked my blessing on your prospective match, as you know, though I am happy to grant it. I appreciate the invitation to your wedding; however, I regret that ill health makes travel on such short notice impossible.*
>
> *Please give Frances my love. I regret that so much time has gone by since we parted, and I hope one day we shall be reunited.*
>
> *Yours sincerely,*
> *Sir Wallace Ward, Bart*

The hand was fainter and shakier than she remembered. But she could hear his voice speaking the words as clearly as if no time had passed. As if they had never fought and he hadn't all but disowned her.

Seven years ago, when her mother died, Frances's father had sent her the rosewood box that had once held Lady Ward's jewels. No note was enclosed, as if he meant to tell her, *I know where to find you, but I have nothing to say to you.* The silence was worse than a reprimand, so on it stretched.

His voice still echoed in her ears, though. Fifteen years ago he had checked her arithmetic with a proud, "Well done, daughter." Twenty years ago, he explained the rules of chess and whist, sure she could master them as well as any male child. Twenty-five years ago, he bounced her on his knee, laughing as hard as she.

She had not thought of these things for a very long time. There had been no point. But now—here was the past, right before her face.

"This is from my father." She could hardly believe it. But it was his hand. His signature. It *sounded* like him, all sternness over hesitant warmth.

She looked up at Henry. "Why did my father write to you?"

"I wrote to him first." He looked self-conscious; his left hand played with the brass buttons on his coat. "Because of the letter you sent me, explaining everything. I could tell it pained you to lose everything you'd grown up with. I wish your father had never forced you to choose between love and family."

She started to lift a hand to his face, but her father's letter crackled in her grip and she abandoned the gesture. "I forced the choice more than he."

He acknowledged her words with an if-you-say-so lift of his brows. "I wanted to let him know you were well. Caro told me your maiden name and even recalled your father's direction. He lives in Ward Manor, just as he always did."

"After all this time," she said. "It seems impossible that nothing has changed."

"I wouldn't say that. He feels regret, as you can see. I believe he wishes to have his daughter back in his life."

He watched her with raised eyebrows, his expression a patient cipher. "Are you glad for this letter, Frances?"

She looked at the letter again. She felt as though her eyes could not truly be open, seeing what was before them. This letter itself. Henry, uncovering her deepest hurt. Seeing how thin her skin was.

But it was real; here was the quaver and shake of her father's pen over the lines. It offered forgiveness and the chance to forgive. To stitch closed a wound that was almost ten years old.

It would always leave a scar. The wound was too old, too ragged, for anything less. Yet it was a healing, even if an imperfect one.

"You wrote to my father," she repeated. The paper fell from her hand to the floor, and she wrapped her arms tight around him in a quick, crushing embrace. "Yes, I'm glad. I'm very, very glad. I can scarcely believe you did that for me."

"I wanted to give you more than myself." His lips moved in her hair, tickling her scalp. "I wanted to help you regain some of the things you lost over the years."

"Is this why you made me wait day after day? For this letter?"

"Partly. I wanted you to get the other letters first

too. I wanted you to have the attention you missed as a younger woman. It's your due by worth as well as birth."

Her head reared back. "All those letters I've been pestered with. You sent them?"

"No, not at all. I merely mentioned to a few influential people how enjoyable your company was. The rest was simply the *ton* doing what it loves best: following a good story to ground as surely as a hound scents a fox."

"That is a terrible analogy if I'm meant to be the fox." She rested in the hollow of his neck and shoulder, liking the scratch of her jaw against the fine woven wool of his coat. "You are fortunate that I am stupid with surprise right now. I'm not even going to chastise you for not sending me the one letter I truly wanted."

He rested his hand on her back, and she breathed into its comforting weight. "What will you do, Henry? Now that you've conquered the polite world?"

"That depends on you. I have a small estate not far outside of London, but I'm willing to stay at Tallant House so I might see you every day if you'll allow that honorable courtship you once agreed to. I'll understand if you won't, after my dueling and my taking offense at the letters you wrote. I've had enough pride for seven men."

"I've always thought you extraordinary," Frances murmured. "The pride of seven men, though—I hadn't expected that much good fortune."

His hand played up her spine, and she couldn't remember how to tease him anymore.

His eyes were lapis lazuli, deep and clear. Even

Frances knew how precious that color was, and she was no artist. "You've told my father I already accepted you."

"And so you did, once. You agreed to my suit just before we had our exceedingly memorable encounter with Lord Wadsworth. But if you wish to part from me, I'll still do what I can to make things right between you and your father. I'll blame everything on myself. Former soldiers can be unpredictable bastards."

"So can artists."

His mouth twitched, and he released her and took a step back. "There's no hope for me, then. But I'll tell you this. Your letter gave me much to think about, Frances. I believe honor is not an act of a day, and it is not destroyed by one failure. It is a matter of intent as much as success. As is trust."

"So the means to the end *do* matter, even if the end is what you wish." She swallowed, but there was a lump in her throat that would not dislodge.

"The means always matter because they tell the world what type of person you are."

His eyes fixed hers, deep and true. "As I said, it's a matter of intent. I was too hasty before when I criticized yours—too hurt, really. But I know you acted out of great kindness. I understand you, past and present, and I trust you for the future. You loved me enough for two women—in person and in letters. If you'll only let me, I'll love you enough for two. It's no more than you deserve."

"It *is* more," she said. Her throat caught. "Damn. I'm not going to cry. That would completely undermine my dignity."

"We can't have that." He patted his chest. "But if you decide to toss dignity aside, I have a handkerchief."

"Because a soldier is always prepared?"

"That, and an artist always has paint on his hands." He cleared his throat. "So. Whether we're artists or soldiers or… I don't know… pig farmers, I believe we'll make excellent allies. If you agree to my proposal, that is. You haven't actually said the words. I may have the vapors if you prolong the suspense any longer."

She smiled. "I almost feel I ought to write it down, given our history. 'HENRY IS TOO DEMANDING.' Though I am too."

They had overcome the weight of loss, the depth of need, the high wall of pride. Compared to those obstacles, love seemed fragile in its beauty.

But when shared by two, it was not fragile at all.

She wrapped her arms around him again, breathing in his clean heat, drawing his solid body as close as her strength could manage. "Yes, I'll marry you. Yes to it all."

⤝⤞

Relief flooded Henry's body. He'd not known how their treacherous reunion would go, whether Frances would want to reconcile with her father. Or with Henry himself.

Now she was nestled under his chin, right as right could be. If he focused, he could feel the shuddery beat of her heart against his own ribs. It was as if they were one body. Thank God, she was willing to forgive.

Although… this didn't quite feel like forgiveness anymore. Forgiveness didn't rub itself against his body with a low, throaty sigh. Forgiveness didn't toy with the buttons on his dove-gray waistcoat. Forgiveness didn't slip them free from their holes.

This was far better than forgiveness. It was love. With a fair smattering of passion to brighten the tone.

Frances slid her hand beneath one layer of fabric, then another. "Madam," Henry said in a mock-surprised voice. "Are your intentions entirely honorable?"

She laughed. "Not at the moment."

"Perfect." When she tugged at his coat sleeves, he flexed his shoulders forward to allow the snug garment to slip free.

With sharp, hungry tugs at his clothing, she undressed him. He helped when he could, twisting his way out of layer after layer, even as his own hand fumbled with the buttons of her bodice. He touched the laces of her stays, and she shook her head.

"Better leave them on. I can't imagine asking Lady Tallant's maid to come help me dress, can you?"

"She's Emily to you now, since you'll be sisters." He tilted his head. "But perhaps you're right about the stays. I'll have to be creative."

He let his eyes slide over her body; at last, he just looked and looked and looked.

Someday he would paint her. Maybe even like this: a secret picture, just for them. Light burnishing her coffee-dark hair with glows of red; her creamy skin warmed by the morning sun. Through the translucent linen of her shift, the form of her body and the shadow between her legs faintly visible. Peeking over the edge of her stays, a semicircle of damask rose—the edge of one nipple, wanting to be touched.

"Henry," she admonished, crossing her arms over her chest as the moment drew out long and slow. But she smiled. And when he touched her forearm, pressed it down, she chuckled and lowered her arms to her sides, giving him an unobstructed view of her again.

Except for those dratted stays. Without removing them, he couldn't take off her chemise either.

When restricted in some way, find another route.

He couldn't quite shed the habits of the military. Right now, they gave him a marvelous idea.

He would find another way in. "Spread your legs," he murmured in her ear.

A flush delicate as a new blossom spread over Frances's cheeks and bosom. She breathed quickly, sharply as she slid one foot along the carpet until there was nearly a yard's span between her feet. Her stocking-clad toes dug into the weave of the rug.

"Perfect." Henry crouched on the floor at her feet. Balancing carefully on the balls of his feet, he lifted the cotton chemise and exposed her sex to his view.

Soft brown curls rich as earth, folds like a budded rose, flushing darker red, drawing his eye. His mouth. He needed two hands, damn it. He released her chemise, allowing the fabric to fall atop his head, and used his freed fingers to part her, opening her for his tongue.

He barely got a taste before she writhed, hips bucking. "Good God, Henry." Nails dug into his scalp, raking the sensitive skin.

"Do you enjoy this?"

"I enjoy it so much that I'm going to ignore how ridiculous we both must look. Will you do a bit more? Or a lot more?"

Laughing, he pointed his tongue, found her hottest part, and licked at it with the gentle pressure he would use on the smallest paintbrush, for the most delicate coloring. The most precious, detailed part of a painting.

This time, there was no subsiding. This time, her fingers wove into his hair, pressing him against her hot flesh; this time she grew wetter for him, and her breath came in gasps. She trembled on her feet, and then she began to tremble all over, and as he tongued her, harder and faster and hungry and thirsty, she came apart in his mouth with shudders and cries.

She sank to her knees at once, wrung out. Henry rocked onto the balls of his feet then sat on the floor and folded his legs before him. They must look even more ridiculous now, facing each other on the morning room floor with their clothes half off.

To his eyes, though, Frances looked beautiful: hair tangled, cheeks flushed, lips inviting.

He just wondered one thing. "Why did it please you that time?"

"What we just did?"

He nodded. "Last time we tried that, you didn't like it."

Frances let her head loll back. "How could I not like that? It's... well, you can guess. You saw how much I liked it."

She folded her arms and rubbed her hands over them again, shivering with a final spasm of pleasure. "Last time, I felt I was doing wrong by you, keeping secrets, and I couldn't forget that." She spread her hands. "So I couldn't forget myself."

Henry brushed tangled hair back from her forehead, traced the straight line of her nose, bumped over her lips, the indentation below them, then her chin. Whisked down her neck. Stopped.

"No more blame. That's all in the past." He leaned forward, kissed her furrowed brow.

"But the past... it doesn't go away," Frances insisted. Henry could feel her tension under his lips.

He sat back. "You're right. It doesn't."

He shrugged his right shoulder, allowing the dead weight of his arm to swing and dangle. "The past is here with us. It shapes the present. It matters." Of course his arm mattered; it would always matter. He would always regret the loss.

Yet without it, there was so much he would never have gained. His life had been routed onto a whole new path—one with obstacles and stumbles, but one he would not have to walk alone. He took a deep breath. "But it mustn't prevent us from finding joy."

Frances looked at her hands in her lap. She smoothed them over the translucent fabric of her chemise, then took both of his hands in her own and pulled them to her heart.

"Can you feel this?" she asked, her eyes deep as a forest.

Henry wanted to. He really wanted to. He longed to. But in his right arm, as always, there was nothing but a blank where feeling used to be.

But in his heart...

"Yes," he said, and he knew she understood.

She smiled, a bit sadly. "How did you get so wise?"

A short laugh popped out. "Wise. Well, I haven't been called that in a while."

She squeezed her eyes shut, holding his hands and pulling them toward her. "You are. Very. Wise."

When she opened her eyes, they were almost nose-to-nose. They breathed the same air, smiled the same smile.

She released his hands. "Very wise. So wise, I think you deserve a reward."

The air of the room was still and warm on his skin. Frances pressed at his shoulders until he was laid out, flat, and his back ground into the coarse wool of the carpet. Sun cut through the window and filled his eyes, and he closed them against the dazzling brightness.

The world was nothing but touch, nothing but the sun, and her fingers gliding over his skin. And then it was her mouth, hot as a fire and wet as a lake. Impossible, yet it was happening. He was buried, and he was flying. He could not stand it; he could not bear for it to end.

His back arched in a silent cry.

His eyes snapped open. "Come with me."

She leaned forward, the tip of her tongue peeking between her lips. "Now?"

"Yes." He could not manage more than one syllable. He could only pull her atop him.

They would go through life together. They could come together too.

He laughed, and that made it even better.

Twenty-Eight

THEIR MARRIAGE WAS SET TO TAKE PLACE IN TWO weeks' time at Tallant House. As a wedding present to the couple, Jem helped Henry obtain a special license. He also sent a reluctant Sowerberry to Winter Cottage for several days, to install a few servants and make sure the small house was ready to receive the newlywed couple.

Four days before the wedding, Henry sat in Jem's study looking over an account book for Winter Cottage. The usual assortment of post littered the broad desk, and Jem whistled as he sliced open invitations and notes and bills with swift flicks of a penknife.

As the knife slit paper after paper, the whistling grew louder, until there was no chance of concentrating on the accounts. As of three years before, Winter Cottage had seemed to be in solid shape, but for all that Henry could tell amidst Jem's auditory barrage, it might have been conquered by mermaids since then.

The whistling stopped for an instant, then drew out long and slow in a piercing fall. Then silence.

"Jem?"

Getting no reply, Henry snapped the ledger shut. Standing, he faced his brother over the back of his chair. "Has something happened?"

Jem's mouth was hanging open as he stared at a paper in his hand. Henry's voice seemed to jar him back to awareness. His face grew faintly pink. "This must be some kind of maggoty humbug. Here, take a look, Hal."

He released the inscribed paper from an unsteady hand before Henry could take hold of it. It flipped open as it drifted slowly to the floor, and from its folds a paper rectangle fell next to the desk.

"What is this?" Henry crouched to pluck up the smaller paper. "A bank draft?"

"I shouldn't have opened it except that it was mixed in with my letters. Sorry about that."

"Wait. It's for me?" Henry rose to his feet and squinted at the paper, wondering if the name was a mistake. "Someone has sent me a bank draft for a thousand pounds. This can't be right. What on God's green…"

Sussex. It came from Sussex, he noticed. "Was there a letter with this?"

Jem handed it over with a nod.

Dear Mr. Middlebrook,

It is my pleasure to send a portion of my daughter's dowry to you, as a sign of my esteem for you and my faith in your honorable intentions. The remainder of the amount—a further eleven thousand pounds—I will gladly transfer to you upon receiving news of your marriage.

This amount has been set aside for Frances since

the time of her birth, on the condition that she marry in accordance with my wishes. Please do not think ill of me for having withheld it from her at the time of her first marriage. I hope it can be of use to you as you build a new life together during what I hope will be many long years of peace.

All my best regards for your happiness.

Sincerely,
Sir Wallace Ward, Bart

P.S.—I should be pleased to receive a letter from Frances if she would care to write me.

"I say, Hal." Jem had sidled over to read the letter over Henry's shoulder. "A dowry for Frances. Who'd have thought you were marrying an heiress?"

Henry shook his head and folded the draft back inside the letter. "Not I."

Well. First a father, now financial security. This was a very fine set of wedding presents for Frances.

For his part, he was happy enough just to have Frances.

❧

Henry did not expect any further surprises that day. An enormous bank draft and a country household run by phantom mermaids were surely eventful enough.

Which was why, when he was sitting at the morning room's desk practicing his penmanship in an endless string of AEIOUs and sometimes Ys too, he was only concerned with trying to ignore the feeling of being watched by the painted figures in the room's mural. The goddess Athena had the look of a wretched termagant.

A tap at the door caught him unawares.

"Come," he called. He sanded his paper, then turned to see who had entered.

"Bart." Henry blinked. "You're back in London? I thought you'd be shooting partridge around Beckworth by now."

Bart held a high-crowned beaver hat behind his back, tapping its fashionably wide brim against the backs of his knees. "Oh, well. I wanted to see how things went with the letter. My letter. Ah, the one I wrote to Mrs. Whittier."

"As well as you can imagine. We're getting married in a few days. Maybe you didn't know, since I sent word to Beckworth."

"Are you? That's excellent. Well done, Hal." Tap, tap, tap, went the hat behind his back.

Henry's brow furrowed. "Bart, you've never been a good liar. I can see you've heard the news already. And you're going to mar the shape of what I'm sure is a very fashionable hat if you keep whacking at the brim. What's going on?"

Bart stared at the floor, then said in a rush, "I understand if you don't want me at your wedding—"

"What?"

"—because our friendship's fallen by the wayside in recent years."

Henry held up his hand. "Bart. Wait. I didn't keep up any friendships in recent years. It just wasn't possible while I was in the military. It had nothing to do with you or our friendship."

The hat flipped in Bart's hands, fumbled, fell to the ground. "Sorry," Bart said in a tight voice as he bent and retrieved his hat. His face was redder when he stood than one might have expected, considering he'd only been bent over for a second or two.

As if he'd been rapped on the head with a candle, light dawned in Henry's mind. Bart felt hurt. And if the situations were reversed, Henry might well have felt the same. How else would he react if an old friend returned after years of silence, let him learn of a serious injury by chance, then largely avoided his company in Town?

It had nothing to do with Bart, just as Henry had said. But maybe he understood his old friend better than ever now. Just as quiet Bart always had, Henry now knew the feeling of separation within a crowd, of light pleasantries weighing heavily on a mind distracted.

And Bart, like Jem and Emily, remembered Henry's best self. He gave Henry another chance to reach out and remember it himself. Bart's unquestioning loyalty meant all the more after Henry's long separation from everyone he knew.

"Bart," Henry said. His old friend had begun to turn toward the door. "Bart, to whom did I entrust the first letter to Frances?"

Bart turned back to Henry, looking puzzled.

"*You*, Bart. I trusted *you*. I knew Frances thought you a kind man, and she would value a letter from you. Your friendship is worth a great deal." Henry smiled. "To me."

Bart's face reddened. "Oh, well. It was—I mean, I was happy to do it."

"Thank you. I am very grateful for that." Henry nodded. "For everything."

It was not the most articulate thanks, but he hoped Bart would understand. If Henry was any more effusive, he would embarrass them both.

"I'm afraid," Henry continued, idly straightening papers on the desk, "that I can't hunt anymore. But I'd still be pleased to go to Beckworth next autumn."

Bart scuffed a booted foot in the carpet and gave a rascally grin. "That's no kind of a problem, Hal. You can help the hounds retrieve the game."

Henry chuckled. "I've been a son of a bitch to you often enough. That might be the perfect way to repay me."

Bart laughed, ducking his head. "Well. I'll see you next hunting season then. I suppose you're busy today."

"Not so busy. Emily's working herself into a frenzy over my wedding preparations and won't allow me to do a thing. There's nothing in the world that makes her happier than mild domestic chaos." Henry motioned toward a chair. "Please, sit."

With another tap of his hat against his legs, Bart sidled to a chair and perched at the edge of it.

"I'll probably see you again long before next autumn," Henry said. "In fact, if you don't have to head to Beckworth immediately, I'd be honored if you'd stay in London to attend the wedding. It will be just for family, here at Tallant House."

"Do you mean it?" Bart leaned forward. The chair tipped, upsetting his balance, and he spent a few chagrined seconds rearranging himself into a dignified posture.

"Yes, of course. Though I should warn you, Emily is determined that any gentleman who attends should wear a striped cravat. She insists they are—"

Together, Henry and Bart chorused, "All the crack."

Bart laughed. "She's right, you know."

Henry raised his hand in a gesture of surrender. He didn't know these things. But it didn't matter. He'd relearn it all in time, as much as he needed to.

Bart twirled his hat on his forefinger. "Do you have time for one more ride in the curricle before you settle down?"

"I'm sure there's time for that," Henry said.

"Where shall we go?"

The old question. Henry remembered running free, not caring what the answer was.

He didn't really care now. Anywhere would be just fine.

"I don't know." Henry let a grin spread across his face. "Where would you like to go? We'll go anywhere you like."

As Bart grinned back, Henry snapped his fingers in a gesture of remembrance. "As long as we stop at Gunter's on the way back. If we drive hell for leather across Berkeley Square, we might be able to bring Jem home an ice before it melts."

"So we shall," said Bart. "I say, would you care to drive the team?"

❧

Henry drove the team. They never broke out of a walk, and horses and men all survived, though the ice was almost completely melted by the time it arrived at Tallant House. Still, Lord Tallant devoured it with indecorous glee.

Four days later, Henry did *not* wear a striped cravat. Yet he and Frances still contrived to be married.

Jem manfully choked back tears during the brief ceremony, and Frances beamed up into Henry's face as he clasped her hands together. She was swathed in white satin, pale as cloud. Hair dark as earth, eyes steady as a tree.

He could not help his flight of fancy as he spoke his vows. She was his world.

After they were pronounced man and wife, the newlyweds and their few guests piled into the dining room for a wedding breakfast that Emily assured them would possess all the pomp missing from the ceremony itself.

She was right. Henry looked over piles of brioche and cakes and eggs and sliced meats with a wondering eye.

"What do you think?" Emily said to Henry in a low voice, as Jem began to pour chocolate out of a silver pot as neatly as any footman.

Henry thought there was far too much food for only a half-dozen people—the same half dozen, in fact, who'd come to dine at Tallant House, cheat at cards, and criticize Henry's fireplace screen.

How much they had been through since then.

"Thank you, Emily. You are very kind." He offered her a smile, knowing she would consider his gratitude the best repayment for her efforts. *Not just now. Always. You are very kind.*

"Chocolate, Em?" Jem held out a cup. Emily pulled a face and shook her head. "Lady Stratton, then?"

Caro took the cup from him as they all arranged themselves around the laden table. "I simply have to tell you all something, though it may not be dignified enough for the occasion."

"Ah—do we have to be dignified today?" Frances made a mock frown. "I hadn't planned on that. After we're done with breakfast, I thought we would all dance a hornpipe on the table."

"Or a minuet," Henry said, nudging his foot into hers under the table until rose stained her cheeks. Henry felt her toes flex within her thin slippers, as if they were turning together again in the center of a ballroom, with eyes only for each other.

Caro set her cup down on the table with a hollow clink. "Dance if you must, but for heaven's sake, hear me out. You'll all *adore* this. Two days ago, I was looking through the sweetest china shop, trying to find a vase to replace the one I was unfortunately required to throw. And who should walk in, just as I was lifting the vase up to look at the potter's marks?"

Bart spluttered into his tea. "Not Wadsworth."

Caro nodded. "Exactly. As soon as he clapped eyes on me—well, I've never seen a man turn so pale or spin on his heel so quickly."

Henry laughed. "Jittery, is he?"

"Awfully. I don't suppose he'll be able to look at a tree for some time either after what you did to him, Henry."

Emily took a dainty bite from a slice of brioche. "I can't say I've got any sympathy for the man. He's had undeserved good luck, timing his humiliations for the end of the season. By next spring, everyone will have forgotten them."

"*He* won't forget," Caro said. "I will do my utmost to make sure of that. Nearly every house has a vase in its drawing room. I only hope I happen to call on someone at the same time as Wadsworth. I shall draw my fingers across the vase and watch him turn pale as a fish belly. It will be…" She bared her straight teeth. "Smashing."

Before Henry could reply, Sowerberry ushered in two violinists and a man carrying an ivory flute. "As you requested, my lady," the butler said with a bow to Emily.

"What is this, Em?" Jem asked.

"A little surprise for our newlyweds," Emily said, failing to keep a pleased smile from her face. "You've only ever had one dance. You simply must have one more before you leave London. It's my wedding present to you."

Frances set her cup down so quickly that a drop of coffee sloshed over the edge. "I was only joking, my lady—Emily. I really didn't plan to dance a hornpipe this morning. Especially not on the table."

Emily dismissed this protest with a wave of her hand. "Not *that*. But you haven't danced for weeks. You simply must dance on your wedding day."

Jem choked on a bite of eggs. "Not in the dining room, surely." Stuffed into the corners of the dining room, the three musicians were beginning to look uncomfortable.

Henry didn't feel uncomfortable at all. At last, he felt a blessed certainty. He'd returned home at last, and he'd carry it with him always.

"No, indeed," Emily said. "When everyone's eaten their fill, we'll return to the drawing room."

Frances lifted her eyebrows at Henry, and he nodded. Certainly, he could dance today.

"All right," she agreed with a wicked half smile. "If Mr. Middlebrook cares to invite me to stand up with him, I suppose I'll agree."

Caro looked equally mischievous. "Bart, we can have that waltz at last, since you won't be pressed into service at the pianoforte this morning."

Bart fumbled his fork. "Yes. Yes, absolutely we could. I'd be—it would be my honor." He turned the pale pink of a tomato's inside.

"Glad you stayed for the wedding?" Henry murmured to his old friend, and Bart shot him a sideways glance, a smile.

This room contained Henry's family, the people most precious to him in the world. Jem and Emily. Bart, close as a second brother. And today it had grown to include Caro, and—dearest of all—Frances herself.

Twang.

Oh. And those three musicians too. One of the violinists had shifted his instrument, clearly wondering when the quality were going to cease this bizarre, buoyant behavior.

Certainly not today.

"I think," Henry said, "I'd like to dance with my wife now. Frances, do you agree?"

He held out his hand to her, and she took it at once, pushing her chair back in a swift scrape and allowing Henry to pull her to her feet. Lovely as any painting. Art come to life.

"I do."

Epilogue

March 1816

"A LETTER FOR YOU, HENRY," FRANCES CALLED AS SHE carried the post past the east wall of Winter Cottage, trailing her hand on its rough stone exterior.

Henry was, as usual, in the garden. He was to be found there every day, unless the weather was cold enough to thicken his paints into uselessness. His art students found many more subjects for study outdoors than in. Besides, he wanted to spare Frances the smell of the turpentine used to clean his brushes whenever they worked in oils.

She brushed through dried grass and found the gravel path to Henry's favorite spot for lessons, amidst a tangle of winter-sere rosebushes and a view of the ancient stone bridge that crossed the creek to the east of Winter Cottage. A frozen crust still blanketed the creek; it was too early for the damask roses to bloom. Soon, though, they would be putting forth leaves and tiny buds. Frances rubbed one of the rosebush's waxy stems between her fingertips. This would be the first time she saw them blossom in her new home.

Crushed stone crunched under her feet as she stepped closer, alerting Henry to her presence. "Frances. Did you say something?"

He smiled as he turned from his canvas and rubbed his arm across his forehead, shoving wind-ruffled hair out of his face. His hand bristled with paintbrushes, all stained with different oils.

"Yes. You've got a letter, I said." She held out the folded missive, but he shook his head.

"Go ahead and open it. I'm still packing up from Ellery Todd's lesson. He's got a good eye, but no interest in learning about pigment and paint. He only wants to draw nude women."

Frances smirked. "Would you have been any different at the age of thirteen?"

"I suppose not. I'm not much different now."

He set the fistful of brushes down on a brightly painted orange-red baroque table, the ornate piece incongruous in this outdoor setting. "Perhaps I ought to refresh my memory. How long, do you think, has it been since I saw a nude woman? At least seven or eight hours."

He crossed the few feet to Frances and wrapped his arm around her, pinning her arms to her side. "Mmm." He pressed his face to her neck, inhaled. "You smell... not like turpentine. Delicious."

She laughed. "I chose the scent just for you, you silver-tongued charmer."

After seven months of marriage, they'd fallen into a comfortable pattern that still surprised her with its easy fit. They spent a lazy—or strenuous—morning together, then taught students each afternoon. Jem and Emily had canvassed the *ton* for promising young artists who needed a bit more study before haunting the Royal Academy as Henry had once done.

Considering the inconvenient location of Winter Cottage just outside London—a bumpy carriage ride back and forth, plus the lesson itself, could take a student half a day—it was surprising that Henry had as many students as he wanted and more than he could take. Knowing Emily, Frances guessed that the sociable countess had pinned down interest by embroidering Henry's military past.

That didn't matter, though. Once proud parents got their curiosity out of the way, they left their young artists under Henry's tutelage because of his talent. His own painting was still shaky, but his eye for color and his patience as a teacher were unmatched.

Frances's memory was an unqualified boon, for she taught students in the history of art, and had the pleasure of being right and giving advice every day. When not teaching, she kept everything else running smoothly: scheduling students, checking stores of paints and pigments, arranging for young Cecil Sharpton to come over from nearby Sidcup to mill paints for Henry when he was getting low.

And when life ran slowly, London was not far away. Close enough for Jem and Emily to visit. Even Caroline had come to stay once.

And Frances's father. He'd come for Christmas, settling his rheumatic bones into a squashy armchair for several weeks and spoiling their dogs with treat after treat. The bustle of the holiday had gone a long way toward filling awkward silences and the distance of long years of separation. Frances wrote to him faithfully now. She would not be lost to him again.

Frances broke Henry's hold around her arms and slid them around his waist, pulling his hips to hers. "Are you finished for the day? I can have one of the servants stow all of your supplies."

He squinted in the afternoon light. Against his tanned skin, his eyes were a startling blue.

"Yes, I've been out here long enough. It's chilly for March. I hadn't noticed before." He bumped his forehead against hers. "You must have been keeping me warm."

"Since I was inside our house all morning while you painted with the aspiring nudist, that's not possible."

"Ah, but every time he asked about drawing naked women, I thought of you."

She raised an eyebrow. "Just open your letter, you wicked man."

He winked at her, then took the fat folded paper from her hand. His brows knit. "This can't be right."

"What is it?"

He flipped the letter to show her its reverse. "It's the Great Seal. Why would I be getting a letter from the Prince Regent?"

"Because Emily hounded him into calling you to court?"

"She wouldn't be so unkind." He tucked the letter high under his right arm and cracked the seal with his left thumb. Such gestures were getting smoother, more natural as the months passed.

His sapphire-blue eyes flicked over the lines of the letter, then he raised his eyebrows and pulled his mouth down in the expression Frances thought of as *well-there-it-is-then*.

Sure enough. "Well. There it is, then." He handed the letter to Frances.

She read the finely inscribed lines quickly. "They want to give you a medal?"

"Waterloo," he murmured. "Always Waterloo."

"They're calling it the Waterloo Medal. But Henry, it's for *you*. For the men who fought at Quatre Bras and Ligny too."

"Then why call it a Waterloo Medal?"

She met his eyes over the thick paper. The loosened wax seal flapped in a faint breeze. "I don't know. Maybe just because it was the last battle. Everyone was so glad when the war was over."

He inclined his head. "That's true. I certainly was."

He folded over the top of the paper in Frances's hand. "Waterloo." He sounded amused this time, as if Waterloo were a puppy that kept yanking the draperies down in a bid for attention.

Frances squeezed his hand. "The Prince Regent might just be amusing himself with pomp or seeking to honor Wellington. But it would be impolite of you to refuse the medal. Being so close to London, we could easily journey for you to accept it in person."

Henry groaned.

She trailed her free hand down his chest, teasing. "And if we give enough notice, Emily could plan a great ball in your honor. You could wear your medal and be the center of all attention."

"You paint a very vivid picture, my dear wife."

She slipped fingers between the buttons of his waistcoat. "Is it to your liking?"

"Some of it. This part." His heartbeat thudded strong under her fingertips, and he flexed his arm to pull her fully against his body.

Frances cleared her throat, tried to summon the companion's brisk voice. "I'm talking about London." The crisp tone was hardly convincing.

He shook his head. "As you said, I'm just glad it's over. I don't need a medal. I haven't needed one for a long time." His fingers found hers, entwined with them. "Although I wouldn't mind going back to London. Students would be glad to call on me in a more convenient location. I could even finish ruining Emily's Axminster carpet with spilled paint."

"She would love that even more than hosting a ball for you."

His eyes crinkled at the corners. When he smiled, it was bright and warm even in the bracing March air. Never that desperate, dented look anymore.

"I would welcome the chance to see Caroline again," Frances mused. "And you could visit with Bart. He'll probably return to London soon."

"You're very persuasive. All right. If you want to go, we'll go." With a quick, fluid gesture, he raised their linked hands and twirled her as if in a scandalous waltz, so that she faced away from him, turned toward the house. He slid a hand down her back and placed a heated kiss just where her neck met her shoulder. She shivered, and not only because the breeze quickened, ruffling her skirts and nipping at her exposed skin.

"Now let's go inside. There's something I need to tell you."

"What is that?"

"Oh, nothing, really. It's just an excuse to get you back into bed." He stepped up to walk at her side toward the house. "Wasn't that a favorite trick of yours before we married? You see, I have a good memory too."

Author's Note

Writing historical romance is a wonderful job for those who like to poke through the details of the past. For this story, I got the chance to study historic paint pigments with fantastical names: orpiment, atramentum, cinnabar. I also asked my medically-inclined relatives questions like, "What kind of injury would take away the use of my hero's arm, but wouldn't require its amputation?" Ah, research.

For the record, Henry has *Erb's palsy*, a type of paralysis due to torn nerves (in the brachial plexus, if you too are medically inclined). Though a recovery wasn't possible during the Regency, if Henry lived today, he could have surgery to correct much of the nerve damage.

Soldiers who fought in the battles of Ligny, Quatre Bras, and Waterloo really did receive a medal. Its name? As Henry says: "Waterloo. Always Waterloo."

As for the chilly spring at the book's end, the year of 1816 was extremely cold, probably due to a massive volcanic eruption in Indonesia in 1815. But in Winter Cottage, we can assume that Henry and Frances found ways to remain quite cozy.

Acknowledgments

I always thank my husband first, because he's been a wonderful support ever since I began writing romance. Thanks, hon—I couldn't write heroes without you.

Many thanks to the Sourcebooks team: my editor Deb Werksman; Susie Benton; and the art, marketing, and publicity teams. It's a pleasure to venture into Regency England with you!

Thanks, as always, to Paige Wheeler, for her wondrous expertise and guidance. I also owe a great debt to my brother, who helped me figure out the perfect way to injure Henry, and to my eagle-eyed beta reader Amanda. Gratitude and huzzahs to my darling family and friends, and to the bright and inspiring authors I've had the pleasure of getting to know over the past few years.

And finally, thanks to my wonderful readers for finding my stories. In honor of Henry and Frances, a special shout-out to all you lefties out there.

About the Author

Historical romance author Theresa Romain pursued an impractical education that allowed her to read everything she could get her hands on. She then worked for universities and libraries, where she got to read even more. Eventually she started writing, too. She lives with her family in the Midwest.

To Charm a Naughty Countess

by Theresa Romain

❦

Caroline, the popular widowed Countess of Stratton, sits alone at the pinnacle of London society and has no wish to remarry. But when the brilliant, reclusive Duke of Wyverne—her counterpart in an old scandal—returns to town after a long absence, she finds herself as enthralled as ever.

Michael must save his family fortunes by wedding an heiress, but Caroline has vowed never again to sell herself in marriage. She offers him an affair, hoping to master her long-lasting fascination with him—but he remains steadfast, as always, in his dedication to purpose and his dukedom.

The only way she can keep him near is to help him find the wealthy bride he requires. As she guides him through society, Caroline realizes that she's lost her heart again. But if she pursues the only man she's ever loved, she'll lose the life she's built and on which she has pinned her sense of worth. And if Michael—who has everything to lose—ever hopes to win her hand, he must open his long-shuttered heart.

❦

New York Times and *USA Today* bestselling author

The Rogue Steals a Bride

by Amelia Grey

———— ⌘ ————

A promise can be a terrible thing...

All heiress Sophia Hart's father wanted was for her to marry a gentleman with a title. She promised him on his deathbed she would do just that. But the only man Sophia wants to spend time with is Matson Brentwood, who makes up for the lack of a title by being dashing and decidedly dangerous. Since Matson crashed his way into her life and her heart, that vow to her father has become an awful burden...

———— ⌘ ————

Praise for *New York Times* bestseller *A Gentleman Says "I Do"*:

"Grey neatly matches up a sharp-witted heroine with an irresistibly sexy hero and lets the romantic sparks fly." —*Booklist*

"Sensual, charming, and touching."
—*RT Book Reviews,* 4 Stars

For more Amelia Grey, visit:

www.sourcebooks.com

Lady Mercy Danforthe Flirts with Scandal

by Jayne Fresina

---— ❦ —---

Lady Mercy likes her life neat and tidy. She prides herself on being practical—like her engagement to Viscount Grey, whose dark coloring coordinates very well with her favorite furnishings. But things start to get messy when her best friend abandons her fiancé at the altar, leaving it up to Mercy to help the couple. There's just one problem. The jilted man is Rafe Hartley—Mercy's former husband.

Rafe has not forgiven Mercy for deserting him when they were seventeen. Their hasty marriage was declared void by law, but in his eyes the bossy little vixen is still his wife, even if the marriage lasted only a few hours. And Mercy "Silky Drawers" Danforthe still owes him a wedding night.

---— ❦ —---

For more Jayne Fresina, visit:

www.sourcebooks.com

The Wicked Wedding of Miss Ellie Vyne

by Jayne Fresina

— ❧ —

When a notorious bachelor seduces a scandalous lady, it can only end in a wicked wedding

By night Ellie Vyne fleeces unsuspecting aristocrats as the dashing Count de Bonneville. By day she avoids her sisters' matchmaking attempts and dreams up inventive insults to hurl at her childhood nemesis, the arrogant, far-too-handsome-for-his-own-good James Hartley.

James finally has a lead on the villainous, thieving count, tracking him to a shady inn. He bursts in on none other than "that Vyne woman"…in a shocking state of dishabille. Convinced she is the count's mistress, James decides it's best to keep his enemies close. Very close. Seducing Ellie will be the perfect bait…

— ❧ —

Praise for *The Most Improper Miss Sophie Valentine*:

"Ms. Fresina delivers a scintillating debut! Her sharply drawn characters and witty prose are as addictive as chocolate!"
—Mia Marlowe, author of *Touch of a Rogue*

For more Jayne Fresina, visit:

www.sourcebooks.com

Lady Vivian Defies a Duke

by Samantha Grace

The Naked Truth

Lady Vivian Worth knows perfectly well how to behave like a lady. But observing proper manners when there's no one around to impress is just silly. Why shouldn't she strip down to her chemise for a swim? When her betrothed arrives to finally meet her, Vivi will act every inch the lady—demure, polite, compliant. Everything her brother has promised the man. But until then, she's going to enjoy her freedom…

A Revealing Discovery

Luke Forest, the newly named Duke of Foxhaven, wants nothing to do with his inheritance—or the bride who comes with it. He wants adventure and excitement, like the enchanting water nymph he's just stumbled across. When he discovers the skinny-dipping minx is his intended, he reconsiders his plan to find Lady Vivian another husband. Because the idea of this vivacious woman in the arms of another man might be enough to drive him insane—or to the altar.

"An ideal choice for readers who relish smartly written, splendidly sensual Regency historicals." —*Booklist*

For more Samantha Grace, visit:

www.sourcebooks.com

Miss Lavigne's Little White Lie

by Samantha Grace

❦

Spirited and determined to protect her young brother at any cost, Lisette Lavigne is desperate to flee New Orleans. There's only one ship sailing to England, though, and the rakish Captain Daniel Hillary will only allow Lisette's family aboard for a very steep price…

Daniel prides himself on running a tight ship, and he knows a lady will be nothing but trouble on a long voyage. Yet he can't help but break his own ironclad rules when Lisette persuades him that being gentlemanly just this once is his wisest course of action…

❦

"Evocative… There is a charm in Grace's prose that will delight readers." —RT Book Reviews

"Grace's fabulously fun debut will dazzle readers with its endearingly outspoken heroine and devilishly rakish hero." —Booklist

"Clever, spicy, and fresh from beginning to end." —Amelia Grey, award-winning author of *A Gentleman Never Tells*

For more Samantha Grace, visit:

www.sourcebooks.com

If You Give a Rake a Ruby

by Shana Galen

———— ⌘ ————

Her mysterious past is the best revenge…

Fallon, the Marchioness of Mystery, is a celebrated courtesan with her finger on the pulse of high society. She's adored by men, hated by their wives. No one knows anything about her past, and she plans to keep it that way.

Only he can offer her a dazzling future…

Warrick Fitzhugh will do anything to protect his compatriots in the Foreign Office, including seduce Fallon, who he thinks can lead him to the deadliest crime lord in London. He knows he's putting his life on the line…

To Warrick's shock, Fallon is not who he thinks she is, and the secrets she's keeping are exactly what make her his heart's desire…

———— ⌘ ————

Praise for *When You Give a Duke a Diamond*:

"A lighthearted yet poignant, humorous yet touching love story—with original characters who delight and enough sizzle to add heat to a delicious read." —*RT Book Reviews*, 4½ stars

For more Shana Galen, visit:

www.sourcebooks.com

Once Again a Bride

by Jane Ashford

She couldn't be more alone

Widowhood has freed Charlotte Wylde from a demoralizing and miserable marriage. But when her husband's intriguing nephew and heir arrives to take over the estate, Charlotte discovers she's unsafe in her own home…

He could be her only hope…or her next victim

Alec Wylde was shocked by his uncle's untimely death, and even more shocked to encounter his uncle's beautiful young widow. Now clouds of suspicion are gathering, and charges of murder hover over Charlotte's head.

Alec and Charlotte's initial distrust of each other intensifies as they uncover devastating family secrets, and hovering underneath it all is a mutual attraction that could lead them to disaster…

Readers and reviewers are charmed by Jane Ashford:

"Charm, intrigue, humor, and just the right touch of danger." —RT *Book Reviews*

For more Jane Ashford, visit:

www.sourcebooks.com

How to Tame a Willful Wife

by Christy English

How to Tame a Willful Wife:

1. Forbid her from riding astride
2. Hide her dueling sword
3. Burn all her breeches and buy her silk drawers
4. Frisk her for hidden daggers
5. Don't get distracted while frisking her for hidden daggers...

Anthony Carrington, Earl of Ravensbrook, expects a biddable bride. A man of fiery passion tempered by the rigors of war into steely self-control, he demands obedience from his troops and his future wife. Regardless of how fetching she looks in breeches.

Promised to the Earl of Plump Pockets by her impoverished father, Caroline Montague is no simpering miss. She rides a war stallion named Hercules, fights with a blade, and can best most men with both bow and rifle. She finds Anthony autocratic, domineering, and... ridiculously handsome.

It's a duel of wit and wills in this charming retelling of *The Taming of the Shrew*. But the question is... who's taming whom?

For more Christy English, visit:

www.sourcebooks.com